HEIBERG'S TWITCH

Robert Wexelblatt

Heiberg's Twitch by Robert Wexelblatt

ISBN-10: 193834930X

ISBN-13: 978-1-938349-30-0

Library of Congress Control Number: 2015948048

Cover painting: "Melancholy" by Edvard Munch, oil on canvas, 1894

Layout and Book Design by Mark Givens

First Pelekinesis Printing 2016

For information:

Pelekinesis, 112 Harvard Ave #65, Claremont, CA 91711 USA

www.pelekinesis.com

HEIBERG'S TWITCH

Robert Wexelblatt

CONTENTS

HEIBERG'S TWITCH

———————————

GULLS wheeled above the harbor, screeched cheerlessly, then stopped. It was as though they had been trapped in the sky. At the end of the breakwater the flag whipped this way and that. Three girls who had been jumping rope down by the main wharf ran to put on their quilted jackets. A couple of old men played dominoes in the café. "For the love of God, shut the door," grumbled the one who was losing. Four boys came down the lane from the school yard kicking a leather ball. They hooted into the wind but the girls pretended not to hear them. The sea churned, turned from grey to copper green. On that northern island it took no more than five minutes for autumn to become winter.

Peter Aakenson, ignoring both the boys with their ball and the girls with their rope, ran past the jetty and straight into the café. He had to lean against a table to catch his breath. "Something's washed. Ashore. Something. Enormous." He pointed to the north. "Bjelsen's Strand."

The proprietor, who did double duty as mayor, shrugged. "Another beached whale that'll stink if it doesn't freeze first."

"Excuse me," Peter replied with dignity, his chest no longer heaving. "I've seen plenty of whales. Besides, it was old Karlson who sent me and you can't say Mr. Karlson wouldn't know a whale if he saw one."

The pensioners rubbed their beards and went back to their game.

The proprietor grew querulous. He was not fond of Karlson. "Well, what if the old fool's seen a beached battleship? What am I supposed to do about it?"

Peter left the café in disgust, eager to tell his friends his news and lead them personally up to see whatever had come ashore on Bjelsen's Strand.

Heiberg lay stretched out under the covers watching Evastina at her cleaning, hoping the place did not smell too sour.

His four-room house lay high above the harbor town. It was built of stone still covered here and there with stucco, an old but sturdy cottage. Five paces behind it sat a stone woodshed half the size of the house itself. Heiberg had ordered the shed well filled before his arrival. The privy was attached to the house by a little walkway that could be covered and heated in winter, detached in summer. This was a sensible feature of houses on the island. At that latitude what filled privies would be frozen for all but two brief months and then people were seldom indoors.

As a child Heiberg had been forced to eat meat. Fearing for his health his parents compelled him to stay put at the table until he had gulped down the bloody gobbets that made his gorge rise. It was more a question of his digestion than his scruples but even before he went off to the university Heiberg had become a vegetarian. To the island he had brought a large supply of canned vegetables and these constituted his staple diet. Fresh food, such as goat cheese and the local bread, was carried to him daily by Evastina. He had been delighted to discover that sometime in the last century Evastina's great-grandmother had spent one summer in the house as a nursemaid to his father and uncle. Once it had been the home of the Heibergs, but already a century ago it had devolved into a summer house. Neglected for years, it had become Heiberg's property the previous winter on the death of his cousin Albert. The notion of moving there had seized Heiberg during the summer as he felt his health failing. His friends considered it a dangerous eccentricity but they could not dissuade him; his heart was set on it. Dire warnings from his doctors had no more effect. By mid-July he had arranged for the most necessary repairs, and toward the end of August he had thanked his friends and physicians for their concern and bid them all adieu.

Long ago Heiberg had calculated how old he would have been the year the girl was born. He could see her in the kitchen and called to her.

"Evastina, do you mind if I ask you a personal question?"

"Yes?"

"When do you plan to marry?"

The girl turned her head. He relished the sight; she did it so pertly. "I've only just turned eighteen, Professor. There's plenty of time for that and besides, I've no such plans."

"You never think of leaving the island?"

"Every now and then. Of course, why not? Perhaps someday. We have people on the mainland. My aunt and uncle and three cousins. I've been to visit them. I may visit them again."

"Didn't you like it over there?"

"I liked it well enough but I was glad to come home. To tell the truth, my cousins were nasty little boys."

"Anyway, Evastina, I hope you will leave the island."

Heiberg said this not so much out of concern for the girl's future as because he knew for certain that he himself would never leave. That is, he spoke out of no more generous impulse than self-pity.

There was little daylight these days and Heiberg had to strain to watch Evastina move about the house. He put his finger to his eyelid and pressed lightly.

"You can't even see where its eyes were," said one woman.

"If it even had any," replied her neighbor, pulling her shawl tighter with a shudder.

The beast might have been the incarnation of all the terrors the women felt whenever their men put to sea. Most left in horror after a single glance. The men, on the other hand, were fascinated by the huge carcass. Above all they wanted it explained, classified, named. The inexplicable made them uneasy, putting out as they did almost every day on the sea, pulling creatures up from its depths. A name is always reassuring.

Those who had come into harbor first built bonfires on Bjelsen's Strand so those arriving later would be able to see as well. That night the shore was turned into a theater.

Some hypotheses were fanciful. "The damned Kraken," insisted one fellow.

"You idiot. Nothing but a sperm whale, though quite a big one, I admit."

"A sperm? Then just you tell me, where's his blow hole, eh? Where are the flukes?"

"How should I know?"

One who knew his Bible objected with respectful awe, "No, no. It's Leviathan."

Of late Heiberg thought chiefly of women and God. He knew that women and God are both consolations but at the same time sources of disturbance, that they are able to be the one only in proportion as they can be the other. In his youth he had run after women, though it would be equally accurate to say that he had run from them. He had thought it his duty to escape from women, that he abandon them for the sake of his work which he believed needed solitude. It was to his work and not to women that he attached what in those days was called Romance. And the work had prospered. Now, at the end of his life, his fame extended beyond his own professional circle.

It must have been the presence of Evastina that started him thinking of women. After all, he saw no one else, no students, no colleagues.

Though he had given his life to theoretical physics, the purest of all the sciences, in his private thoughts Heiberg had never entirely freed himself from the all-too-human superstition that dwells in the unmentionable depths of even a physicist's imagination. He had always conceived of his powers as flimsy reeds that must be carefully protected. This had much to do with his rather fitful sexual life; for his model was, in a sense, Samson. To give oneself to a woman, to let oneself go in the comfort she provided, could cost him his strength and bring to an end that power that was as tenuous as a human hair. Nevertheless, it was not only in his youth that he had run after women, or allowed himself to be pursued by them. He had satisfied his desires in middle life too, but always without relaxing. With women he remained a fist that might permit itself to be held tenderly and stroked, but which would never, never unclench.

In those days it had been women with whom he contended most and now it was God. Ever since he had first entered into real consciousness he had fervently wished to understand the physical framework of the world and had pictured his career as an arduous game. God was a useful construct, the worthy opponent whose stratagems it was his vocation to decipher; for there is a kind of comfort to be had in believing even in a Deity whose leading attributes are slyness and evasion. The God of physicists is as stern as that of the stiff-necked Hebrews and not a whit less jealous.

Heiberg had a friend from his undergraduate years who had also been occupying his thoughts of late. Erasmus Jacobson conceived, to judge from his verses, a quite different picture of God from Heiberg's, just as he had a different view of women, judging by his three marriages. What interested Jacobson was what he called the Human Condition, complete with capital letters. Their friendship had eroded over the years, worn away by separate careers. But now the differences in their orientation toward life that had seemed so rudimentary fifty years before struck Heiberg as merely vain. *To the one gate there are many paths.* It was a line from the poem Jacobson had dedicated to Heiberg on the occasion of his winning some academic prize. The physicist might have rated the poet's gesture more highly had his old friend not gone on to publish the poem. But now this line about the Gate kept running through Heiberg's head and he recalled with shame the needlessly acerbic letter he had written to Erasmus at the time. What had he said of this line?

"Perilously near to 'all roads lead to Rome' for a Lutheran like yourself, isn't it?"

There was consternation among the fisher folk. But at least the dead beast did not stink. The weather had grown too cold. Already the field ice was descending from the polar regions, rolling right up to the island like a grey stippled carpet. Soon darkness would embrace the island, the boats would be pulled ashore, and, except for the ice fishers and seal hunters, life would move indoors.

It was Evastina who told Heiberg about the thing that had come ashore on Bjelsen's Strand.

"You've seen it for yourself?"

"No," she admitted.

"You know, Evastina, there was once a philosopher who reasoned that because hair grows out of our heads, our heads must be full of hair. You see? One must examine all the evidence before reaching a conclusion. To do otherwise is always a capital error." Heiberg tapped his own bald pate three times as he had done when telling this story to his classes.

He was rewarded by Evastina's laughter, which he loved to hear; but then the girl spoiled the moment by narrowing her brows and moving closer. He knew that face. "You don't look very well today." Heiberg pressed himself against the pillows and coughed. It wasn't the decline of his health that disappointed him, only that Evastina had ceased to laugh.

The girl came every morning at nine and then again at six to prepare his supper. He paid her once a week and, in his opinion, far too little. After the first week he had offered to double her salary but she refused, pointing out that her father would object because "It wouldn't look proper." Nor was there any question of their financial arrangements remaining private, for it appeared that too would be improper. Heiberg felt, notwithstanding his consciousness of the difference in their ages, rather flattered by the mention of impropriety.

Here is this dutiful child, he thought as he watched her move about his house, but where is God? Perhaps Jacobson is right and each calling really owns its own relation to Him, a path all its own that winds up at the same Gate. Once every profession had its patron saint. What a lovely idea, thought Heiberg. A patron saint is virtually a household god, but then the prettiest as well as the most suspect aspects of Christianity are precisely those that derive from Paganism.

A physicist thinks of God as the Creator in a more literal sense than other people. What fascinates him is the God who is in the details, the God who is in this sense indistinguishable from the Devil. In Heiberg's private cosmology the Devil was as much a Creator as the Deity. He could never decide which was responsible for the curvature of space-time. To see God as a gigantic displaced parent did not interest him at all; it was too sentimental. That was the God of Jacobson, a loving, adjudicating parent, as much mother as father. For Heiberg the cunning of the universe was the cunning of God, his opponent in a lifelong game of hide and seek. To him God *was* cunning. And women?

Could he have loved a girl like Evastina, a girl without cunning or, at any rate, only the endearing variety proper to a young girl? Would he have done better to have married, and to have married such a one? Would she have had him? Heiberg wondered if he were merely indulging in romantic fantasies at an age and in a condition when all that ought to have been well behind him. Was he deflecting his fear of death by turning to the dregs of lust? His pride rebelled and he girded up his loins, so to speak, to concentrate on the serious work of dying.

He was alone most of the day. To be continuously alone is to be beyond consolation, and yet in the face of death there is something truthful about solitude, honest and elemental. Death is outside the human circle. More than once he had pictured Evastina discovering his cold body one morning at nine o'clock or one evening at six. The image made him shudder for her sake, though he was surprised to find that it excited him. Would the girl touch his hollow chest and thin legs?

With their heads crammed into fur hats and their bodies bundled in woolens five men tramped up the icy path to Heiberg's house. Evastina, having just completed her morning duties, met them on the way.

"Good morning to you, Evastina," said the mayor. The others stood back and touched their caps. Even though they had known her all her life, the two youngest were embarrassed by the girl simply because she had grown to be so pretty. As Heiberg represented to them the sophistication of the great world, so the girl personified loveliness. To them the old man and the young girl stood, so to speak, as reproaches. Knowledge and beauty were forms of power they could get along without, but to be face to face with either made them feel ignorant and clumsy.

"The old fellow isn't dead yet, is he?" asked the mayor jerking his head to one side so that the others would be able to hear his witticism over the wind. Evastina made it clear that she did not appreciate this joke, though in a way it pleased her by confirming her as the authority on the great man. Over the last months she had discovered the value of this status. She had been careful not to squander the little she knew of Heiberg, letting drip only a trickle of information so that the people down below would suppose she knew far more. But it was not entirely because of the prestige her job conferred on her that she felt protective of Heiberg; she was genuinely concerned about him. It was owing to this concern as well as curiosity that she turned back and followed the men up to the house and, on a sudden impulse, prevented the mayor from knocking.

"He's very ill and has to keep to his bed," she said. "He shouldn't come to the door. The wind's too cold. Best let me go in first. I don't want him to be alarmed."

"Really, you could almost be his mother, Evastina," quipped the mayor, who was in a facetious mood. This was because he had argued against appealing to Heiberg during the ad hoc meeting at his café the night before. Nevertheless, when the issue went against him he felt it necessary to his position that he himself lead the delegation. The fishermen grumbled at this but, as the owner of the town's only café, the mayor had his way.

As it happened Heiberg had climbed out of bed shortly after Evastina's departure. She had stoked up the fire to warm the house for him and left a pot of water on the stove in case he wanted tea. What he had in mind was to give himself a bath. He had not felt strong enough to have one for three days.

Evastina was surprised to see Heiberg out of bed, standing

near the stove in nothing but his long underwear. Heiberg too was shocked. He just gaped and put his finger to the corner of his eye.

"There are some men who've come up to see you, Professor. I thought I'd better—"

"Men?"

"The mayor and four others. Quick. You'd better get back in bed. What on earth were you up to anyway?"

"Just a bath. You may not believe it but I *do* bathe occasionally, Evastina."

"A bath? But it's still far too cold in here," Evastina chided, grabbing a blanket from the bed and throwing it over his shoulders.

Heiberg was irked and began to cough.

"See?" she said with kindly fury. "Just listen to that nasty cough."

"What on earth can they want with me?"

"You can't guess?" She was in motion everywhere, picking up the book of Jacobson's poems he had dropped by the bed, smoothing his sheets, plumping up his pillows.

"Now get in and I'll stay and make tea."

Heiberg did as he was told, feeling less like a child than as if he and Evastina shared the tacit solidarity of a married couple preparing for unwelcome but unavoidable guests.

Only after he was settled and well covered up did Evastina consent to open the door. The men trudged in, stamping their feet. The mayor growled about being kept waiting in the cold, pulled off his gloves, and blew ostentatiously on his fingers.

Evastina went to the kitchen while the men surrounded Heiberg's bed. Of course the mayor did the talking. He explained about the thing on the beach. This he did clumsily and Evastina was pleased to note that Heiberg did not make things easier for him by mentioning what she had already told him.

"... And so, Professor Heiberg," the mayor wound up rather lamely, "it seemed to us that you might be able to tell us what it is."

"From the little you've just said I can hardly tell a thing. Do you men have anything to add?"

Three of the men shook their heads.

"Maybe you could come and have a look for yourself," suggested the fourth.

"That's impossible!" Evastina thundered from the kitchen. "Can't you see he's not well enough to go out now the weather's turned?"

They were all abashed. Everyone knew that Heiberg had come to the island to die. It was obvious. He smiled at the men and gave a helpless shrug as if to say, "What can I do? Women rule us all." Aloud he assumed a professional tone, "If I'm to tell you anything I'll need better information. To begin with some accurate drawings. And a number of technical observations and three or four measurements."

Evastina carried in a wooden tray with mugs of tea for everyone. "I'll see to it for you," she announced. "I'm quite good at drawing."

The two youngest fishermen blushed.

In his late twenties Heiberg developed a condition that plagued him for weeks on end. He finally consulted an eye specialist. This worthy gentleman listened to Heiberg's description of his symptoms with a knowing smile and, when he had finished, nodded twice, leaned forward on his leather chair, and put his hands on his knees.

"Your condition's not in the least uncommon or likely to have serious consequences, though I grant the persistence of the muscle contractions for several weeks is unusual. Unusual and, for you, doubtless unpleasant. As a scientist you'll appreciate knowing the name of your malady. It is called Eyelid Myokymia, which is a sub-form of the uncontrolled spasm of muscle tissue called in general Myoclonus. As you say, it's not particularly painful in itself but a considerable annoyance all the same. In cases more extreme than your own it can manifest itself as a distorting twitch and even occluded vision. The sole treatment in these instances is to inject the muscles of the eye with a relaxant compound. This yields only temporary relief and, frankly, is out of the question in a case as mild as yours."

"So I just have to live with it?"

The doctor shrugged good-naturedly.

The fact of having lost control over even so small a part of his body as an eyelid was all but intolerable to Heiberg. He had tried rubbing, warm compresses, darkness.

"The condition is often exacerbated, some even say triggered, by specific behavioral factors. These include lack of sleep, the consumption of caffeine, stress, smoking, and eyestrain."

"Of all of which I can boast."

The doctor grinned as though Heiberg had just said something droll. "I thought as much. Well, you *could* try sleeping more, reading less, giving up your briar and your coffee. It might help, but then, to be perfectly frank, it might not."

"No rewards even for renunciation?"

The doctor threw up his hands in a paroxysm of mirth. "Your condition is what we medical types call *idiopathic*, Dr. Heiberg."

"A fine word!"

"Indeed it is, one which places a decorous cover over the unplumbed abyss of our ignorance, you might say."

Heiberg left the expert having gained nothing but a very slightly augmented vocabulary.

His condition continued to trouble Heiberg, sometimes waxing, at others waning and, worst of all, without any determinable pattern. He was never free of it for more than a week. Anything might set it off—brushing his eye while washing, a prolonged stare, late reading, even just waking up. He took to studying his face in the mirror, fascinated by the vibrating muscle below his right eye clenching and unclenching all on its own, as if it contained a tiny beating heart. After fifteen minutes or so this twittering made for a slight pressure on his eye to which he responded by placing the tip of his forefinger on the offending muscle and pressing lightly. While this gesture did not by any means end the contractions, it did ease the pressure a little. Before long this gesture became unconscious, itself a sort of tic.

One evening at the end of a university banquet Heiberg found himself seated next to Evald Hanson, an emeritus professor of chemistry. Hanson was asking him about the latest theories on the nature of light—waves or particles or both?—when he observed that Heiberg kept pressing his finger to his eye.

"A twitch, eh?"

"I'm sorry. Myokymia of the eyelid. It's driving me crazy."

"I can well believe it. I myself suffered from myokymia when I was your age. Perhaps it's a sort of occupational hazard."

"Perhaps so."

Hanson stubbed out his cigar and turned his head toward Heiberg. "Would you care to hear an odd story?"

"Certainly."

Hanson took a sip of port before beginning. "When my own twitching began it was much worse than yours appears to be. I honestly thought I'd lose my mind. Everybody noticed it, you see, so it was an embarrassment to me in company as well as an irritant when I was alone. If people mentioned it I was chagrined, and if they said nothing it was even worse. One day I went to buy a new suit. My tailor was an old Jew named Feingold. I had been going to him for years, ever since my father took me to him for my first suit. He was almost an uncle.

"'That twitching in your eye,' he said, 'it bothers you?'

"I answered him rather sharply. 'Of course it does.'

"'You've been to see a doctor then?'

"I told him that I had but that nothing could be done for me.

"'I thought as much,' Feingold said, and he proposed that I visit a certain rabbi, a refugee who had only recently arrived in the city.

"I assured him that it would be pointless. 'Not only am I not a Jew, Feingold, I'm an atheist.'

"The tailor shrugged. 'Suit yourself,' he said, 'but this rabbi is said to be very wise. Over there in the East they know plenty of things we don't. Let me just give you his address. Perhaps you'll change your mind.'

"Not wishing to offend Feingold, I took the slip of paper he pressed on me, put it in my pocket and promptly forgot all about it. However, a week or so later—another week of unrelieved torment—I was clearing out my pockets before having the suit cleaned and there was the address of the wonder-working rabbi.

"You can well imagine what sort of condition I was in when I tell you that I actually went to see the man. It turned out to be a remarkable experience."

Hanson paused to summon a waiter and fortify himself with another glass of port.

"And did this miracle rabbi from the East cure you?" Heiberg asked facetiously as the old man's glass was being filled.

"No, but listen. I found him living in one room in a building next to the old synagogue; you know, the one near the custom house that burned down it must be twenty years ago. The room was so crammed with books it was a wonder anyone could live in it. I had expected an old man with a long white beard and a fringed prayer shawl. I had always assumed rabbis were all old men, but to my surprise this one was a young fellow of about my own age.

"I knocked and he let me in. He cleared a space for me on the couch that must have done duty as his bed and offered me some tea which he served not in a cup but in a glass and then he began chattering amusingly about his neighbors who kept chickens in their apartment. I was fascinated by his accent and his exceptional vitality. I listened to the whole story of the poultry without interrupting. Only then did he ask me why I'd come.

"I couldn't hide my embarrassment at being there; in fact, I decided to make up some story or other and get away as soon as possible. But, of course, he noticed my twitch and interrupted whatever cock-and-bull story I was telling him. 'Now, now, you're here because of your eye, aren't you, Professor?'

"I was astounded and complimented him on what I took to be his preternatural insight. He laughed and observed that skeptics are the most gullible of people because they don't know what to believe. The remark was impertinent but made with such good humor that I too had to laugh. Of course then he told me that Feingold had already informed him about my case.

"'Judging by your hesitation, Professor, would it be fair to say that you are, in a certain sense, here against your will?'

"'That's putting it a little strongly,' I said.

"'Then I apologize. You must forgive me. I am merely a humble immigrant while you are a famous professor, a man of science. Let me tell you a little story. If it fails to enlighten at least it may amuse you. Once, in the university town of Lvov, a great scientist, not unlike yourself, was walking through the streets with his students trailing behind him when they came on a little Jewish boy who was hurrying to the yeshiva, the study house. Perhaps the professor was amused by the boy's comical appearance or maybe he wished to take the occasion to make a point to his students. In any event, he grabbed the boy by the shoulder like this.' And here the rabbi actually clapped his hand on my own shoulder, held me fast, and put his face right up to mine like this. "'Look here, my little fellow," said the scientist as he took a coin from his pocket. "I'll give you this gold crown if you can tell me where God lives." The boy, quite undaunted, looked up at the man and answered him in a loud voice, "And I'll give you two crowns if you can tell me where He doesn't!"'"

Both Heiberg and Hanson laughed at the story, though it was not entirely clear at what or whom they were laughing.

"Wait. There's more," said Hanson. "The rabbi looked me in the eye and told me that there was no cure for my twitch because it was an expression of a portion of my soul that I had denied and was trying to bury. I still remember the quaint way he put it. He said, 'The watch that we have mislaid goes on ticking for a time even though it's lost,' or some such thing. Then he added something. He said, 'But I will tell you this. There is one way and one way only to get relief from your twitching and this is a kiss on the eye from a woman who loves you.'"

"Just like the Flying Dutchman," Heiberg said mockingly. "How romantic!"

Hanson nodded and smiled. "I told him I'd already tried warm compresses but he only laughed at me.

"'Either you've willfully misunderstood me, Professor, or, as I suspect, you are being ironic. It isn't the warmth or the moisture of her kiss but the love the woman feels for you that will do the trick.'"

Old Hanson was exhilarated by telling his tale. With an almost triumphant gesture he turned his stiff torso toward Heiberg, who could see in the candlelight every wrinkle on his face.

"Well, what do you think?"

"It really is a fascinating story."

"And *true*, Heiberg, a true story."

"I assure you I didn't think—"

"No, I mean the rabbi was right—at least in my case. You see, shortly after that I met my wife. One night after a skating party I offered to see her home. We were in high spirits but she quite astonished me when at the door of her house she got up on tiptoe and kissed me right on the eye. Just imagine. No doubt she was aiming for my cheek, as she's often insisted, but you'll understand when I say that the pleasure of that moment of surcease was ineffable. Naturally I recalled what the rabbi had said, what I had mocked and even now feel rather silly mentioning to you. I remember that as I was leaving he cited a text. 'It is written that to have married a good woman is already to have fulfilled the Law.' A very Jewish sentiment but I hope it is true, for our engagement was announced within a month's time. Regine and I have been happily married for nearly forty years."

"Please accept my belated congratulations. And what about the twitching?"

"The rabbi was right there as well, I suppose. It didn't leave me entirely until around the time I was appointed to my chair. And even today, seeing you . . . Still, just as he promised, I could always find a few moments of solace thanks to Regine."

God, women, science. No doubt it was because his mind had been trotting behind this formidable troika that Heiberg recalled Hanson's story; for it involved all three. He thought almost with shame of how he had made use of it, of the rabbi's oriental wisdom.

The first time was a few months after his conversation with Hanson at the banquet. He had begun an affair with a young woman of beauty and intelligence, an archivist at the University library. One night, exasperated by the contractions in his eyelid, he asked her if she could stand to put her lips on it. She willingly agreed and at once the twitching ceased.

"Oh, I can feel it," she cried. "It tickles."

The very next week Heiberg had broken off the affair.

He was not a marine biologist. Any fisherman on the island knew more than Heiberg about the sea and its denizens. He didn't even like to eat fish. Four generations earlier his family had given up life by the sea for the complicated professions of the city. He might have told the islanders, but could they be expected to distinguish between one species of scientist and another? Wouldn't they think he was simply too lazy or too preoccupied with his dying to trouble himself with their little mystery? Why should he undermine their faith in him, however tentative, however misplaced? After all, he was flattered by it. If they believed he could tell them something worthwhile about some dead animal, why should he protest ignorance? Besides, he really did intend to make an effort through Evastina. He reasoned that, in the end, when the time came to throw up his hands they would be no worse off and, who knows, perhaps more prepared to accept the mystery of the world and the limitations of human science.

The latter was a lesson that Heiberg himself had been learning all through his career, one which his approaching dissolution was driving home. Theoretical physics has its proper ironies, he had said in one of his last lectures. A good physicist, he advised his students, must grasp that scientific knowledge has limits but at the same time never presume to know what these limits are.

Heiberg was surprised by the devotion with which Evastina threw herself into her researches. Her visits were now filled with reports and revisions of those reports. He had to examine her preliminary sketches, which he thought genuinely excellent, and reply to her requests for further directions. Soon she herself was proposing measurements and additional physiological investigations.

From Evastina Heiberg learned that the creature was approximately seventeen meters in length, predominantly black in color, with eyes set forward on a rounded head at the end of an elongated neck, rather than on the sides, as with whales. Its mouth had three sets of teeth which, from Evastina's drawings, he could tell were those of a carnivore. Instead of the flukes of a whale its body tapered to a single lateral fin three meters across and shaped something like a manatee's. It had a huge set of gills and, astonishingly, a curiously depressed aperture on the dorsal surface that, though apparently too small for the purpose, might have served as a blow hole. From one unmistakable indication Evastina concluded that the beast had been a male. The body itself was now completely frozen.

Perseus had faced nothing more terrifying in defending Andromeda off the Joppa coast.

One day Heiberg, examining her rendering of the monster's head, said, "Evastina, you ought to have become a scientist yourself, or an artist."

The girl blushed with pleasure. "I only want to help you."

"No, I mean it. You've done extraordinarily well. Believe me, nobody at the University could have done better."

"And yet?" added the girl, catching something in his tone.

Heiberg broke into a terrific fit of coughing and when it had passed he said, "Excuse me. And yet I'm baffled. I've no idea what the creature is."

Unwilling to give up, Evastina suggested that she might get some of the men to saw the creature open so that she could draw its internal organs for him.

"I'm afraid that would be no use. For all I know it may be something never before seen, a new species."

Her face lit up. "Do you really think so? A new species?"

"It's possible."

"Then what if I were to send my drawings to the University? You could tell me where, I mean who should see them."

Heiberg was surprised again, not so much by the girl's ardor or her altogether sensible proposal as by the pang of jealousy he felt, as if he were a failed Perseus, as if Andromeda had saved herself. Another fit of coughing covered his discomfiture. Evastina ran to fetch him a glass of water.

His eye had begun twitching again; it had been twitching incessantly for five days. It felt like a punishment, as though God had chosen this cunning way to get back at him for his presumption and vanity, for seeking to see and know but never to love. *And I'll give you two crowns if you can tell me where He doesn't*, the Jewish boy had said to get the better of the professor in Lvov. *Even a lost watch ticks*, said the rabbi to Evald Hanson. And now there was this colossal beast that he could not see except through the clear eyes of a girl and about which he understood nothing at all.

Evastina, who desired knowledge more than he did, who had far more of the romance of science in her than remained to him, came back into the room with the glass of water and Heiberg said aloud, "Perhaps the beast is death." He was not even speaking to the girl; he had only meant to allow himself a bitter and self-pitying joke, but as soon as the words were out the idea seized him.

Evastina had never looked lovelier or more vital than now, when she began to cry for his sake, as if he were the Flying Dutchman. He watched her tears with fascinated delight.

"Evastina, my dear," he whispered, "forgive me. I'll tell you where to send your drawings. I'll even go to see the beast for myself. Yes, I want to go to Bjelsen's Strand with you. We'll go over everything together. And I'll take you to the University. And I want to smoke my pipe again too. Why not? But please, please would you do me one very great favor?"

She brushed at her tears. "Yes?"

"Do you think you could give me a kiss right here, just on my eye?"

The Tale of Pu'i Chu-wo,

from an Old Manuscript

1.

IN the west of the Kingdom of Ch'in was a poor village called Rich-in-Stones. True enough, the land was hard to farm, the climate harsh, water scarce. Yet, as peasants always do, the people of Rich-in-Stones complained only among themselves while, to outsiders, they extolled the virtues of their village. Here Pu'i Chu-wo was born. Because he was the only boy, his four sisters served him, his grandparents indulged him, and his parents placed all their hopes in him. Nevertheless, Chu-wo was not spoiled. For one thing, his family was too poor to afford silk robes, carved jade, or even wooden toys; for another, Chu-wo was embarrassed by his exalted position in the family, particularly by the dutiful attitude of his sisters; he thought they ought to resent him. When he reached the age of ten, however, he did make use of his status by insisting that he be spared some hours of work in the fields each day and permitted to study instead. His father grew angry and was against this idea, but his mother and grandmother argued for the boy. "Ambition is good if it is matched with ability," said the grandmother, who spoke in proverbs. So it was that the sole luxuries in the family were Chu-wo's books, paper, ink, brushes, and, for most of a year, the board and salary of an itinerant scholar who tutored the boy.

"He is a good lad and intelligent enough," said the tutor on the day he took up his staff to depart. "Let's hope he will also be wise."

When he was of age, Chu-wo, weighed down by the expectations of his family and, indeed, the entire village, left Rich-in-Stones for the capital, where he hoped to obtain some minor position in the service of King Tan.

The day before Chu-wo arrived at the castle, a clerk who had worked on the tax rosters was fatally struck on the head by a loose roof tile and, because of this misfortune, Chu-wo was, after formally pledging his allegiance to King Tan, taken on as a replacement.

The boy proved diligent and dependable, intelligent, chaste, and polite. He turned down a bribe that was offered to test him, then a much larger one as well. With delicacy, he rebuffed an offer from one of the Assistant Chamberlain's lesser concubines, which was not a test but did much for his reputation. Thus Chu-wo was promoted until he was brought to the notice of King Tan himself, who had him summoned.

Chu-wo pressed his forehead into the floor.

The King was in a jovial mood that day. "Your superiors say you are intelligent," he said to Chu-wo. "Tell me, then, what is it that everybody does at the same time, kings and peasants, great lords, sows, and even granite boulders?"

"Grow older, Most High."

Everyone laughed which pleased King Tan, who then asked the young man where he was born and how he had come to the capital. Chu-wo explained his background.

"Your village has an amusing name. Here are some rich stones," laughed the King who handed his Chamberlain three silver coins to give Chu-wo before dismissing him.

These coins, and all the money Chu-wo was able to save, he sent back to his family in Rich-in-Stones.

Two months later King Tan was distressed by a report that the people of Ku'an had driven off his tax collectors. The most remote and backward province of Ch'in, Ku'an was on the northern frontier with the barbarians and was itself deemed in the capital to be only half-civilized. The people there were just as poor as those in Rich-in-Stones. Chancellor Feng suggested to King Tan that he send the clerk Chu-wo to Ku'an.

"Surely he is too young and inexperienced. Besides, it will be dangerous," objected the King.

"The young man has distinguished himself, Most High. He is looked on with favor by his superiors and has quickly achieved preferment. Tax collection is the business of his department. Moreover, the fellow is low-born and from the provinces himself. He may know how to deal with the louts of Ku'an."

Feng, who had been keeping an eye on Chu-wo even before the incident of the riddle, did not intend to do him good in this business; quite the contrary. Mean as were Chu-wo's origins, Feng saw in him a potential rival and, as he did with all such men, he intended to arrange that he should lose favor. If the young man failed in his commission, or if the people in Ku'an did away with him, so much the better. If, improbably, he somehow succeeded in extracting their taxes, then half the credit would go to Feng.

King Tan called Chu-wo to him. Again Chu-wo pressed his forehead into the floor of the audience chamber. King Tan gave him his commission.

"You will have a retinue of six warriors. They are all I can spare. See that you bring back to me something of real value."

"As you wish, Most High."

The journey to Ku'an was difficult, the weather contrary. It took Chu-wo and his small retinue most of a month to get there. The warriors were anxious the whole way, but Chu-wo calmed them by each night telling them one of the tales he had heard from his grandmother. He chose only those stories in which brave soldiers are rewarded with treasure and peasant girls become queens and live in pavilions with names like Willow Branch Colonnade and Chamber of the Celestial Iris.

In Ku'an the peasants were silent and looked at the seven men resentfully as they rode by. When Chu-wo arrived in Wu, the capital of Ku'an, he installed himself at the Inn of the Two Medlar Trees and had his warriors put on a display of their martial skills in the market square. When they had finished he said sternly to the crowd that King Tan could, if he chose, send ten thousand such men to Ku'an. He then sent couriers to summon all the chief men of the province to meet with him in the square in three days' time.

While he waited, Chu-wo walked about the town and spoke to the people in the common way he knew from his childhood in Rich-in-Stones. He chatted about this and that—weather, crops, the dishonesty of the last governor, whether the King's taxes were too high, and what was going on among the barbarians across the frontier. These were the topics he chose with the men, but he spoke with women as well. He asked these who the local beauties were and they all bragged about an unfortunate girl named Mei-lei, whose father had recently died. Even by the standards of Ku'an, she was so destitute that, notwithstanding her surpassing beauty, no man would marry her.

On the third day, most of the men he summoned had gathered, grumbling and looking sour. Chu-wo, dressed in the stiff silk gown and sash of a court official, stood above them on a dais he had ordered to be built for the purpose. He sternly looked over the men then asked one of his warriors to hand him the tax roster for the province. He looked to another of his retinue and snapped his fingers. The warrior, perplexed, came to his side. Chu-wo whispered into the man's ear and pointed across the square to where a dumpling-seller had set up his booth. Perplexed and somewhat reluctantly, the man went to the dumpling-seller's brazier and returned with a burning brand from the fire beneath it. Chu-wo had the scroll unrolled by two of his men then lit it in three places. In shocked silence everybody watched the tax roster go up in flames.

"The King will cut out your tongue; he'll slice off your hands and then lop off your head," hissed one of his men. Chu-wo ignored him and addressed the crowd.

"I will return to the capital without your taxes. I have burnt this year's roster at King Tan's direction because he feels in his heart how hard things have been for his people here in Ku'an."

There were cries of amazement; blessings were heaped on good King Tan.

"But," said Chu-wo, "there is one thing of great value from Ku'an that, with your consent, I would like to take back to our King. That is the girl Mei-lei, with whose widowed mother I will leave five jin of gold."

The chief men of Ku'an thought this an excellent bargain.

On Chu-wo's return to the capital, Chamberlain Feng was quick to denounce his failure to carry out the King's commission. He looked forward to Chu-wo's humiliation, to seeing how harshly King Tan would deal with the upstart. Would it be banishment, torture, or instant execution? Feng would have to apologize to the King for his warm heart that led him to trust too readily in the good reports he had received of Chu-wo.

The audience chamber was full. Nobody liked to miss the chance to witness another's humiliation.

"Explain yourself," demanded King Tan.

Chu-wo, forehead flat against the floor, did so.

"Most High, Ku'an is even poorer than people say. There was a flood in the spring and then drought all through the summer. They have also suffered from raids by the northern barbarians. Even if you sent an army to strip the land, the tax roster of Ku'an still would not be satisfied by half. However, you asked me to bring back something of value. I have brought you two."

Feng scoffed at Chu-wo's being taken in by the excuses of the people of Ku'an and at his unheard-of arrogance. The rest of the court followed suit.

"What things?" thundered the King.

"The first is the loyalty of the people of Ku'an. I told them that King Tan had remitted their taxes for one year out of compassion for the hard times they have suffered. They were grateful beyond measure, Most High, and, unless I am mistaken, this good will shall prove its value before long. The peasants of Ku'an say that the barbarians are making preparations to invade Ch'in. Before we left, the warriors and I gave the people some advice on that matter."

The King, though intrigued, was not yet mollified. "And what is the second thing of value you've brought me from Ku'an?"

"May I rise, Most High?"

"On your feet."

Chu-wo backed from the chamber and returned moments later leading the incomparably lovely Mei-lei, whom he had suitably attired for presentation to the King. Though terrified, the girl controlled herself as Chu-wo had instructed her. She looked as serene as a spirit from another world, a vision.

Chu-wo was neither punished nor rewarded. He was sent back to his tax rosters and his status remained uncertain.

Two months later the barbarians did attempt to invade Ch'in. As they passed through a defile in the mountains they were stopped by the people of Ku'an, who rolled huge boulders down on them. Chu-wo and his men had shown the peasants how to use fulcrums to move the rocks and where to place the them. Many barbarians perished, and the survivors fled back to the north.

When news of this event reached the capital, King Tan, who delighted in his new concubine, sent rich gifts to the people of Ku'an and elevated Chu-wo to the rank of minister. Half of his handsome new salary he sent to Rich-in-Stones; most of the remainder he dedicated to the establishment of a hospital for the poor.

2.

THE crafty Feng was furious at Chu-wo's success and set in motion a plot against him. He had a rumor put about that Chu-wo had not remitted the taxes in Ku'an but had struck a deal with the richest men of the province to pay a quarter of the sum directly to him. How else could he afford to endow a hospital, let alone to support the poor poets and scholars everybody knew flocked to him? There were those who defended Chu-wo; but, as Chamberlain Feng had influence over King Tan and was notoriously vindictive, people were reluctant to cross him and soon even Chu-wo's friends fell silent.

Finally, Chu-wo was summoned by the King.

"You deny this report, Chu-wo?"

"I do, Most High."

"Chamberlain Feng says it is so."

"Then the Lord Chamberlain is mistaken."

"He produced two men from Ku'an who swear he is not."

"I am not worthy to argue in your presence but, with respect, Most High, two men may be persuaded to speak untruths."

King Tan drew his brows together. "I had one beheaded in front of the other. The other did not change his story."

"I grieve for them both," sighed Chu-wo into the floor.

"Mei-lei alone defends you."

"I am glad."

"That means nothing," said the King. "You did her a good

turn. She's naïve, still a child. But for her sake I have chosen to banish you. Leave the castle tonight. If you are not out of my kingdom in three days' time even Mei-lei's weeping won't save you."

So Chu-wo left Ch'in in disgrace and crossed the border into Shu, the land of Duke Tsien.

Tsien was an intelligent and prudent ruler. He appreciated the proverb that says the mouse must keep a close watch on the elephant. He had spies in Ch'in so the abilities, character, and fate of Chu-wo were known to the Duke. He sent men to seek out the exile and fetch him to his castle.

No longer was Chu-wo sending good things to Rich-in-Stones, supporting poets, or wearing silk gowns; yet once again he found himself pressing his forehead against the floor of an audience chamber.

"Chu-wo," said the Duke.

"I am here, Lord."

"Are you able to tell me the meaning of a verse from Laozi?"

"I can only try."

"Good. The verse is, *The scholar wears rough clothing and carries jade inside.*"

Chu-wo nearly raised his head.

"What is its meaning?" asked the Duke in a pleasant voice.

"People used to say it was because scholars dressed in woolen coats and carried their manuscripts against their hearts in jade bindings. The true meaning is that the genuine scholar cares little for shows of wealth and much for wisdom and uprightness. Likewise grammar."

The Duke laughed. "Well, your clothing is certainly rough but I wonder, do you carry jade inside, Chu-wo?"

"I hope to, Most High."

"On your feet then."

That very day Chu-wo swore an oath of allegiance to Duke Tsien, who made him one of his ministers. The Duke had reason to be pleased by his act. He received nothing but wise advice from Chu-wo. Every task assigned the man was executed efficiently and with justice. He became popular at court for his good manners, learning, and sound sense, but also with the common people, who petitioned him by scores, saying, "See how he dresses and how he talks? He's one of us." Indeed, Duke Tsien allowed his new minister to dress in rough clothing, except on formal occasions, when he sent Chu-wo the finest silk garments and insisted that he wear them.

And so for two years events flowed as smoothly in Shu as the Yangtze in summer. Then a serious crisis arrived. King Tan of Ch'in sent a demand that Duke Tsien of Shu cede Wen, his richest province, or there would be war.

The Duke's spies had kept him abreast of developments in Ch'in. For instance, they informed him that after Chu-wo's exile Chamberlain Feng had risen to become First Minister and wielded more influence over King Tan than ever. He also knew that Mei-lei, the lowest of Tan's concubines, was the one he loved best. The spies had hinted that something seemed to be brewing but failed to caution him, or to discover, that war was imminent.

The Duke called a conference of all the ministers of Shu, also his provincial governors. He informed them of the peril, and solicited their advice.

Everyone was shocked. Relations between Ch'in and Shu had been peaceful for as long as any of them had been alive.

"The population of Ch'in is ten times that of Shu," said one minister at last, a man who always stated the obvious.

"Most High, you should send all our forces to the border at once," said the governor of Wen. "Perhaps a pre-emptive attack will make King Tan think again."

Meanwhile, Chu-wo was troubled. His scrupulous conscience reminded him that he had, after all, sworn allegiance to both Duke Tsien and to King Tan; exile did not cancel his oath. His mind was also at work. One of his correspondents in Ch'in kept him up to date with court gossip and, combining this information with that of the Duke's spies, Chu-wo had formed certain suppositions that now seemed substantiated.

"Most High," he said to the Duke, "I humbly beg to be sent to Ch'in as your special ambassador."

"A terrible idea!" roared the bellicose governor of Wen. "To send a special ambassador will only confirm our weakness."

"Our weakness needs no confirmation," the Duke replied sensibly.

"The King of Ch'in will execute Chu-wo as soon as he shows up in the capital, if he even gets that far. He was banished on pain of death," pointed out the Minister for Public Works.

"Ambassadors are sacred and immune," answered the Duke.

"With respect, Most High, can you be sure? King Tan has threatened us without cause. To trust him may be unwise."

"No more can Chu-wo be trusted," chimed in the governor of Wen. "Did he not swear allegiance to the King of Ch'in?"

Chu-wo remained silent, surprised that the governor of Wen had thought of the very thing that was so perturbing him.

Duke Tsien looked hard at Chu-wo. "It's true that you would be risking your life."

"Certainly," said Chu-wo in a firm voice. "But my purpose is to prevent a war which would cost the lives of thousands."

"And what of your two oaths?"

"Most High, to preserve the peace would, in my opinion, serve the great rulers of both Ch'in and Shu, as well as their people."

In the end, Duke Tsien decided both to fortify his border with Ch'in and, despite his misgivings, to send Chu-wo to King Tan as special ambassador.

When Chu-wo beheld the gray battlements and red tiles of King Tan's castle towering above the blue spruces and green pines, when he glimpsed the ladies of the court gossiping in the gardens under their scarlet and yellow parasols, the couriers dashing between offices and the clerks deep in conversation as they strolled outside the walls, he was overtaken by an unexpected nostalgia. There were so many people here he missed, including the King.

The passport furnished him by Duke Tsien was a particularly gaudy document that quite cowed the border guards. Chu-wo, himself impressively clothed, and his escort of twelve knights in burnished armor, were not delayed on their way, except by the peasants who gaped at them passing on the road. Those who recognized Chu-wo enthusiastically called out his name.

At the castle gate Chu-wo was separated from his retinue, who were disarmed, their horses led to the royal stables. A flunkey conducted him to the smallest of the guest apartments. Chu-wo, in his most commanding voice, told the fellow to convey the message that he wished to see the King at his earliest convenience. He was kept waiting two hours, but he made good use of the time. He sought out an old friend, one of the castle laundresses, and asked if she would be able to deliver a letter privately to Mei-lei. "You must not show it to anyone else," he cautioned her.

She was so pleased to see Chu-wo that the old woman couldn't resist patting his cheek. "Anything for our boy from Rich-in-Stones," she said, shoving the letter under her skirt. "Oh, how we've missed you!"

King Tan received Chu-wo formally with all his court. First Minister Feng stood close by his master's side. Chu-wo again pressed his forehead into the floor of Tan's assembly chamber, and the familiar scent conjured up many memories.

"Well, we see the Duke of Tsien means to insult us by sending back one we have sent away," said the King.

"No, Most High, not to insult, but to forestall an unjust and unnecessary catastrophe for Ch'in and Shu."

Feng whispered into the King's ear. "As you know," said Tan, "we demand the province that sits on the untenable border between Ch'in and Shu. If you are here to turn Wen over to us, good; if not, then we will take it."

Chu-wo then delivered a short oration, studded with erudite quotations, on the miseries of war and the blessings of peace. No one paid much attention to this and Feng made disparaging noises throughout. Then Chu-wo addressed King Tan directly.

"Most High, the Duke of Shu has entrusted me with an important message meant for your ears only. I humbly beg a few minutes alone with you to deliver it."

Feng called this unheard-of request an outrage. "The thief will murder you!"

With far more calm than he felt, Chu-wo offered to strip and show he concealed no more weapons than he did violent intentions.

King Tan hesitated. Feng objected again and Chu-wo saw the King look furtively at his First Minister with a mixture of fear and suspicion before making up his mind. Then, with an impassive face, he declared, "We will see Tsien's ambassador alone. Clear the room."

Only ten minutes later, Chu-wo backed out of the audience chamber and returned to his apartment, where he found food and drink.

Soon after nightfall, Chu-wo, wearing his rough clothing, secretly slipped out of his apartment and stealthily made his way to the women's quarters. In the empty Chamber of Three Paradises he found King Tan and two huge guards waiting for him.

In silence, the four men then passed behind a peacock screen, squeezed through a tight doorway, and made their way down a narrow interior corridor into a large closet which had been cleared of its contents.

Minutes later they heard a conversation between a man and a woman, the Lady Mei-lei and Minister Feng.

"At last," said Feng. "How you've made me burn!"

"Do you really love me?"

"Since the day you first arrived from that hell-hole Ku'an and with a fire you've stoked to a blaze. Who'd have thought a sty like that could produce such a perfect ruby."

"Lord Feng, I have endangered my life by permitting you to come into this room. What are your prospects? If I consent to your pleadings what will become of me?"

"Ha! So that's what's been worrying you, is it? Mei-lei, I am a crafty and ambitious man, the kind of man who always arrives at his destination. Just look at how easily I got rid of that upstart, Chu-wo, and established myself as Tan's First Minister. And now I've arranged this pleasant little war with Shu."

"Pleasant?"

"For us."

"In what way?"

"In the way of making you my queen. Listen. King Tan will lead the army to attack Shu. Of course he won't be in the forefront, at the point of greatest danger; however, he will be on the field where there are always risks. I have an archer in my employ, a most excellent bowman. The fortunes of war are unpredictable and a stray arrow can accomplish wonders. When Tan is dead it will be easy to dispose of his young heir and make myself king—and you, pearl plucked from a midden, will be my queen. And now—"

Together King Tan and Chu-wo pushed down the screen

behind which they were concealed. It crashed to the floor. The two guards quickly seized Feng. No torture was required for the former first minister to divulge the identity of the treacherous archer and his other confederates. All were beheaded.

Needless to say, there was a great banquet and no war between Ch'in and Shu.

What had Chu-wo written to Mei-lei and what did he say in private to King Tan? The latter may be guessed but here is the former:

> Honored Lady Mei-lei,
>
> If I am brief I hope you will pardon the discourtesy. Time is short as well.
>
> Unless I am mistaken, you have long been pestered by Minister Feng. You chastely refused his attentions and prudently concealed them from our master.
>
> Much depends on what I am going to ask you to do—not just your precious life and my worthless one, but the lives of thousands in Shu and Ch'in, and, as I believe, King Tan's as well. You must be brave.
>
> I want you to arrange an assignation with Feng tonight at the fourth watch and in your own bedchamber. Beforehand, please open the door of your large closet, clear it of everything stored there, and place a screen before it. You need also to see that the lock on the entrance to

the interior corridor is undone. When the First
Minister comes you will ask him if he loves you.
He will, I am sure, say that he does.

Then you must ask him about his prospects, his
plans for your future together.

You will not see me, but you will not be alone.
I implore you to think of the people of Ku'an
and do as I ask.

Because she had always been grateful to him and because she
had pleaded for him with King Tan, Chu-wo had reason to hope
that Mei-lei would follow his instructions, but persuading King
Tan to do so was more difficult. He made good use of the gossip
he had received, his own intelligence, and also the sincerity with
which he spoke. As for King Tan, he had missed Chu-wo and
had begun to doubt the story of his corruption, which Chu-wo's
successor had been unable to confirm. He was never at ease with
the ambitious and jealous Feng and he admitted that the war
was Feng's idea. But the point that convinced the King was one
that touched nearer his heart.

"Most High, when I was slandered—by Feng, of course—who
was the only person who defended me?"

"Mei-lei."

"We know how vindictive your First Minister is, how little
he can endure being opposed. Yet nothing happened to Mei-lei."

Not only was peace between Ch'in and Shu preserved, it was
made durable when, some years later, Chu-wo made the arrangements for Tan's oldest son to wed Tsien's second daughter.

EDITH FEVRIER

———————————

CHANCES are I'd never have met Paul Hanley except for a midweek robbery on Hyde Park Avenue. Bank of America branch office, broad daylight, less than professional. Paul wasn't the sole witness, just the only one worth talking to. Paul made up for the terrified, inarticulate, vague, contradictory others. In fact, he was a marvel. And he was only eleven and a half years old.

When I got to the scene at 1:15 the uniforms hadn't even lined the kid up as a witness, being preoccupied with three hysterical tellers, one shaken manager, and four panicked customers who'd all been inside the bank. When I asked if anyone had seen the getaway, Sergeant Pinkney looked at me like a large pig that's received a tiny nudge, and insisted it had all gone down too fast and anyway there wasn't anybody on the street at the time. I looked at the ceiling. This was Hyde Park, not Los Angeles. Pinkney was porcine in all respects except native intelligence.

So it was Paul who found me, literally pulled at my sleeve.

"You in charge?"

He was short for his age, pre-growth-spurt, slight but wiry. His face was mobile; it looked like a hoodlum's one second, a choir-boy's the next, and then an imp's after that. His red hair was shading to brown and he had the sharpest pair of blue eyes you've ever seen—or that have ever seen you.

"Who wants to know?" I asked him. I could see he liked that come-back.

"Paul Hanley," he said, and held his hand out and up.

I told him my name and we shook on it.

I pointed to my watch. "So, Mr. Hanley, why aren't you in school?"

"Suspended," he said succinctly and shrugged.

"You get suspended often?"

He considered for a moment and allowed as how he got suspended pretty regularly.

"And you walk the streets?"

He pulled a face. "Oh yeah, sure. Like my mother's going to let me prowl Hyde Park. I'm supposed to be home, of course. She's working. She's *always* working. Two jobs. I just felt like a walk."

I looked down at him and nodded, as if joining him in a male conspiracy against mothers.

He looked worried. "You won't tell her, will you?"

"That depends."

"You mean on whether I help you catch the robbers?"

"We'll see," I said, a man reluctant to promise what he can't perform. Then I suggested we go outside. I told the uniforms to go on taking statements from the other witnesses and they gave me dirty looks. Pinkney even made an unmistakable noise.

There were no benches so we settled on the curb, not quite eye-to-eye but closer. My experience is that boys like Paul don't much like it when adults do a knee-bend, raise the pitch of their voices and smile at them like idiots. It was just as well since I later learned vocabulary-building was one of Paul's specialties and he probably knew the literal meaning of *condescending*.

"So," I began, "you saw the robbers?"

Paul didn't care for rhetorical questions. "Think I'd be bothering you if I didn't?"

"How many?"

"Two."

"You saw them coming out of the bank?"

"Sure. Wasn't here when they went in." He pointed across the street at a store that sold cigarettes, magazines, candy, and lottery tickets. "I was right over there when they came out."

Questioning children is tricky but no more than debriefing adults. If you get it right, if they see you mean business and let them know you'll accept no fantasies or embellishments, they can be helpful, though, in my experience, never in court. Questioning Paul Hanley, however, was something else again.

"Moving pretty fast, weren't they?"

Wrong tone again. He gave me a pitying look. "Wouldn't *you* be?"

"The car?"

"Van," he corrected. "Five, six year-old Ford Econoline. Blue. Rust over the left rear fender. Dirty. Stolen probably."

"Why stolen?"

"Well, it had New Hampshire plates. You know, *Live Free or Die*. HBL964. They must have been over the border recently, I figure. I mean nobody from New Hampshire's going to take their van to Hyde Park to knock over a bank."

I acknowledged the level-headedness of this judgment with a nod. "Look, will you wait here a minute?"

He shrugged his narrow shoulders. "I'm suspended."

I went over to my car and called in the information on the van and practically skipped back to the curb.

"Okay," I said, getting back on the curb. "Anything more?"

He spread out his hands, as if revealing a treasure. "I'd say they're both in their twenties. Thirty at the outside. One of them runs funny—not exactly with a limp, but kind of crab-like. You know? Left leg shoots out a little sideways. Probably a bad hip. I'd look for a hockey player. The other one, the one who drove, he's got these just enormous ears. The buzz-cut doesn't help. The other one's vain, the hockey player."

"Vain?"

"Conceited. Proud of his looks. *Vain*. The minute he was in the car and pulled off the ski mask—they both wore ski masks— what'd he do but pull out a comb. His hair's long, below the ears, black, straight, but with curves. Irish."

"Irish?"

"What they call *black* Irish, because of the hair. *Really* white skin. Also his hoodie was bright green. And it wasn't new or anything."

"Height?"

"About five-ten or maybe eleven. And the guy with the big ears, the driver? He needs glasses for distance. Put them on soon as he started the car. And they weren't sunglasses. Dumbo's got bad skin too. Acne." He paused and frowned at me, his brow puckered by the suspicion that I wasn't taking him seriously. "Shouldn't you be writing this down?"

"Later," I said. "Anything else?"

"Oh sure. They're from here. Boston, I mean. Revere or Everett, I'd say." He looked over furtively to see if he were pushing it too hard. "Maybe Chelsea, Charlestown."

"They spoke?"

"The one who wasn't driving, pretty hockey boy, yelled at Dumbo. *Move yah ass, retahrd. Come awn. Let's get a fuck outta heah.*" It did sound like Revere. "Also, I think it's not their first robbery, but *is* probably their first bank job."

"How's that?" said good, slow Doctor Watson.

"Well, first, don't you have to work your way up to a bank job? Second, because they weren't nervous enough but also they weren't *not* nervous, if you know what I mean. And then there's the guns. Handguns. Black ones."

"What about the guns?"

"Not loaded."

"Why do you say that?"

"Because they both just tossed them in the back of the van with the loot. Chucked them in. Well, you wouldn't do that with a *loaded* gun, would you? *I* wouldn't."

"You wouldn't, eh?"

"Look," he said as I started to get to my feet.

I sat back down. "Fire away."

He was desperate to keep me there. I was glad to oblige. "Okay. Where's your partner?"

"Went home sick this morning."

"Hangover?"

I didn't reply.

"So . . . what *kind* of detective are you?"

I laughed. "Not bad."

He exploded with hilarity, spewing air. "No. I mean what *rank*. Sergeant, lieutenant, or captain?"

"Lieutenant," I said. I took out my badge, which he looked at the way a radiologist does an MRI. Then he nodded and handed it back.

"You know what *lieutenant* means?"

"Tell me."

"It's French for place-holder. Like *God's lieutenant on earth*, which is what kings used to claim they were."

"You don't say." I stood up. So did Paul.

He wouldn't let me go. He grabbed at my arm. "Only two more questions. Okay?"

"Why not? You're already suspended."

"Are you, uh, married?"

"No. Not any more."

He nodded, all compassion and sadness, bowed his head like a skinny little Buddha accepting the tragic nature of life and gave my ex-marriage a couple seconds of respectful silence.

"Last question. Got any cigarettes?"

I drove him home. It was just three blocks, second floor of a triple-decker on Dana Avenue. I took him to the door and knocked. Nobody there.

"Told you," he said with satisfaction.

"Phone your mother as soon as I leave."

The boy crossed his arms. "Not supposed to. Unless it's an emergency and this isn't an emergency. I told you, she's working."

"Tell her—" I stopped. His face was pleading, appealing, and appraising all at once. I gave in. It was too hard not to. Besides, I couldn't force him. "I shouldn't interview you unless your mother's there."

"Now this *is* an emergency," he said.

"Let's go," I sighed.

We didn't even leave a note.

On the way to the station on Pingtree we passed by Saint Aloysius Gonzaga School. He pointed it out. "The Temple of Learning," he said.

The trip to the station proved unnecessary. Garcia, behind the desk, motioned me over when we got there and told me that the perpetrators of the great Hyde Park Bank Job were already in custody, the money recovered. They hadn't even ditched the stolen van.

"Were their guns loaded?" I whispered.

Garcia looked at me funny. He shrugged. "Dunno. Check the report."

I put my finger to my lips and nodded toward the kid. "Who were they?"

"Pair of dirt bags from Everett, both had sheets, but nothing this ambitious."

"Thanks."

Paul's eyes were big, taking in everything he could, cops, posters. I escorted him into an interrogation room and wrote down his statement. He was having the time of his life. I took the report to be typed and got him a soda. He talked about his mother. "You'd like her," he said. When the statement was put in front of him he took his time poring over it. Finally, he signed it with a flourish, a victorious general putting his name to the surrender document after a jolly war, John Hancock mocking King George's myopia.

"When's your suspension over?" I asked, taking the paper from him. I would toss it later.

"Tomorrow. They never give you more than one day. Could become a habit."

"So, it's back to Saint Aloysius in the morning then."

He looked at me sideways. "You Catholic?"

"Not any more."

He laughed. "Just like being married."

I put my hands on the dented metal table and began to get up.

"You know anything about Saint Aloysius Gonzaga?"

"Nope."

He gazed up past me, and recited: "*I am a crooked piece of iron and am come into religion to be made straight by the hammer of mortification and penance.* Nobleman's son, our Aloysius. Dad didn't like the whole religious vocation bit but Mom loved it, as you can imagine. At nine little Aloysius vowed himself to perpetual virginity and, according to both Sister Rose Emelda and Bishop Butler, was spared by a special grace from any fleshly temptation. In Rome he volunteered to look after the sick during a plague, caught the fever, kicked the bucket at twenty-three. Irresistible role model, right? Sister thinks so."

I'm ashamed to say I was thinking about how Aloysius might have benefited from being "made straight" in another way and about how it's always the saints who have the worst consciences, how sensuality and asceticism aren't opposites, about Paul's defiance of Sister Rose Emelda which I found I admired.

On the way back to Dana Avenue he was jumpy, twisting and bouncing.

I pulled over and turned to him. "What's the matter?"

He looked at me, looked away, rubbed at his pants. "I had a pretty good time today."

"I'm glad."

"I mean *really* good."

"You'd make a fine detective."

He shot a fluorescent grin at me. "Think so?"

"They caught the robbers."

"They *did*? So .. ?"

"I told you I'm not allowed to interview you without a parent present."

He considered. "So then, why did you?"

I gave the child a childish answer. "Because."

He nodded. "Where were they from?"

"Everett. First bank job."

"Ha! *Told* you."

"Yep. That you did."

"Want to meet my mother?"

"What?"

"Want to meet my *mother*?"

I started up the car.

"She's beautiful. She's smart. Patient too. I mean she puts up with me, doesn't she? You'd really like her. She's voluptuous."

"What?"

"*Voluptuous.*"

I knew I shouldn't but I asked anyway. "What about your father?"

"Unfortunately dead. He was biking. Teenage girl hit him. She wasn't texting or anything, just a bad driver. Five years ago. I can hardly remember him." The closer we got to his house the faster he talked. "Mom has to work two jobs. The second one—waiting tables at Cherrystones on weekends—that's to keep me at Saint Aloysius but she won't admit it. *Ironic*, huh? Anyway, the seafood's pretty good there, I mean at Cherrystones. You know, I think if I had only about a thousand dollars I could turn it into a *million* doing foreign currency trades; I mean, I've looked into it and it's not all that hard. But I'm only eleven and a half and they won't even let me have a job as a busboy. It's *legal* for Mom to work *two* jobs but I can't do even *one*." He blew a raspberry at the Law.

"You're on your own a lot?"

"I guess."

"So—what do you do?"

"I read. I get into trouble at school. I witness bank robberies."

"Why were you suspended?"

"You won't believe me."

"Everett," I said dryly.

"Okay. It was for hitting Warren Lynch."

"Why'd you hit Warren Lynch?"

He crossed one thin leg over the other, the raconteur settling in. "Lynchie's not a bad kid, really. We're more or less friends, in fact. I was just stopping him from picking on this shrimp, Carl. Calling him stuff like dork and gay and shoving him around the schoolyard. I *asked* him to stop, asked him nicely *twice*, but he wouldn't so I hit him."

By now I was pulled up outside the house but Paul was happy to keep on talking, even about his sins.

"So all of these suspensions of yours are for fighting?"

"Oh no. This is the first one for that. It's usually for ticking off Sister Rose Emelda."

"You got something against her?"

He shrugged. "Suppose I must."

I pointed at the house. "Time for me to be off. Thanks for all your help, Mr. Hanley." I held out my hand.

He didn't want to shake it, not yet. "Want to come in?"

"Sorry. Have to get back to work. Crime waits for no man. So long. Take care. Thanks again."

As he was getting out he said, "You're not going to tell my mother about this. I mean we got a deal, right?"

"When would I do that?"

"When you come to dinner," he said with a leprechaun's grin. Then he jumped out of the car and slammed the door.

Paul Hanley may or may not have been a prodigy, but he was nothing if not persistent. He called the station and left messages for me. *Tell him this is his star witness and I may clam up unless he meets me halfway.* That was a good one. Even better: *Tell him this is Hanley and I've got a line on something big going down at Cherrystones so he'd better call back.*

Over the next couple of weeks I drove down Dana Avenue a few times when I was alone, going off duty. I told myself it was more or less on my way home, which was a two-bedroom apartment in West Roxbury, far larger than I needed; the phrase *rattle around in* sometimes occurred to me. Paul's block had no kids playing in the street. There were old people inching up and down the sidewalk with plastic bags pulling their arms down like plumb-bobs. Could have been a few punks on the block, judging from the beat-up Camaro and Trans-Am and a pair of Harleys but I never saw them.

One afternoon I spotted Paul letting himself in. He had to put down about a dozen books to get his key out. I honked.

He spun around, squinted, shouted "Hey!" and ran down the steps. You'd have thought I was a Christmas tree on Christmas morning.

I didn't get out of the car, or turn the engine off, just rolled down the window. "How's it going, Mr. Hanley?"

"Well, actually, kind of dull. Didn't get suspended the whole of last week or this one, so far. Haven't seen even one bank job."

"Sounds boring."

He rolled his eyes. "You get my messages? You didn't call back so I'm asking."

I tapped the steering wheel. "You shouldn't do that."

"*I* know I shouldn't. *Obviously*. It's a risk/reward thing. So look, you want to come in?"

"On my way home."

One hundred watts dwindled to twenty-five. "Oh." Then he said cunningly, "Well, if you're off duty then I don't see why you can't come inside. You know, just for a minute."

I had to admire how the kid used logic like a battering ram.

"Come on. I'll show you some Edith Fevriers," he said. He pronounced the name in the French style—*Aydit*, as in Piaf.

"What?"

"Aw, come on. You'll see why I get suspended so often."

The apartment was attractive, homey and very clean. It smelled good—a woman smell I remembered. There was a large and, in my opinion, very interesting painting over the beige couch. Inside a frame of light oak a woman in a fringed vest reclined on another couch, a gray one, beside a small blue radiator. The empty floor and walls were yellow, separated by curved red lines that somehow made the whole thing balance, even though the woman and the couch were squeezed all the way on the right. It shouldn't have balanced, yet it did. Some trick of geometry I couldn't figure out. The furniture and rugs weren't expensive, but everything looked all right. I spotted a photograph in a silver frame on the mantel. A smiling man with olive skin and dark, wavy hair.

"He looks Italian but he wasn't," said Paul.

I went over to the round oak table and put down the books I'd carried in for Paul. They didn't look like kids' books. One was on genetics; there was a history of the Dark Ages and a heavy biography of Theodore Roosevelt. I was amused to see among them *The Casebook of Sherlock Holmes*.

Meanwhile Paul was pulling out an album. "Here's a picture of my mom."

I saw where he got the red hair.

"It's recent," he assured me as if I might think he was pulling a fast one. "Want something? Coke? Mom keeps iced tea in the fridge. Home-made."

"No, thanks. I'm fine."

He headed for the kitchen. "Suit yourself. I'm having an iced tea."

"Who's Edith Fevrier?" I called after him.

"Wait a minute."

I heard the refrigerator door open, ice clinking against a glass, the door shut, then open, then shut again.

"Mmm," he said, sipping as he went over to the door where he'd dropped his backpack. He put his glass down on the floor and began fishing around inside.

"Sister Rose Emelda is, as you might have guessed, Old School. We're in a war."

"A war?"

"Well, that's what I'd call it. A war of national liberation, a war that you get after a declaration—you know, of independence. I'm the Ewoks; she's the Empire." He stood up with a fistful of papers. "I drive her nuts. Half the time I don't even try."

"Why?"

"If she were any kind of teacher at all, I wouldn't. But she isn't, so I do. I got on fine with Sister Alberta last year and Mrs. Halloran the year before. Honest. But Rose Emelda's out to get me. One time she got me suspended for talking in class even though it was actually Marsha Venanzi. I didn't mind taking the blame but it *was* kind of insulting. I can't wait for my voice to change."

"How about your grades?"

He waved the silly question off in a way that said his A's were straight. "It's just memorization, pretty much. Here." He peeled off the top paper and handed it to me.

It was a mimeographed exercise sheet.

Grade 6-A   Sister Rose Emelda

WEEKLY VOCABULARY DRILL

Use each of the following words in a sentence.

Encumbered	Obstreperous
Anxieties	Emporium
Disport	Meander
Oblivious	Amorous
Languid	Paltry

Next to this surprising list of words in a tight, copybook hand was written, in bright red: *Paul Hanley, this simply will not do. It is not acceptable. See me at the end of the day. Sr. R.E.*

Below, in his big John-Hancocky hand, Paul had written:

Edith Fevrier, lonely but encumbered by few anxieties, meandered through the Jardin des Tuileries, oblivious of the disporting children in sailor suits, the amorous young couples tangled on the grass, the languid, gossiping nursemaids, until at last she came to the chair upon which sat the man who had begged her to meet him, the obstreperous Monsieur Jules Lussac, proprietor of a paltry leather-goods emporium in Montparnasse.

I handed it back with a rueful look.

"I didn't actually get suspended for that one. I read the directions and told Sister that, so far as I could see, I'd fulfilled the assignment. I also gave her definitions of all the words, including *proprietor*."

"Still," I said.

He handed me another exercise sheet. On this one Sister Rose Emelda had written, again in red and bearing down somewhat harder, *Paul Hanley, you are insufferable. You are to give this exercise sheet to your mother and let her read what I've written.*

This time the words were:

Anteroom	Beget
Choleric	Decibels
Ferrous	Glabrous
Harlequin	Correspondent
Advocate	Remonstrate

Paul had written:

*Edith Fevrier patiently waited her turn in the lawyer's ante-
room where she could hear the ferrous tip of the glabrous harlequin's
walking-stick as he paced the floor, raising his choleric voice to many
decibels as he remonstrated with his advocate that he did not beget
the child of Madame de Meuble and so should not be a correspondent in her husband's divorce action, no matter what she claimed.*

"That one got me grounded," said Paul proudly, handing over
another sheet. "Here's the one that got me suspended."

Saturnine	Manifold
Vitriolic	Stentorian
Rhizome	Pullulate
Transmogrify	Orate
Iniquity	Abominable

*Edith Fevrier was shocked by her son's saturnine teacher as she
orated her vitriolic sermon in stentorian tones, her distaste for her
charges pullulating like a rhizome through the ranks of desks, her
transmogrified countenance turning ever more rubicund as she
accused them of manifold abominable iniquities.*

It wasn't easy to keep from smiling. "She *is* a nun," I observed.

Paul favored me with a disappointed look over the top of
his iced tea glass. "I don't object to her vocation," he said. "The
vocation's fine, but not the *education.*" He paused for another sip,
then added, "You sound like my mother."

"Your mother—?"

"Yeah, my mother." He bounced up from the couch spilling

a little tea on his shirt which, speaking rapidly as he was, he ignored. "Look, I want you to do something. I want you to go to Cherrystones Saturday night. You're free, aren't you? You could take somebody if you wanted but I want you to go and just *look* at her, at my mom. You've seen her picture now, the red hair and all, so it'll be easy to pick her out, even if you don't get one of her tables. You could sort of, you know, *reconnoiter*."

Reconnoiter. Sister Rose Emelda could have been proud of her pupil's vocabulary. Should have been.

"I don't know," I said in a slow-motion verbal stumble.

Paul didn't in the least mind making me uncomfortable. As an eleven-year-old without boundaries he relished it. Discomfiting grown-ups was, after all, just one of his talents.

"Order the baked scallops," he recommended.

I am a man whose divorce was more amicable than his marriage. Captain Connor tried to cheer me up when the news got to him. *Sorry to hear it. Shit, it's more common than flat feet around here.*

What kind of men go to restaurants alone, especially on Saturday nights? Pathetic ones. Sad and forlorn ones.

I did go to Cherrystones, to my own amazement, and even ordered the scallops. I looked out for Paul's mother and watched her work. I could see she was a good waitress. She was obviously tired and the uniform wasn't exactly flattering—nevertheless, all the same, notwithstanding . . . well, and so on.

The following Tuesday Garcia brought me a square cream-colored envelope with my name on it in fancy script. With something between a grin and a sneer, he let me know it had been hand-delivered by my "star witness."

Paul had splurged on the stationery and worked hard on the calligraphy. The paper was thick, the color of melted coffee ice cream. The language was direct, formal, and brooked nothing so uncouth as a refusal.

The pleasure of your company is
requested at dinner on Sunday.
Any time after four p.m.
45 Dana Avenue, Second Floor
No R.S.V.P. required

At the last minute, as I imagined, he had scrawled a post-script in his familiar handwriting:

This invitation is from me but it wouldn't hurt to bring something.

Well, a boy loves his mother that much, what could I do?

LAR

MY father placed him in a sort of bird cage, flush with the wall just outside the bathroom. For Father this was at eye level but for me the location was exalted. Even as a child I was a little dubious about this god who seemed small and in danger of shattering, however high. He was rather chubby and thoroughly bald; he looked like a grocer in an exotic robe. The god stared over my head straight at the opposite wall on which nothing ever happened. I thought he must be terribly bored. Even I could see he was fashioned out of clay, not badly made, but still of clay.

Father would give the god a nod on his way into the bathroom and another on the way out. These nods were casual rather than ceremonial or reverent. Without making a fuss about it, he let me know he approved of my doing the same. As it pleased me at that age to please Father, I too nodded and even tried to do it with a sort of conviction. When I was little I assumed every house had one of these gods, perhaps even the same god, and that nodding outside the bathroom was normal. For some months I believed that something might go wrong in the bathroom if I neglected to acknowledge the god, such as being sucked down the bathtub drain or flushed down the toilet. I quickly realized this was childish.

"Where's your god?" I asked my friend Victor the first time I was permitted to visit his house. "In heaven, idiot," he said. "Not outside the bathroom?" Victor punched my arm and we went into his room to play. Later, when I asked to use the bathroom, it felt odd not to nod, and so I did, furtively and to nothing. That night I asked my father to tell me about the god. "He looks just like your great-grandfather," was all he said, as if that covered the matter. "But what does he *do*?" I wanted to know. "He protects us," said Father. I wanted to know how he protected us and what from, but Father never explained how the clay figure that looked just like my great-grandfather protected us or from what.

If only I had had a brother or sister, especially an older one, then I could have shared the god and whatever protection he was providing. I imagine us hugging the god to us, our special secret. Father, to my chagrin, made no secret of the god. All of his friends knew about the statue. I had seen the way they gave mocking nods as they went to relieve themselves during a card game. I was embarrassed because they were humoring my father. I imagined them entertaining their families with stories about their crazy friend and his son.

Only once did I hear my father speak to the god. I had been asleep for some time and so, I thought to myself, it must be the middle of the night. The middle of the night fascinated me; it was something I had never seen. The middle of the night was a secret time so it made sense that it was then that Father spoke to the god outside the bathroom. I woke up and heard his voice, crept out of bed, crouched by the door, peeked into the hallway. The light was dim but I saw Father still in his white shirt leaning with one arm against the wall, his mouth close to the little cage. His voice was so low I couldn't make out anything he said. So, as children do, I listened for the music beneath the words: anger, love, suspicion, joy, anxiety, despair. I decided my father must be asking the god's advice about something important, something to do with money, or with me. It seemed reasonable to me that Father should ask the god's advice. After all, I deduced, the god existed for us, not vice versa, and if the god's only reason for being was to protect us, then his advice was bound to be sensible.

The next morning I thought it best not to mention my spying to Father. Instead, I asked with what I thought was nonchalance just how powerful our god was. "He can't change the weather or the results of football games," said Father in that brusque way he had, especially over breakfast. Whatever he told me about the god, something was always lacking so I understood things as best I could. For example, I understood that our god was, so to speak, a personal matter, our god and nobody else's, and this seemed to me at once comforting and disappointing. However, it was hardly in line with the official monotheism about which I had picked up a good deal at school. That afternoon I looked up the Ten Commandments in the encyclopedia and was startled by the first one. "Thou shalt have no other gods before me." This was ambiguous. It could mean there are no other gods but also that there *are* others, just that they are only secondary ones. It was all right to have your own god so long as you didn't over-estimate him.

That night I asked my father, "Can he do miracles?" Father was only half paying attention and replied, "I suppose that depends on what you mean by a miracle." I persisted. "Well, how about getting a test all right when you haven't studied?" Father just made a face at me over his coffee mug. Maybe he doesn't know, I thought. So the next time I had a test I deliberately didn't study for it but tried asking the god for an A+. It didn't work. I was angry but concluded that tests must be like weather and football games and that our god, being of the second rank, wasn't all that powerful. He might be *a* god, but certainly not *the* god, the one who comes before all others. Years later I was reminded of this in college when an irreverent guy I knew showed up in my room one night claiming he could prove he was God. "Go ahead," I said with a sigh. "Well, whenever I pray I always wind up talking to myself." Childishness can express itself as disbelief as readily as belief, but, in either case, childishness always wants miracles. I suppose it's in the nature of a child to want the law suspended. To blame a clay god is childish. What is adult is to blame yourself.

Mostly, though, I didn't think about the god at all. He was simply another fixture, like a lamp or a chair, far less important than the television or the car, which actually did things. He was like another picture hanging on the wall. As I grew older and taller the god came closer but this didn't increase my interest in him or my respect. Still, there were moments when I couldn't help noticing him. I remember one afternoon when I fantasized a whole society of such gods, each protecting its own household, each devoted to a single family. But these families were bound to compete, I figured, to come into conflict. What then? Wouldn't the tensions of the ordinary world simply be duplicated in the divine realm? *The divine realm*—what a misleading phrase, because the whole point about a household god is that there is no such thing as the divine realm, that the godly isn't distant but nearby, not sublime but commonplace. By then I had learned more about what people believed and knew this wasn't conventional theology. My father's cage enclosed what some would dismiss as a superstition and others condemn as paganism.

Ours was a relentlessly masculine household. My mother

was never spoken of; it was one of our tacit rules. It was just my father, myself, and the bald god in the cage. Few women ever came to our house and none stayed long: my aunt, a cousin once, on rare occasions the wives of my father's friends. As I began to grow up I realized how isolated and confining our routines were. Our big events were few and unimaginative, a day at the aquarium, an afternoon of bowling, a movie matinée. We never traveled or paid visits. My social life was centered at school and, as my adolescence dawned, I craved more of it. I began to notice girls and, to my delight, some of them noticed me back. Notes were passed, messages whispered. The world was suddenly full of ineffable promise, brighter sunshine, greener grass. But I was shy and clumsy. This is why I blurted something to Marcia Rogers about our god. It wasn't so much to make myself more interesting but simply to say something. She wanted to see him immediately. It wasn't difficult to arrange; I merely had to get her into and out of the house before my father got home from work. Still, I was hesitant. My reluctance had less to do with the little cage outside the bathroom than with the prospect of being alone in the house with Marcia Rogers. At some level I felt this was just the sort of situation from which I needed protecting and not only was the chubby deity not protecting me, he was the occasion of my needing to be protected.

Marcia took charge, suggesting we arrange things for Friday after school. She would skip band practice and I would sneak her into the house. I prayed that Mrs. Przbyl and Mrs. Thomas wouldn't see us and decided to use the back door. I succeeded. Marcia was excited and, as soon as the door closed behind us, began to giggle. The next thing she did was order me to kiss her. "But," I stammered pathetically, knowing I would never forget this humiliation, "what about—?" The kiss was sudden and while not a triumph it wasn't a fiasco either. Marcia had evidently been preparing, had given thought to a sort of physics I'd never contemplated. "Good," she announced triumphantly, pushing me away. "Now you're my boyfriend. It's official. Okay, where is he?"

She took my hand and I led her upstairs to the hallway. Marcia on tiptoe looked into the cage, put her finger fetchingly to her lip, but the moment she opened her mouth I knew she wasn't the girl for me. "But he's so *cute*," she squealed.

What did I want? What had I hoped for? I hardly knew. Years later, when I was really in love, I found the answer the moment it was given. She was named Leda, a fine classical name. Leda and I were together for a whole year in college and, when things looked serious, she even came for a visit. She dumped me soon after, it's true, but that was well after the night she got up from our clutching on the couch to go to the bathroom. My mind was not on the god. "Come here," she called down from the landing. "What's this?" I shrugged and smiled nervously. "Our household god," I said apprehensively. "A household god," she breathed. "What could be better?"

During my time at college I had two dreams about the god. The first was during April of my sophomore year. I was not faring well. My grades were down, my social life had yet to begin, I had a lingering head cold, I couldn't decide on a major, and my father had had his first heart attack. The college girls had emerged from the long winter like so many flowers, in shamelessly short skirts. I took to wearing a necktie to hold my head on. In this first dream I stood before the little cage, eye to eye with the statue. I denounced the god, called him feck-less, declared I'd never believed in him, that to believe was itself a form of stupefaction. He let me go on using my fancy new vocabulary, listened impassively even to my threat to pulverize him, then he took a bar of his cage in one little fist and pulled his face right up to mine. This startled me into silence. When he spoke his mouth didn't move. "You're not entirely wrong," he said in a surprisingly high, mild voice. "Belief is often a kind of sleepwalking. Your not being sure of what to believe has always kept you alert. It's what I like best about you." I awoke feeling comforted.

The second dream came in my senior year and was even stranger. This time I approached the god reverently, looking up, as I had when still a child. I told him I needed his advice, pleaded for it, in fact. My father had had his second attack. He was dying and I was about to graduate. My grades were impec-cable and my needs were great but Leda had just dumped me.

In the dream the god spoke verses at me, gnomic couplets. I asked him to repeat them and when I woke I wrote down what I could remember:

> *Let those in, but stay outside;*
> *close the door, but not too wide.*

> *Bestir yourself while you're at rest;*
> *your worst is better than your best.*

> *Beware the patch around the hole;*
> *you're well-heeled now, save for your soul.*

The car's gassed up, the sky's bright blue;
the clock runs backwards, three to two.

One meal a day makes not a fast;
the unstruck match is made to last.

Leave rooms that cough, they seethe with germs;
fish you can catch are full of worms.

You'd have two legs if you could dance;
don't wear a skirt beneath your pants.

Endure the weather, bear the news;
forget the church but clean the pews.

Let people in after you go;
if they say yes, then you say no.

I still have the page of notebook paper on which I scribbled this down. What can I say? What the god said seemed full of meaning but without sense whereas my life struck me as sensible enough but without meaning. I suppose what I wanted was for the god to point the way for me, yet this wish was only a kind of wavering.

A short paragraph in my father's will is devoted to "the statuette that hangs beside the bathroom door," a neutral, unmetaphysical designation that told me something of my father's caution. Since he had left everything to me, with his attorney as executor, the paragraph was superfluous and must have baffled the lawyer in much the way I had once puzzled Victor. Father's last word on the matter of our little god was a solemn command. He wrote that, as his legatee and beneficiary, his wish was that I make this object my particular care, placing it safely in my current and all future domiciles, and, upon my own death, pass it on to any issue I might produce. The language was as stunning as the presumption.

"An heirloom?" asked the curious attorney after reading me the paragraph.

"Not exactly." I saw no reason to spare the lawyer my candor. "My father believed—or at least he always told me—this statue was our household god, a graven image in the likeness of his grandfather."

The man looked at me disapprovingly over his reading glasses. It was precisely what I wanted, that look.

I did keep the statue but not the cage, which I've replaced with a glass box. I have affixed it to the wall outside my bathroom; nowhere else seemed quite right. I look at him from time to time, my impotent protector. While I cannot overcome my irony, my alertness, I suppose I've come to believe what Leda said, though with an amendment. There's nothing better than a household god except a household god in which you believe or, what is almost the same thing, a god who believes in you.

KOLWITZER'S FATHER

1.

THE day they announced the Prize I downloaded a photograph of Nathan Mullhorn. In this picture Mullhorn appears every inch the shrewd captain of industry he was, sleek and predatory, hardly at all the philanthropist he likewise was. The old plutocrat is seated behind a mammoth desk looking up imperiously, as if at a secretary he'd just summoned. With a green felt-tip I drew a heap of cash on the desk, dollars tumbling to the floor like rose petals. "Cecilia, send in Kolwitzer," I wrote underneath and pasted the picture over the label of a bottle of Veuve Clicquot. Before heading downtown the following morning I phoned work and announced I'd be late.

It was around nine when I buzzed Kolwitzer. I figured he would probably have been up late celebrating, might even have stood drinks for his bohemian pals in one of the funkier East Side bars. It took a while before he let me in. Robert had always been a late riser. Back in our sophomore year he'd given me a key to his dorm room so that I could wake him up for final examinations. He didn't mind sleeping through classes or midterms.

Kolwitzer regarded nothing about the body as trivial and at the age of eighteen was already spinning off theories to justify his habits. "The body has its proper rhythms," he'd lecture in the apodictic tone he affected even then. "It's always a capital error to violate them, invariably a form of self-betrayal, particularly for the artistic temperament. The Industrial Revolution made people perform by clock and calendar instead of sun and season. The systematic damage is incalculable. Why else should population have increased geometrically and good art barely arithmetically? Sleep's a great general and should issue orders, not obey them." Robert would deliver these lecturettes mock-professorially; perhaps he was lampooning his father. Anyway, what was notable wasn't that he liked doing as he wished but his insistence on giving reasons. I suppose this was part of what fascinated me about him, along with his unpredictability. Robert was apt to launch an analysis of anything, from a classmate's gait to the national debt. As we walked around the city he would do things like break into a Gershwin tune (complete with tap dance), declaim Aristophanes, or criticize the hexameters of Arthur Hugh Clough. At eighteen Robert was a young man with a narrow, intense face and hair that, like what was under it, seemed to be flying off in all directions. Yet he could also be stiller than still, a ruminative spider pondering profundities in the middle of an infinite web. I've never known anyone as purely *alert* as Robert Kolwitzer. He made me feel like Dr. Watson, two steps behind and anxious about his sanity, but neither jealous of his talents nor displeased to be commonplace.

Robert was wearing sweatpants and a T-shirt. He wasn't sleepy but rather exhilarated, maybe even a little manic. He grabbed my bottle of champagne and laughed and laughed at the label.

"Wonderful! Fucking brilliant!" He gave me a hug, something he'd never done before, not even when I'd loaned him money.

"Well, you're obviously pleased with yourself," I said.

Robert threw himself down on the open sofa-bed. "Pleased with myself, eh? So you think I'm delighted because I'm a success?"

"Well, *aren't* you? I mean officially?"

"An official success? Not at all. I'm like the French Revolution. Remember what Chou En-Lai said when he was asked whether it had been a success? He said, 'Too soon to tell.'"

"Well, there's *some* proof. There's the cash."

"Ah, yes." He rubbed his hands together greedily.

The Mullhorn Prize is given annually to "a young artist of promise," as the great benefactor's will puts it. The selection is organized by the Mullhorn Foundation and transpires completely in the passive voice. Nominations are solicited, deliberations carried out, a decision reached. The panel never meets; no member knows the identity or even the number of his or her colleagues. The final decision is proclaimed at the end of March and received by a more or less interested world. The prestige of the Mullhorn Prize is owing to the quality of its past recipients—which is to say its predictions—but just as much to its mysteriousness which is perceived as proof against politicking and gives each year's announcement the character of a papal election. Certainly, the choice of Robert Kolwitzer was a bolt from the heavens. Even I, a humble laborer in the venal vineyards of Wall Street, could come up with a dozen more accomplished candidates. But Robert had done a lot of different things, done them well and, what's more, had provided cheeky interviews about them. Journalists liked him not because he was cooperative or forthcoming but because people wanted to read his interviews.

When asked to describe the intention behind his theater-piece *Oedipus at Coney Island* he called it "a defensive action so retrograde that it looks avant-garde. It's conceived as an entertainment aimed at the next stage of evolution. The idea came from a box of Cheerios. *Oedipus* simply states yet again that the original sin is the conviction that the original sin was committed against us. *Non aequus est* is a gripe that rolls down all the ages, renewed by every generation of three-year-olds. Why put the Cyclone on stage? Formalism. Roller coasters and dramas are both structured in accord with the male sexual response. Every decent thrill-ride requires a build-up just as a revelation demands a prior concealment. A climax is just a climax, but a falling action isn't always an ending." And so forth. Mystifying, allusive, disconnected but always amusing.

Robert once confessed to me what he desired from his audience. "I want people to say *out loud*, 'Look how easy it is for him to knock that outhouse together' but I want them to say *to themselves* that it must be pretty hard to knock together an outhouse like *that*."

Robert Kolwitzer's maiden gallery show was a gallimaufry, a declaration of scope. There was a startling sculpture of a thoughtful, emaciated corpse which he called *Professor Golovin, Carcinomatotic*, a wittily fantastic installation he titled *Miniature-Golf Hole Devised by an Inebriated Pythagorean*. There were four small paintings in distinct genres and styles: a photo-realistic portrait of an exceedingly old woman, a neo-classical landscape with a punk band in the foreground, a post-Impressionist still-life with rotting fruit, and a vaporous abstract that recalled the way Turner painted weather but, somehow, without the moisture. In fact, Robert called these collectively *Four Pictures From A World Without Atmosphere*. The chief work was a mural daubed right on the gallery's largest wall. This piece, *Susannah and the Elders*, attracted the most comment not only owing to its size but because it was thought to be political, which, as they say, "excited considerable comment." I don't doubt the effect was shrewdly calculated by Robert; he always calculated shrewdly, though without being petty or self-seeking in the ordinary sense. ("I'm far too ambitious to settle for money and fame," he once told me.) The mural showed about a dozen "elders" leering at the viewer but no Susannah at all –an unsettling conceit but hardly an obscure one. The political angle derived from the repellent aspect of the elders, their dress, and what, apart from unpleasantly ogling into the viewers' space, they were doing with their hands. Scientists, men in business suits, generals, computer geeks—all were assembling what looked like fanciful weapons, passing money, and stepping on severed limbs. ("People ask you how you think the world's going," Robert explained. "It's generally smart to tell them—*bad*!")

Robert may not have been quizzed about the world but he was asked what he was *trying to say* in this mural and, disgusted by the phrase, replied with a brick wall of language. "Trying? To say? The most profoundly political, authentically apocalyptic art is invariably the most a-political. Like Camus, I'm way too patriotic to be a nationalist; like Dostoyevsky, I think civilization's only achievement is to increase the range of sensation. My ambition isn't to make social comments but to be a pane of glass. The meaning of any artistic act floats about, declaring its independence from the intention behind it, especially *the intent of the studio*, so to speak. *Intent* is indispensable, intention superfluous. The former's a motivation, like hunger, the latter like a menu or, better, a restaurant review. In my opinion, intent is no proof of intention. The ideal work of art would be one sustained on style alone yet no such ideal can or will ever exist. Ideals, like rock crystals, are boring, inanimate, and dead. Just think—what if *you* worked for a newspaper in Heaven? What would there be to write about? Don't you agree?"

Robert was fond of ending interviews with challenging, rhetorical questions. Unnerving interviewers delighted him. He recognized no distinction between creation and destruction, so long as neither claimed to be "pure." He thought the phrase "constructive criticism" oxymoronic and saw critics as parasites. On the other hand, among a gaggle of whining artist friends I once heard him quote with approval a Mexican writer who complained his nation suffered from having millions of superb poets but not a single decent critic.

"So," I said, "last night? A crowd of sycophants parade you on their shoulders through the East Village?"

Robert rolled over on his bed and put his hands behind his head.

"As a matter of fact, there *was* something of a mob," he admitted. "After an hour I sent them away. I thanked them but said giving prizes to artists was like giving awards to mothers. Virtuosity in childbirth? Besides, what if the Assembly had given a prize to Socrates? What if Pilate had crowned Jesus with laurel rather than thorns?"

"Not very gracious of you. Or humble. Want *me* to go?"

"Not yet."

I checked my watch. "Too bad. I'm late for work."

He smiled. "Fair's fair. So am I."

"You know, no matter what you say you *do* sound happy."

He looked sideways at me with that wry, suspicious smile of his. His hair was mussed and he hadn't shaved. The studio was a mess, too small for everything that went on in it. "*La chambre fait l'homme*," he'd said the first time he showed it to me.

"Your father?" I asked carefully.

"Hasn't phoned."

Kolwitzer's father taught European history at Columbia University which is where his son and I met. "Tuition remission," Robert instructed me during our first dinner together as freshmen, "is a variety of nepotism." In my third year, much against Robert's wishes, I took a course with his father. It was titled simply "1848." Professor Kolwitzer was an erudite and intelligent man, in his teaching more thinker than scholar, not the sort to be reduced to crawling between lines of old texts. His lectures brought the revolutionary year to life; they were full of "for instances" and peopled with big boys like Mill, Marx, Metternich, and Manzoni. He spoke ardently of the students and workers at their barricades, of hopes dammed up since Waterloo bursting out in a kind of continent-wide lyricism of action. He made us listen to Verdi. His lectures could also be operatic. The professor was patient even with foolish questions but sharp with the lazy who didn't do the reading and downright sarcastic with those given to glib generalization. Robert had warned me that his father was a strict grader both in class and at home. "I believe it comes from living with ideas whose time is past," he said derisively. In fact, his father was a comparatively easy grader. I got an A-.

Robert took out a couple of wine glasses while I popped the Veuve Clicquot. Happy New Year.

"Champagne at nine-thirty in the a.m. Must be a first for you," he teased. It pleased Robert to pretend that I was strait-laced. Once, when I'd dared to reproach him for something he'd done that I considered nasty, he retorted that the greatest force for virtue in the universe was cowardice.

"The first time on a working day," I replied as I filled up our glasses.

"Quasi-touché."

I handed a glass to Robert and raised mine. "To this year's most promising young artist," I declared pompously. "So, what exactly are you promising?"

Once again, he laughed. "You'll see," he chortled. The prize seemed to have made him almost giddy. "No, no! Wrong toast." He cleared his throat. "To Nathan Reardon Mullhorn's millions and the philosopher's stone that transmutes commerce into art!"

We clinked. We drank.

"That stone works both ways," I cautioned. "Watch out that your art doesn't turn into commerce."

"My, my. You're quite *on* today, pal. Mm."

He gave me a rundown of who'd phoned, emailed, stopped by, and which of his friends had maintained a dignified silence. There was no further mention of his father the professor.

"It really is disconcerting," Robert philosophized, "to be

congratulated over and over for this Mullhorn thing. What are people so delighted about, anyway? Why do they beam down on me like fluffy clouds on the fair-haired lad? After all—"

I knew him of old and begged. "No dialectics, Robert."

"No, really. I mean is it for my past achievements or the greater accomplishments sure to come? I don't think so. Oswald Balisser nudged and winked away as if I'd pulled a fast one, diddled some brass out of the squire. Fred acted as if I'd just got laid. And speaking of the women, they looked at me the way traders do at an IPO. But, you know, what touched me most was what old Marcini said to me. You remember old Marcini, don't you?"

"Sure. Buzz cut, big sweater. Crusty old cuss."

"*Very* crusty. Survived *both* the Marine Corps *and* Citigroup. *Soi-disant* mentor to the young, self-appointed conscience to the middle-aged, darling of the rich, and neo-classicist to all."

"When did old Marcini show up?"

"He swelled the early throng. 'Robert,' he said, big arm over these ectomorphic shoulders, 'you've got to *do* something with this. It's time to stop playing the smart-ass teenager full of dreams and yearning to spite everybody. Dump the adolescent negative self-definition. Not that all that isn't a fine pose in its way. The alienated pubescent bourgeoisie is the backbone of high culture. But don't think for a minute you've *proved* anything to anybody you'd *care* to prove things to. It's put up or shut up now, kid.' After that the old lech got stinking drunk and felt up all the girls."

2.

ROBERT and I were mulling over an old classmate's engagement. "To become a husband and a father the one *sure* way," he said.

"Sure way?"

"To stop being a son."

Robert's death was senseless and seemed to confirm his view of things. I can picture him with a bitter smile pointing at my chest. "See? See? In a car, like Camus." Neither Camus nor Robert was driving. But there was a difference. Camus bought it in a flashy sports car, Robert in a grimy New York cab, crushed by a fire truck in a hurry.

The idea of calling on my friend's father, on my old professor, actually scared me. But it was one of those ideas you know you'll have to carry out. As soon as the notion took me I could already see myself sitting in his office, in the center of all those books, as if I were again a junior perplexed by Kierkegaard's feelings toward Bishop Mynster. When my own father died a couple of years after we graduated, Robert sent me some verses inside a particularly mawkish Hallmark card.

> To turn ache into consciousness,
> Find health inside the malady,
> Transmute defeat into success,
> Change death to immortality—

This is a culture's cruelest task.
Prometheus' gift to help us cope
Was to fashion an eyeless mask
And blot out sorrow with blind hope.

Mere alchemy can't refine lead;
Magic's a meretricious fake.
We must look to ourselves instead
And in shared grief some solace take.

Well, I wanted some of that brand of solace and could think of no one else from whom to get it but Professor Kolwitzer. And yet what Robert had done in that last month, the climax of two decades of twisted relations, made a condolence call feel impertinent. Knowing how close I was to his son, would the old man even see me? I couldn't just show up on his doorstep, could I?

Of course I had seen Professor Kolwitzer at the funeral, which had been generic and perfunctory. This was apparently the way the professor wanted it, since he'd made the arrangements. He himself didn't speak. The affair was held at a suburban funeral home. Such as it was, the eulogy was delivered by a childish man who identified himself as the family's Unitarian minister. ("Their *one* is so very, very close to *zero*," Robert had once quipped about his religious education.) I couldn't recognize my friend in the speech: nice boy, good student, loving son, terrible loss. Wham, bam. Not a word about his work. I mean the deceased could have been anybody, even me.

After this inanity I joined the line filing by Professor Kolwitzer. He looked old and unwell but stoical, an unapproachable figure who'd prepared himself to be approached. I kept thinking of this morbid Chinese proverb, "Happiness is when the grandfather dies, then the father dies, then the son dies."

When I phoned Professor Kolwitzer's office I half-hoped he wouldn't be there, that Columbia had sent him off on compassionate leave or something, that he was on a cruise to the tropics. When we were juniors and I was taking "1848," Robert had told me his father wasn't any good at vacations. "He's a complete homebody who'd rather read about a place than see it. The only form of social life my father can tolerate is teaching, where it's clear who's got the power. Once *that's* settled, my father can be as *charming* as you keep assuring me he is." When I asked why he didn't take a course with his father, Robert guffawed. "Oh, I couldn't ever take a course with him. That would be too cruel, even for me. Hell, it'd knock the old man for too much of a loop."

"Yes, of course I'll see you." The familiar voice sounded almost eager. "Actually, I think I ought to. I'm truly grateful to you for calling. I've been wandering around the house, you see, picking up his old things . . ." He trailed off as if he had disclosed too much. I made a note of this because the point of our meeting, at least to me, was precisely revelation. There was a lot I wanted to know. What really happened with Robert's mother? Why had my friend tried so earnestly to hurt his father? *Had* his father been hurt? It never occurred to me that my old teacher might wish to learn something from me.

He didn't want to meet either at school or at his home. "Some place neutral," he said.

"A bar?"

The place wasn't crowded. We took a booth. With a nervous

grin, the professor said it reminded him of Ivan Karamazov having it out with Alyosha.

I decided not to beat about the bush, certainly not Russian literary ones. "Tell me about Robert's mother."

"What did he tell you?"

I answered frankly. "He told me you drove her away."

He smiled faintly, nodded once, took a deep breath.

"When Robert was six my wife ran off with a man quite unlike me. You might say an anti-me." He paused to squirm. "Look, maybe my wife lacked a maternal instinct. I suppose it's just as possible that she changed her mind, her heart. In any case, our relationship began to go wrong the moment she found out she was pregnant. It shocked Leda, terrified and disgusted her. She bawled her eyes out that first night while I—well, I was completely over the moon and couldn't hide it. She saw this and got angry. I guess she offered silent prayers to Saint Spontaneous. She probably thought of an abortion but didn't have the nerve for it. I don't know. Perhaps at first she thought what I did, that her misery was just hormones or because of the surprise. Robert was what they call *unplanned*. I've had almost three decades to think about it but I still don't really know. In any case, Robert and I were *both* rejected. Inevitably, he mythologized her and her leaving, also her return. Leda had her own kind of nobility, though; once the papers were signed she never attempted to contact him or me again."

"Not even . . ."

"No, not even when he was killed. Not since either, if you're wondering. As for Robert, you could say he had his mother's pride. I mean that he was too proud to search her out. Yes, he was always terribly, terribly proud, just like her. Haughty. But it's also possible he was afraid to confront her and risk his precious mythology. Robert wasn't averse to taking risks, as I'm sure you know, but he needed to be in control of the risks he took. As a child he'd do dangerous things but only if they were *his* doing, climbing trees, biking in the rain, getting into the whiskey. In my opinion—I don't know about *yours*, of course—that's also the way he operated as an artist."

I had to admit that there was truth in this, that controlled risk-taking was part of what Robert thought an artist was supposed to do—to risk and to mythologize. He wanted his fate in his own hands. Well, everybody's concerned about their own fate, but how many consider that of their cab driver?

"What *did* Robert think about his mother?"

"He never talked to you about her? I'm surprised. And you his closest friend."

"It was usually *you* he talked about, Professor."

He nodded, again that wan little smile. "Robert was never what you would call whole-hearted. I expect that even as he was composing the romance about his mother he also knew it was—what?—a bubble? He preferred bubbles—his art—to life. Perhaps I was just a burster of bubbles. In history, as in physics, one ugly fact can explode the most beautiful theory. Robert wasn't a liar but he loved theories and despised facts. That's one reason why he was stuck in aesthetics, forging things and ideas but never really committing himself to either. In my opinion, that was his weakness as an artist. In the long run, either he'd have grown out of it or he'd have despaired. Perhaps that last month of his, his *mensis mirabilis*, might have been the turning-point. Robert was the most purely *intentional* person, wasn't he? Maybe that's what he had in mind, getting all sorts of things out of his system—above all *me*."

I noticed that almost everything he said about Robert was qualified, *probably* or *perhaps* or *maybe*. Robert himself spoke in this way only at his most whimsical. He'd make these little speculative essays into the nature of things. But more often he spoke in the opposite fashion, broadcasting *obiter dicta*, loving his theories, just as his father said, but believing them for about five minutes.

"You loomed large for him," I said tentatively.

The professor corrected me. "You understate matters," he said. "I had to make a tremendous effort not to argue with my son. This wasn't because we saw the world so differently—perhaps we even saw things much the same way. It was because from puberty, or even earlier, Robert battened on polemics as the most *dignified* way to speak to me, the one that bolstered his amour-propre. What I mean is that Robert argued with me *on principle*. He believed a son with anything in him *ought* to battle with his father. I know he didn't despise me, though at times I'm sure he hated me. Hatred is so close to love that you might almost think that the capacity for love is the prerequisite for hatred. Our war was a religious one, furious battles over little points of doctrine. No quarter for the infidel."

This reminded me of Robert's contempt for his father's Unitarianism. "Last Church of the Vanishing Lukewarm Christ," he called it. "It makes ethics the earth and religion a tiny moon."

"You say I loomed large for him. It was more than that. I

know. I was indispensable to him. I was all at once his subject, muse, and audience, the door against which he devoted his life to pushing. That he preferred this door to be shut saddened me because I wanted it open so much. I'd have gladly thrown it open the second he stopped pushing. Look, Robert knew perfectly well I was only his father, an ordinary man, but he insisted on casting me as the one and only gigantic Father. He abstracted and inflated me to suit his conception of himself. Who better to subvert than a father? He needed to be a victim, and who's more oppressive than a father? Above all, he needed to be heroic. From Zeus to Prince Hal, Freud to Luther, Scarlatti to Alexander the Great—all his heroes had despotic fathers to overcome."

"He *could* be cruel," I admitted.

"Oh, I don't complain; I don't even claim that he did me an injustice. If I can use a fancy metaphor I'd say that he willfully bent my love out of all recognition on the anvil of his ambition. He's dead and I'm not. *That's* all I want to complain about."

I could see the man was becoming carried away by his own words, by the feelings that overflowed them. I let him go on.

"You know, when the police came to tell me he was dead I didn't say anything. I was shocked but the *terrible* thing is that I wasn't surprised. I'd had these, these presentiments. I'd imagined his death even more often than I suppose he had mine. What's more, what *I* imagined was a *real* death whereas what *he* imagined was only imaginary, part of the story in which I'd driven away his mother and tyrannized over him."

Here he paused, waiting for me to say something. I had an odd recollection. "I was once on a streetcar with Robert. There was this woman tearing at her knitting. He pointed to her and said that his life was like that, that art is knitting and life just unravels it."

"Yes, that's just like him." He paused for a sip of tepid beer. "We did love each other but in a way the mathematicians call incommensurable. No common denominator. *My* love made me think about him; *his* made him think of himself. That's how it was, maybe how it always is with sons. I never thought of my own father's troubles, but he thought of mine. All I wanted was to be Robert's father, to *rejoice* in being his father. All *he* wanted was to be an artist. And to him to be an artist was to be in rebellion, and whatever he rebelled against *had* to be *me*."

He straightened up. "Now I have a few questions for you. First, I want to know about Robert's personal life. Were there women? Men? Nobody?"

"Nobody, as far as I know."

He nodded. "He had a distaste for the body. That's why he was obsessed with digestion. He didn't like bodies. Back in high school he wrote this term paper about digital technology and how it was going to make bodies obsolete, how it would translate personality into image. He thought that was wonderful. It was a kind of hygiene gone mad but he was prophetic. My students call a face-to-face conversation 'meat-mail.'"

"Robert told me that abstract painting was the artistic equivalent of genocide because for both the human body is an embarrassment, a sort of infestation of life. He said for the Greeks the body was not yet too corrupt to bear the weight of the ideal. He blamed Hegel."

"That's because I wrote my dissertation on Hegel."

"It's possible, I suppose."

"So no—lovers? None?"

I shrugged. I shook my head.

I was being discreet. Robert took seriously that anecdote about Balzac crying "There goes another novel!" each time he ejaculated into a mistress. His libido, like everything else, was tossed into the hopper of his art, sacrificed on its altar. Neither passion nor seed was to be wasted. "Nothing," he once told me, "makes me more furious than a wet dream." When I objected to so much self-denial Robert replied sharply that while *my* task might be to experience the human condition *his* was to illuminate it. "And they don't put the lights in the middle of Yankee Stadium," he said. "Anyway, sex leads to fatherhood. It's what it was *designed* for. The Big O's just life's cunning little way of tricking us into getting what *it* wants by making us think we're getting what *we* want. It's a mug's game."

The professor sighed.

"What else?"

"I guess I'd like to know what he meant to achieve, apart from slandering and destroying me. And I want to know if he was a good friend, whether he ever did anything at all unselfish."

"On the first one, I never really had a clue. As to the second, yes."

3.

WHAT his father called Robert's *mensis mirabilis* began on the very day of the Veuve Clicquot when he was interviewed by one of the savvy, patronizing blondes of morning television. Apparently someone had thought the Mullhorn Prizewinner would make good filler on a slow news day. They came to him; they wanted a location shoot in the prodigy's studio.

Blonde: So *this* is your studio, Robert? Excuse me, but it seems so *small*.

Robert: Infinite riches in a little room.

B: What?

R: In these matters, size doesn't count.

B (giggling uncomfortably): You're teasing me.

R (looking her over): Au contraire.

B (shaking her shoulders, jovial yet getting down to business): Well, congratulations.

R: For what?

B: (uncertain) Winning the prestigious Mullhorn Prize, of course.

R: I see. Have you considered it might be a clerical error?

B (with an edge now): Oh, come now, Robert. From what I hear, false modesty isn't in your line.

R: Dear Lady, I assure you false modesty is a thing to which I can only aspire. How about you? Are *you* modest?

B (aside and angrily): Cut! (to Robert) Look, you can have fun if you like but bear in mind that I can make you famous. I can also make you look like a total asshole.

R: That hardly seems a modest thing to say. Incidentally, I don't believe I caught your name?

B: I can leave right now.

R: Madam, suit yourself. I didn't invite you over in the first place. However, I wouldn't mind making a short statement to your loyal audience.

B (nonplused): A *statement*?

R: Challenge, actually. You should ask me what I'm going to do with the prize money. I thought that's why you were here. Following the money. By the way, would you like me to paint you? In costume it's two grand but nude would be gratis.

B (pissed off yet resigned): Turn the camera back on. So, Robert, what do you plan to do with the prize money? Get a bigger studio? Some decent clothes? A haircut?

R (to the blonde): Thank you for asking. (to the camera): I plan to use the money to produce four major works, all in different media, in one month—*this* month. That works out to one per week.

B: And the money?

R: Oh, most'll go for coffee, gambling, and bleached blondes, I figure. But I'll probably blow the rest on art supplies and renting out space. For what I have in mind, size *does* count.

I called Robert after seeing an edited version of this on TV the next morning. He told me what had been cut out.

"You're a slow worker," I warned him.

"Am not. In fact, I work so fast you can hardly see me doing it. I just take long breaks. If I skip the breaks I can do it easily, one hand tied behind my back, on my head."

"But why? Why *try?*"

"Why not? I'd like to make the Mullhorn panelists look good. I want to push myself. It's like having only fourteen lines to say something new about unrequited love. Look, just hang up on me, will you. I've got to get to work."

Robert rented a large third-floor space on Warren Street in a building that was about to be rehabbed. A big shot who'd bought a couple of his pictures put Robert in touch with the developers, a special deal. He could do whatever he wanted there for a month, but then he'd have to clear out.

Robert worked all the time, determined to transcend himself or flame out. He willed himself into a state of hyper-inspiration. He simply couldn't not produce. Never before had I gotten so many e-mails from him and most were not the usual updates or gossip but poems in prose or verse, most sent between 3 and 5 a.m. Here's a for instance:

Took an imaginary trip tonight. Went to a hotel in the Midwest, Cleveland or Chicago or some-place, and sat in the bar nursing my whiskey. Here's what it was like:

The piano in the bar unfolds note by
note its melancholic missive of
American regret, insouciance
of deep sofas, Old Spice and Shalimar.

Somewhere inside hunched shadows cower
joy of the joyless and the hopeless' hope.
Upstairs, businessmen phone sleepy wives
or expensive girls, but most are teased

by their computers' protestant lap dance.
It's a byproduct, happiness, no *ding-an-sich*:
closing bigger deals, grabbing more power,
imagining defunct love was *dans le vrai*.

Money goes round like blood or single malt.
Decorated with old decisions, in
the bar everybody moves to a bouncy
profit motif, staff and customers alike

in this febrile economic foxtrot
from which good whiskey renders a flitting
forgetfulness rather than respite—as if
an eight ball could escape solitude or shock.

The backdrop of tranquil jazz, clinks and whispers,
foreground of orders and gags, confessions
and come-ons, might nearly persuade you that
everyone's unique story is the same.

Another:

    Walked down to the river at dawn and came on
that plaque, the one that quotes the end of Gatsby, a

novel that begins with one father's wisdom and ends with another's bewilderment. America, Amerika. Kafka has the Statue holding up a sword, not a lamp.

In the mood to scribble these crypto-patriotic lines. Another game of singles, with a net; perverse national anthem.

> Goethe praised with envy
> but didn't emigrate;
> Donne conceived a body
> nude, ripe to copulate.

> Millions in the lottery
> and millions insecure;
> Marx's diagnosis
> was better than his cure.

> Virtue's road is rocky
> and hand-grenades get hurled;
> intractable is the
> nastiness of this world.

> No doubt those rough Dutch sailors,
> many centuries dead,
> were awed by what they glimpsed
> just like Fitzgerald said.

Week One: *My Father's Breakdown*

For his first piece, the simplest, Robert rented a large-screen TV and bought fifteen full-length mirrors which he broke into shards. The TV he programmed to change stations according to what he solemnly called an "aleatoric algorithm." Behind the TV he arranged the mirrors in an arc that looked crazier than any funhouse. He insisted that the angles had been carefully calculated, his way of saying he knew what he was doing. The space had a fifteen-foot ceiling. On the wall above the mirrors, using more rented electronic equipment, he projected a scrolling "explanatory text," a pronunciamento consisting entirely of declarative sentences.

Television constructs reality. It doesn't mean to. For the writers each TV show is unitary. For a viewer with a remote control it's the purest form of juxtaposition. For one there's the reinforcing of expectations. There is beginning-middle-end, smooth technique and progression. The program is life. Life is programmed. For the others there's disintegration, collage. *My Father's Breakdown* is an invitation to watch the watching and the watchers watching as you watch the watching, watching you watch. TV alone realizes all the aims of Surrealism. Professional wrestling next to vaginal deodorants. The Infomercial patiently awaits your return from the precincts of Elsinore, Tombstone, suburbia, the ghetto. Hamburgers elbow famine. Here we extol television. Here we anathematize television. Repose is disturbed. My father breaks down. He is breaking down into his constituent elements. This is what you look like when you look at what you're looking at. By the age of fifteen an American has witnessed 15,000 violent deaths.

Mr. Rogers introduces a chainsaw massacre. TV magnifies what is divided. The unity of TV is not political. TV is soporific. TV dissolves integrity. TV uses people up. TV gets us through our worst nights and dullest days. TV is friend, pastor, teacher and mortician. Whatever you are looking at already belongs to the past.

Television constructs reality . . . .

It took him only three days. By the fourth he was already hard at work on his second project.

Week Two: *My Fathers' Unconscious Hands*

This time the paternal was pluralized; this time Robert mounted a play. He hired two actors, set up a raised platform ("thirty-five planks and a passion") and covered it with a heap of junk. The "fathers" were, in the immediate sense, Sophocles, Shakespeare, Matthew Arnold, and Franz Kafka; in a second sense, Creon, Kings Hamlet and Claudius (with Gertrude as ambiguous mother?), Rustum, and Hermann Kafka. In a third sense, I suppose all of them are Professor Kolwitzer. Robert fashioned from the jumble of lifted passages and collected debris a drama of non-sequiturs unified by one undefined emotion. The critic who wrote that his aim was "absurdist mystification" had it wrong. His father had it right; Robert was never whole-hearted, never single-minded. He wanted to dramatize cultural collapse but also continuity, to set out precious fragments as one might

diamonds against a foil. The play, like its sources, is both impersonal and intimate, contingent and eternal, picking at while also
drawing together the sides of a wound, a spasm of implosion
and a spurt of release. When asked about the play Robert was
able to reply honestly that he had not created a play. "Try as I
might, I can't help making contemporary art. That means my
task is to juxtapose ruins and rifle the past. *My Fathers' Unconscious Hands* is really just an anthology."

In addition to the dialogue there was stage business. After
declaiming each speech the actors would throw a random object
from the stage, jettisoning comforting illusions, dumping baggage.
And there was a soundtrack, too. I was able to pick out bits
of Mahler, Brahms, Rachmaninoff but, at the end, there was
some unfamiliar music I found arresting. Robert told me later
it was the finale of Alban Berg's *Violin Concerto*, which, he said,
describes a soul spiraling up into heaven over the Bach chorale,
It Is Enough. The end of the piece now seems prophetic, the title
could serve as that of some future biography. Here's the finale,
flat on the page but on stage, ferociously cathartic:

> A. Dearest Father, you asked me recently why I
> maintain that I am afraid of you.

> B. I am thy father's spirit,
> Doom'd for a certain term to walk the night.

> A. I am your son, sir; by your wise decisions
> My life is ruled, and them I shall always obey.

> B. Art thou so fierce? Thou wilt not fright me so!
> I am no girl, to be made pale by words.

A. I'll tear you apart like a fish!

B. You put special trust in bringing up children by
      means of irony, and this was
most in keeping with your superiority over me.

A. Your extremely effective rhetorical methods in
      bringing me up, which never failed
to work with me, were: abuse, threats, irony, spiteful
      laughter, and—
oddly enough—self-pity.

B. You'd be an excellent king—on a desert island.

A. Surely, to think your own the only wisdom,
And yours the only word, the only will,
Betrays a shallow spirit, an empty heart.

B. Not even your mistrust of others is as great as my
      self-distrust, which you have bred in me.

B. Father, forbear! For I but meet today
The doom which at my birth was written down
In Heaven, and thou art Heaven's unconscious hand.

The play ran for only twenty minutes ("I left time for commer-
cials," cracked Robert) and proceeded by a sort of accretion of
pathos which owed a good deal to the actors' skill—their diction,
physical grace, the ability to project heavy objects and weightier
feelings while hitting the audience only with the latter. I believe
that Robert arranged these tragic shards so as to approximate the
trajectory of a doomed relationship, the history of a distended

adolescence. His goat song is likewise a love song, an incommensurable one.

Week Three: *My Father's Sex Life*

This large piece is a bastard work—some would say the work of a bastard—mixing photography and painting. Its dimensions exceed discretion, fairness, decency. The focus of critics was exclusively on what one of them, handling the piece with tongs, called "the unusually vile subject matter." The consensus was that Robert had simply aimed to shock, that the picture had no further aesthetic aim and was, in the most exact sense, a-moral.

I believe Robert wanted to hurdle every inhibition. The images, as few bothered to note, are not his own, but plucked from the air of our times. They are ogled—by whom? *His* father? *All* fathers? Hadn't he said that sex leads to fatherhood? To me, what the critics said was silly, though I grant that the terrible, fascinating images might lead an observer who didn't know Robert to call the work shameful and the artist shameless. In fact, Robert was anything but a-moral. A hurdler must believe in the hurdles. His job is to jump them without loss of momentum. Did Robert want to insult his father? I can't deny it. He had given the entire month over to this task of calculated affront. In this case, though, I think what he wanted was to show off his color sense. The pornography was perhaps just a particularly provocative *donnée* and, I have to admit, grudgingly, an aesthetically alluring one. Here beauty is degraded but it is nonetheless beautiful. To see beauty in degradation makes the viewer ashamed.

Robert's work is never without an idea; in fact, he admitted the idea was what propelled him. But a profitable idea, for him, had to run on more than a single track and it could never remain abstract. "A good idea's like a drowned gangster," he once joked. "It's got to have a pair of concrete shoes."

My Father's Sex Life. Sex was a problem for Robert. He talked about it a lot when we were undergraduates. Talked only, so far as I know. Artistically and intellectually, he preserved the highest standards—why not emotionally as well? He was a Romantic, a Platonist who demanded love and was disgusted by sex without it. It appalled him that his peers *collected* conquests, that so many men and women were two-bit Don Juans, regarded intercourse simply as a bodily function, spoke of regular coitus as a kind of salutary workout. *O Tempora! O Mores!* Robert had a Ciceronian side and was, to put it plainly, a prude—albeit a prude with a singularly filthy mind. He was the opposite of shameless.

He had taken a piece of hardwood six-foot square and divided it into a grid. "It's very satisfying. William Penn probably felt the same way when he was laying out Philadelphia," Robert joked in an e-mail. He searched through pornographic Internet sites, printed out sixteen pictures, blew them up, painted over them in interesting ways and fixed them to the grid. What first snagged the eye were the startling lines and colors. From a distance it seemed a kind of action painting. The colors sometimes swirled into vapor and at others were concentrated to a dazzling density. Here they were lurid and iridescent, there pale and diaphanous. The piece evoked a minor sensation in the press. Critics debated, moralists fulminated, and tabloid reporters stalked Professor Kolwitzer who said (between clenched teeth?) "No comment."

"I'm rather pleased with the brushwork," said Robert to me

at what he mockingly called the *vernissage*. I was becoming more concerned about him. He looked awful, eyes too bright with raccoon-like circles all around them, arms too thin, posture like a depressive's. He greeted everyone who showed up, then slumped in a corner.

The next night brought another emailed poem, the last. "No time to explain this bagatelle," he wrote, "not that it requires exegesis. It should be called *My Father's Field*," he wrote, though the field was clearly his. "Finally had an idea for the last piece. Not much time. If only one could always live this way!" But what the poem says is that he couldn't maintain this exaltation, that, even before he had finished, he had begun to crash.

> Down by those boulders
> the fence peters out
> like a vein of lead.
> The boards still left are
> gray as the rocks. You
> can see just where he
> stopped, though not why.

Week Four: *My Father's Death*

Robert's final work was a sculpture. He fashioned a life-sized plaster convict and stretched him out on a metal table, arm extended for the lethal injection. In a nice touch of circularity, a soupçon of Eternal Recurrence, he had recycled the full-length mirrors. Now the viewers were all witnesses to an execution, victims' families there to relish the *lex talionis*, voyeurs of the legal system, but still art-lovers, trend-setters. Despite the title, there was no mistaking the features of the prisoner's face. This was Robert's version of Michelangelo inserting himself into *The Last Judgment*. It is his only self-portrait.

4.

A S we were making ready to leave the bar Kolwitzer's father, my old professor, suddenly asked if I knew where Robert had been going that morning, why he had gotten into that cab.

I admitted I'd never thought about it.

"He was coming to see me. Where else?"

THE COMPOSER MOSTOV

Imagine two dozen famished cats attacking a drum
and bugle corps. You can get music as good from
a radiator and far better from a cash register.

—from a review of the Second Symphony

M OSTOV'S widow loved to tell the following story at
dinner parties.

It was shortly after the premiere of George's *Second Symphony*.
No, I'm not in the least surprised you don't know it. You'll see why.

A young man came to the house. He identified himself as a
music student, a post-graduate—he made quite a point of that—
and claimed he had been on the road for two days. I believed
him because he looked exactly like a graduate student who had
spent forty-eight hours on a bus or hitchhiking, all scruffiness
and hair and torn blue jeans, but with the *sweetest* face. He
begged to see my husband. "If I could have the honor," he said
in that almost heraldic way Americans have when faced with
nobility. Well, nothing of this sort had ever happened before. I
invited him into the living room and ran to tell George. He was
out in the garden cutting back the forsythia. This was a pastime
he found particularly satisfying. "Forsythia's easy to prune and
you can bend it anyway you like and, even if I overdo, it never
harms the thing," he used to say. He could be so gentle, like
an animist. I actually caught him one afternoon apologizing
to the shrub. For a time he was mad about the work of Jung
and Pauli. You know it? Well, I don't either, really. Something

about physics and psychology being somehow mixed up with each other, the inner and outer knotted up in some discoverable tangle, that coincidences are profoundly meaningful and so on. My husband was a man of wide interests and it all went into his music, of course.

Anyway, when I told George a young admirer had shown up on our doorstep he frowned. No, he *scowled*. I said, "Look dear, I can't send him away. I *won't*. The boy says he's been traveling for two days just to see you. On a bus, I think." Well, George growled like a bear but he headed for the house. Up to a point, I could usually get him to do what I wanted.

After I pushed him in the direction of the living room I went to make tea, being careful to leave the door open so I could listen.

I heard the boy jumping to his feet, heard him stammering with awe—yes, awe at the genius!—but George helped him not a bit, not with so much as one word. I swear I could hear him just *staring* at the poor boy.

Finally the boy got to the point. "Mr. Mostov," he said—and it was so sweet, so shy—"I just *had* to come, to see you. It was a duty, a compulsion."

"That sounds literary," George said. Imagine, his first words. "*That sounds literary.*" Of course, my heart went out to the boy. Maybe he didn't notice the criticism or he just ignored it. Either way he pressed on, gamely.

"Three nights ago my life changed. I was at the first performance of your *Second Symphony*. It was—well, I hardly know what to say. I was so moved, so excited. I could hardly sit still. I had to see you, tell you."

I kept waiting for George to say something, anything. So did the poor graduate student.

"Mr. Mostov, I can't tell you how much I admire you. I'm a composition student myself, you see."

Oh, it was a regular train wreck. George just left the boy bobbing around in that ocean of love, waiting for a rope, an inner tube, a wine cork, anything at all. It was agony.

I hurried up with the tea.

As soon as I joined them I could see George was in a state. He was probably yearning to get back to whacking forsythia but I shot him a warning look. He crossed his arms like this. I made him stay but I couldn't force him to talk. The boy must have thought he was out of his mind, a crazy genius, like Schumann.

I was determined to help so I asked the boy the first thing that came into my mind. I asked him what he particularly liked about the symphony. Well, I could hardly have chosen a worse question. He must have been writing a whole essay in his head on that bus ride. Trying to look at me, but unable to keep his big, soft eyes off George's stone face, he went on and on about technical details, as if he'd memorized the score, then proceeded, with an apology for his temerity, to what he saw as "the inner significance" of each movement and what he wasn't too shy to call the "colossal spiritual progression to the final fugue."

It was terrible. George was, so to speak, more silent than ever. I mean his silence was louder and louder and it hurt more and more. What a shambles. I can't even remember how I got the boy out of the house.

Well, as soon as he was gone George began doing just what I

was afraid he would. He marched into his study and tore up the score of the symphony, then all his notes. He got on the phone to his publisher and furiously cancelled his contract. Finally, he called the conductor of the premiere and demanded he destroy his own and every last one of the performing scores. In short, he did everything possible to blot out the symphony.

You're surprised? But it's quite simple. George was devastated by the boy's praise. If someone, anyone, could love what he wrote after hearing it only a single time, he was convinced he'd failed. After his orgy of destruction he was exhausted and despondent, of course. I followed him up to the bedroom and told him the piece might be among his greatest. Was it so bad to be understood, or even misunderstood? "No," he said. "To be misunderstood is painful. It's like being told to shut up when you have something urgent to say. Not to be understood at all is all right. But that adolescent understood everything all too well. He knew precisely what I was up to. It had to have been too simple, too popular, too sentimental, or just too derivative. Well, whatever it was, it's garbage now."

•   •   •

The difference is that, while Beethoven went deaf,

Mostov makes his audience wish they were too. If

this is the music of the future I'm selling my stock.

–from a review of *Symphoniaci*

Emma Folkes knew what she had in the envelope was going to make big news in her world. Though only twenty-two she was wise beyond her years. For instance, she knew how little that world was but also how little its littleness mattered. Everyone moves in a little world, she believed, as well as the great big one and, of the two, it is the little one that counts the most, except in cases of national emergency. This was hardly a national emergency but she was certain it was going to be a local one. So she cradled the manila envelope she was carrying to the Office of the Music Director and Permanent Conductor as one might an infant or a bomb. She supposed Harald Sigurson would raise his voice and swear, as everybody knew he made a point of doing at least twice at every rehearsal, again for the sake of his reputation.

Emma had gotten her job as assistant orchestra manager less than a year earlier, at the end of the long, idle summer after her graduation. It pleased her to know, even for the few minutes it would take her to walk from the Trustees Conference Room to his lair, something that the redoubtable Maestro did not. Rather to her surprise, she disliked Sigurson. She hadn't expected to, quite the contrary. But Emma judged people with the severity of the young and found the conductor arrogant, hypocritical, and overrated. He liked to paint himself in interviews as a passionate advocate of living composers and new music, but Emma knew this was untrue. What Sigurson liked was doing what he had always done. Before she was born some famous critic had branded him a Mozart/Haydn specialist and he had believed it. Sigurson delighted in keeping his seraglio of rich ladies happy with war horses done tastefully. Most of these dowagers did not read his interviews where, in effect, he blamed his conservative programming on them. However, Mrs. Newman, the newest, liveliest, and wealthiest of the predominantly female trustees, did read at least one of these interviews. Emma had given it to her herself, with the key passages highlighted. Two days later she sent a one-word e-mail to Mrs. Newman: "Mostov."

Mostov read the letter calmly, his expression fixed and then, with a lordly gesture, held it out across the table to his wife. They were having vegetable soup and homemade rye bread for lunch and Mostov's wife, in her amazement, hit the heel of her hand against her soup spoon which rose in the air, made half a flip, struck the side of her bowl, and clattered on the floor.

"But George!" she gasped. "This is the price of a new roof, plus a year's groceries."

"Approximately," he said, "plus the services of Mr. Grillo."

Grillo was the piano tuner.

"Did you know anything about this?" she asked suspiciously.

He shrugged.

"You didn't apply or anything?"

"My dear, it doesn't work that way."

"Oh? So how *does* it work?"

"Same as with art theft. It's always an inside job."

"Mr. Expert. So, you know somebody on the inside?"

"Of course not. It follows that somebody must know *me*."

"You'll accept?"

"Naturally. I'll write a reply after lunch. Would you type it out for me?"

"So long as you get it to me before two. I'm meeting Doris." She blushed. "We're going to get our hair done. Now I think

I'll have mine colored."

Mostov squinted at his wife's still mostly brunette head like a lookout searching the horizon for land. "What a splendid idea! Have you picked a color yet?"

He dropped everything to work on the miraculous, opulent commission, the first he had ever had. It was to mark the famous orchestra's centennial. It was an easy birth, a wonderful opening out. Ideas fell on his head like rain so that he could scarcely keep up. Though in his own style, Mostov's booming, irascible voice, his plan was to incorporate a series of half-concealed homages to a century of musical rebellion and protest. He would bow before his heroes which is the only way to be rid of them. As for the title, he decided almost at once not to call the piece a symphony, but rather *Symphoniaci*, the Latin for orchestra. He intended it as a subtle tribute.

As a condition of the commission, Mostov was obliged to deliver the score in person and be present at rehearsals. This meant a cross-country flight, during which he drank three Bloody Marys and went through the entire score. He was well satisfied with it. He could think of no improvements, not even to the woodwinds, which had given him so much trouble, or the long passage alluding to the Vienna Serialists.

Emma met him at the airport. They hit it off at once because she was holding up a sign that read Maestro George Mostov.

"So, you think I'm a master, Ms. Folkes?" he asked in the taxi.

"Not until the fifteenth time I listened to the *Tantalus Suite*.

A friend of mine from college sent me a tape he got from a music student who made it at the premiere."

"The only performance, actually." Uncharacteristically, he could not help asking. "And the first fourteen?"

She declined to reply, merely smiled and checked her watch. "We have a couple hours to kill. What would you like to eat?"

"Good corned beef on seedless rye," he said precisely and enthusiastically, "and a sour tomato." After a pause during which he gave in to the unaccustomed spirit of openness inspired by Emma, he added, "Those first fourteen times. It sounded like a man rattling a cage, didn't it?"

"Yes, I guess so."

"Well, Ms. Folkes, I carry that cage inside me. For me, that's what music is, cage-rattling."

Emma was too young not to share most of the story of his commission over lunch. On the other hand, she played down her own role and Mrs. Newman's up.

Mostov, already fond of the girl and therefore eager to deflate her image of him, whispered, "I wonder if it would surprise you to know, Ms. Folkes, that this is the first premiere that won't come out of my own pocket."

Emma took Mostov to meet Mrs. Newman in the Trustees Room at two o'clock. She was waiting alone at the end of the long mahogany table but, despite her slight build, she was not dwarfed. Anyone could see she was a woman of strong character, a woman you didn't mess with. A swimmer, she took good care of herself. Her hair had gone half gray, cut short and not overstyled, and it became her. She wore a simple but expensive sundress and exceptionally fine shoes. They looked to Mostov as if they had been carved by Bernini. He was fascinated by these shoes and almost asked her to take one off so he could examine it. He loved all things well made.

The conversation was brief and to the point. Mrs. Newman took one look at Mostov and knew better than to engage in small talk.

"Your music is regarded as difficult, Mr. Mostov. No one could call it popular. Will this be true of our commission as well?"

Mostov raised his eyes from her shoes. "I have a little nephew. Every night my sister reads him the same bedtime story. He loves it. On my last visit I brought him a new book and was permitted to take him up to bed and read it to him. He cried. He hated it. He wanted his old book."

"I see."

"New music isn't difficult, Mrs. Newman, but listening to it is. Painters teach us to see, philosophers to think, composers to listen. It's never easy to see what wasn't visible last week or to think what wasn't thought last year. And it's no easier to listen to something that's never been heard before. People resist. It's to be expected. People like pretty and pretty's always familiar. That's why the women in the magazines all look mass produced. Maybe most of what we call ugly is just unfamiliar beauty."

"How interesting," said Mrs. Newman.

"You're kind of short for a Swede" was the first thing Mostov said when he was introduced to Harald Sigurson. The meeting was, of course, a disaster and the rehearsals a series of catastrophes. The conductor swore so much that Ms. Folkes' boss, the orchestra manager, decided that the open rehearsal on Friday afternoon would have to be closed to the public.

It was no surprise to Mostov when Sigurson claimed to have come down with flu on the night of the performance. The terrified concertmaster tried his best.

. . .

I may confidently report that this new American
concerto is out of the ordinary, like the Black Plague
and the two world wars. Both orchestra and soloist
labored mightily indeed, though to no gratifying
effect. I was put in mind of a gymnast with piles.
            —from a review of the *First Piano Concerto*

"But I assure you it *is* absolutely necessary. Without it, how can I play? How could I know how to?"

"Did you sleep with Chopin?"

"That is entirely different, obviously."

"You don't play Chopin?"

"Please not to be so idiotic, Mostov. You deliberately miss the point. With a dead composer one is not giving first life to a work. One is like a child who admires a great-grandfather and does her utmost to understand him. It is at best resurrection, at worst an admiration from afar. But it is not giving birth. To give birth there is a prerequisite."

"Does this rule of yours extend also to conductors?"

"Well, if one is collaborating . . ."

"Critics?"

"Now you are being crude, Mostov. I am not at all pleased with you."

"I'm a married man."

"So? What do I care? Am I making you un-married?"

Mostov was in a pickle. Here he was alone in Prague with its cupolas and spires, city of Janáček and Čapek, of Kafka and Tycho Brahe, but, as Maria Panalova was reminding him, the town where *Don Giovanni* was first performed and loved by high and low. Mostov was no Don Juan. Wasn't that obvious? Yet here was this blue-eyed, vivacious, thirty-year-old insisting he make a fool of himself. Either way he would be a fool. She was ferociously serious and this single-mindedness was like a thick carapace through which she could not see him. She was not even insulted by his reluctance, only exasperated by his pig-headedness, his unwillingness to see things her way. She had her rules, she said, as no doubt he had his. Naturally, as a fellow artist, she expected him to understand and also to sympathize. She was not a whore. Or, if she was, she was a whore for music, a holy whore. Composition, she told him, may be solitary and celibate but, as far as she was concerned, performances—at least first ones—called for copulation. A metaphor made flesh.

When he signed the contract with the pick-up band of under-employed former wards of the state that called itself the Bohemian Philharmonic, he had left it to the local agent to choose the soloist. He had his specifications, of course. He or she had to be good, not hide-bound, open to fresh ideas, and strong enough to treat the piano as the percussion instrument it was. Maria Panalova's salary was not too high and she played well, but there had been nothing in the contract about sexual intercourse.

"Look Mostov, you want me to play your concerto. I *want* to play it. I really do. If you like I will present you with a list of the other composers who have shared my bed. It is what you call no big deal. But, I reiterate, absolutely necessary if I am to perform."

They were seated in the Café Magus. Mostov sipped black coffee; with determined nationalism, Maria had ordered slivovitz. The city around them rushed to and fro earnestly trying to become Western. Like Maria, it was impatient to give itself, albeit provisionally, leaving plenty of room for later irony. As its citizens collected Coca-Cola and Starbucks, Yankees caps and hamburgers, Maria accumulated composers. It would certainly be more interesting to read her little list than Leporello's.

Mostov had been in Prague once before, long ago, back in the bad socialist epoch. Every evening as he came through the rococo lobby the manageress of the hotel sent her daughter over to offer him Pall Malls; a pack was worth a fortune in those days. The girl was very pretty in her Young Pioneer outfit with its scarlet bandana. She looked like a living poster. With her back to her mother she made it clear that she regarded him as a devil, a capitalist dog, a white slaver. He always thanked the girl and turned down the cigarettes.

"I want you to marry her. Then you will take her to Hollywood where she will become a star," the mother had frankly explained on his last day.

"But, Madam, she's what? Twelve?"

"Fourteen!"

Between the cunning naïveté of that manageress and the principled promiscuity of this pianist lay thirty years. Maria might have been the Young Pioneer's classmate.

"You know," he said, "what you say about living and dead composers is interesting. I write so-called New Music because, after all, I can't write old music. But what I really want is to be one of your great-grandfathers. It's not easy—maybe not even possible—to discern the lasting in the new. So many supplicants waving their petitions before the judge with his long beard. Suppose then you indulge me. Consider me as dead as Chopin."

She pouted at him.

"No, it's not so far-fetched. I'm older than Chopin was when he died. I'm asking you to resurrect, as you put it, what may or may not die. My coming to your bed would show you nothing of how you should play the concerto. Rather than chalking me up on your blackboard, I would be grateful if you played as if you really wanted to make love."

She shot him a furious look, then shrugged and hefted her plum brandy.

"You know Prague was once a city of magicians and alchemists."

"Yes, but Kepler lived here too."

"There's something in that. Science wants to murder magic. But I insist on my magic. You, Mostov, are as unsympathetic as Kepler. Do you know the story of the hand that hangs in one of the three naves of the old Jakobskirche? In the night a thief tried to steal the ornaments from a statue of the Virgin, but as he grasped them his hand was paralyzed. He was found in the morning. Everyone believed the Virgin had laid hold of him, held him tight. No one was able to move his arm and so the hangman was summoned to cut it off. When the thief came out of prison he became a lay brother. This was in the year 1400. Two hundred years before Kepler. You are a materialist, Mostov, probably even a Freudian. He had cramp due to a mother-complex. Yes?"

"No, I believe in magic too, but the magic is in us, not statues, not even in sex. What froze that thief's hand was shame and guilt and a longing for justice. As you said, everyone believed in the miracle, especially him."

"Then you think it was a relief to him to have his arm chopped off?"

"Certainly. Losing his arm rescued him. He became a monk. Losing his arm redeemed him. It saved the man from mutilating himself."

She was indignant. "Are you saying that putting your thing in my thing would be a mutilation?"

Mostov shrugged. "No, only that I too might be paralyzed, and I don't care to have anything cut off. Your offer's generous and tempting. But I prefer you up on your pedestal, just like the Virgin, only playing my concerto."

· · ·

The new quartet again confirmed Einstein's relativity
theory. While the players raced through their score
in a mere half-hour, we listeners aged a century.
At the end, a few members of the audience, presumably

close relatives of the composer or musicians, offered
some light applause and were spontaneously pelted with
balled-up program notes, mine included.

—from a review of *String Quartet No. 1*

Their bungalow was small, with only the one bathroom. So, when Mostov's wife laughed so hard she wet her pants, that's where she ran to.

Though he too got the joke, Mostov did not feel like laughing. In fact, he felt queasy. When he was young a girl he liked but who treated him badly told him she couldn't see him any more. He was heartbroken and relieved at the same time. He felt something like that.

Jessica Tam, his agent in Los Angeles, telephoned with the news at lunchtime. "Isn't it fabulous?" The woman was so excited that her voice sounded full of bubbles. Twenty minutes later Tony Heiberg, Mostov's *other* agent in L. A., called and, though less effervescent, was every bit as elated. "Wow!" he exclaimed.

When he hung up on Heiberg, Mostov turned to his wife and her raised eyebrows. "It appears," he explained, "that I've been nominated twice."

"What? You mean *both* . . ," but then she had completely broken up.

Mostov looked ruefully at the bathroom door. He wanted desperately to go back to working on his string quartet. He felt that if he worked hard enough on it the quartet might save him from this muddle. What worried him most, what nauseated him, was that Jessica and Tony were bound to find out about each other. He dreaded embarrassment and felt like a child watching a rather neat house of cards beginning to buckle. Why, he wondered, does stability have to be so precarious?

It had been some years since the first check had come in, and, after all the joy and mental spending, Mostov's wife had looked at him with big, sympathetic eyes.

"Doesn't it bother you that you can get paid so much for this . . . this merely entertaining people and not a dime for your serious work?"

He heard the plop of a drop of disappointment; and, even though it was quickly swallowed up in the ocean of his love, Mostov felt that he had overestimated her a little and that hurt. He decided it was time for a lecture.

"Yes, that's an ancient complaint with which I don't agree. The world's much smarter than its whining artists. It only pays for what it wants or needs. What I write for the movies is entirely for others. It exists because of them and it's only of them I think while writing it. I have to; they want their emotions engineered and have no interest in freeing mine. So, it's proper they should pay for my services on their behalf, just as they do for dry cleaning and trash removal. If they didn't pay me I wouldn't do it at all. I'm vain and if I had more money I'd do only what suits me. That's the secret. Infinite selfishness. What you endearingly call my serious work is completely selfish, written to answer my own needs. When I jump into the darkness I don't sell tickets, and I don't care what other people think."

"You don't? Not at all?"

"Let's say I *aspire* not to. There's a story about César Franck.

He was sixty-six years old when he finished his only symphony. Franck went to the premiere alone; I suppose his wife was ill. Anyway, when he got home, she couldn't wait to ask him how it had gone, by which she meant how it had been received. Franck replied with satisfaction that it sounded just as he thought it would and went to bed."

Mostov's wife frowned. She knew that she was being criticized. "That's almost solipsism, George."

"You're right. But a lot depends on that 'almost'."

Antal Cerven, Jack Reese. He had chosen the names out of a twelve-year-old phone directory for Chico State University, first one, then, a year later, the other. The book had been there when they moved into the bungalow, elevating one side of the refrigerator. A large disk was pressed into the pulp so that the two names appeared to have haloes around them.

The idea of two pseudonyms and two agents to represent them was born out of financial desperation. Mostov never felt quite right about it. He had chosen Jessica and Tony for his agents, a man and a woman, in order that he would not make a mistake on the phone. They worked at separate agencies, one in Hollywood, the other in Century City. Still, it was entirely likely that they found themselves competing to get him the same job, Cerven versus Reese. Mostov tried not to think about this.

He was good at scoring films because he never confused the work with art. He knew about Nathanael West and Scott Fitzgerald, who both wound up in Hollywood; in fact, both were laid out in Pierce Brothers Funeral Home almost side by side. West was cynical about the dream factory and so he churned out the required crap for the third-rate studio that hired him and wrote *The Day of the Locust*. Fitzgerald, the inveterate hero-worshiper, idolized Irving Thalberg and mixed up his talent with his MGM job, in the end leaving *The Last Tycoon* incomplete.

Art is long; movies are short. Comparatively.

Both agents knew who he was, of course. They had to know; they cut the checks, the cash that hired string quartets and Czech orchestras. They had to know who he was, but not each another. Neither had any interest in his real work, of course, nor did Mostov ever mention it to them. He only wanted paying jobs for Cerven and Reese. Occasionally he would have two projects at the same time, but arranging recording schedules was not so difficult, especially when his services came to be sought after. To have a couple of successes in Hollywood is like being Samson growing hair. People stay out of your way, and Mostov could do a good impression of a lion with a honeycomb inside him.

What if he won? What if Cerven got the Oscar? What if Reese did? Jessica and Tony had already begun pressuring him.

"Drop the secret identity, George," pleaded Tony. "I'll arrange a press event. It'll make a great story."

"What are you talking about? Of *course* you'll go to the ceremony," shrieked Jessica. "You *have* to take your wife. I mean think of the fun she'll have picking out a dress. You couldn't be such a bastard as to deny her that!"

"I'm going to have to find two people to stand in for me," he said to his wife over dinner. "It's the only way."

It had begun to rain late in the afternoon, first hard then

steady. When it started they could hear the big, individual drops hitting the tiles but later all merged into one stream.

Mostov's wife looked at him over the stir-fry with gimlet eyes.

"No," he insisted, shaken. "What? You want the *dress*?"

Still nothing, just the rain falling on the roof, just her gaze.

"Look, I'll probably lose anyway," he said brightly. "There are five nominees. I'm only forty percent of them. Three to two odds, almost a sucker's bet."

She took a bite, chewed, but kept looking at him.

"Are you going to say anything?"

"I like watching you try to scrape the success off. I still think it's hilarious."

"That's all? That's *it*?"

She considered, sucking on her lower lip, as though to keep from laughing. "I guess so."

"Then you don't care?"

"About a dress?"

"The dress, the celebrities, the press, the show—about *going*?"

"Oh, maybe just a little more than a rat's ass. Let's say a rat's torso."

Neither laughed. The rain fell. Mostov brooded. He was miserable, but, in spite of himself, was unable to extinguish a spark of exhilaration. That spark was what made him most miserable. He would have liked to take it outside and let the rain extinguish it.

His wife went on sucking at her lip. "I know," she said suddenly.

"Why not ask Jessica and Tony? They're already there anyway."

"What? To stand in for me?" It was impossible. He saw one of them in front of the crowd, the cameras, the whole world, blowing his cover—worse, letting the *other* one know. All the same, the idea appealed to him because it was at least an idea. His wife had hit on the most logical solution.

He lowered his head like a child. "Do you think I could . . . that I could get them to promise to keep my name out of it?"

"I can't see why not. They're not selling the un-sellable Mostov, you know, just those two hot properties, Cerven and Reese. *Those* are the names they want, as they'd say, out there. You could remind them of that. And the ten percent." She shrugged. "Play hardball if you have to."

Mostov felt the knot loosen in his gut and broke into a broad smile. Outside the rain was falling on the forsythia. Apart from unconditional love, the thing he most craved from his wife was permission.

"The quartet's coming along rather well," he remarked almost contentedly, and reached for the pitcher of iced tea.

Four Cinematic Episodes from the Life of Paul Bronn

I.

AN ant squeezes a man between its pincers and hoists him off his feet. We have seen this man behaving well; we know the sound of his voice, the way his face changes when he is worried or pleased; we believe him to be good and noble. But now he kicks helplessly, twitches, screams, and dies. There have been bomb tests and the ant is the size of a ranch house. There are thousands of these ants and they have made it all the way from ground zero in the Nevada desert to the sewers of Los Angeles.

The movie was *Them!*, ably directed by Gordon Douglas in 1954 during which year Paul Bronn pleaded with his mother to let him see it.

"No," she said.

"Aw, why not?"

"*Them*—I found out who *they* are. It'll frighten you, Paul. People screaming in the theater, terrified children."

"I'm not frightened."

"It's not meant for children. Anyway, why do you want to see it so much?"

How could he answer? He was eight years old. How could his mother even ask such a question? Of course he wasn't afraid of seeing giant ants; he was afraid of not seeing them. The previous Saturday his two best friends had gotten permission to see *Them!* and all they could talk about the whole week were imploded house trailers, flame throwers, and twittery ant noises which they imitated impressively while holding out their arms for lethal hugs. Not only did Bronn feel left out, he wanted to see these ants for their own sake. *Them!* was a cultural event of the first magnitude, one of the best of the what-have-we-unleashed-the-army-and-air-force-are-helpless-monsters-bigger-than-Rhode-Island-whole-cities-stomped-to-rubble-scientists-in-white-coats-explain-it-just-might-work-mega-death-averted-this-time movies of the fifties. Of course there was still an Un-American Activities Committee so the movie, presumably not scripted by any writers on the blacklist, had a chauvinistic, xenophobic political subtext which eight-year-old boys might not pick up other than subliminally. "Them" is what the Russians and Chinese were called, the Red Menace, the communized, interchangeable, hymenopteral swarms in those huge land masses that had outlawed God and individuality and who were also, it was often repeated in portentous tones by figures of authority, infiltrating *us* (or U.S.) from below. Them versus Us. *They* too must be burned out, their ideological queen tracked down and destroyed. Perhaps there was such a subtext but it was not part of the movie's appeal to Paul, who only knew it was crucial that *Them!* be seen by him, and on Saturday.

The argument ran all week, kept alive by Paul. He even appealed to his father who steadfastly refused to arbitrate. In fact, he would take no position either way, which exasperated both advocates. Paul's mother naturally felt she was entitled to her husband's support, while Paul felt his father's indifference as a betrayal of their common masculinity.

"Sorry, Paul. I've got to work this Saturday or I might just take you myself," his father had the gall to confide on Thursday morning. "But look, it's best to humor her, you know. Besides, maybe she's right." This cowardly speech left Paul indignant. In his opinion, *Them!* was men's business, like football and carburetors and hand-to-hand combat.

So it was Paul versus his mother, irresistible force against immovable object.

When supplication proved ineffective, Bronn moved on to bargaining. He would do the dishes for two weeks and keep his room tidy forever; he wouldn't ask for anything else, not even a new bike; he wouldn't ever again shout out numbers while she was going over the bank statement; he would turn up promptly whenever she called him in for dinner. Name it, he would do, or not do, it, just as she pleased.

Paul was an only child. He wore her down.

She gave in at almost the last minute, on Friday afternoon. "All right, all right," she said, "but on one condition."

Overjoyed he agreed, "Anything!"

It was a big condition, a humiliating one, but he had to accept it. She would go with him and they would leave the very first time he looked away from the screen.

"I don't want you having nightmares. Your uncle had them for *months* after he saw *King Kong*. I'm not going to have you *traumatized*," his mother declared.

Paul didn't understand exactly what *traumatized* meant. It was a word his mother used fairly often and always in connection with him; it was clearly something from which he had to be protected, like polio. He supposed, from her ominous tone, that to be traumatized must be pretty awful. It seemed to be not merely a source of bad dreams but a way of becoming crazy for the rest of your life. In fact, Paul never forgot how his mother had worried about his being traumatized. In his teens he supposed the word must come from *Traum*, the German for dream, but then he found out that *trauma* actually derives from the Greek for wound. Nevertheless, he held on to the idea that there must also be a hint in it of dream, the bad dream. There was his trau-matized uncle having nightmares about enormous apes. What, then, are movies? Movies are dreams that can wound, or so his anxious mother believed at least. However, at eight Paul had no fear of trauma, wounds, or nightmares, and nothing seemed to him less conceivable than that he would ever in any way resemble his Uncle Bert who was bald and fat and collected matchbooks.

So that Saturday he went to the theater to see *Them!* with his mother seated beside him, a scarcely endurable embarrassment since the place was full of kids. He kept his eyes on the screen and prayed for the lights to go out, obliterating the audience's mocking scrutiny of him and his mother and, in the fullness of time, they did.

Nothing in the glorious movie surprised him; he had heard it all from his friends. What did surprise him was that his mother squeezed his arm at all the scary spots. It was she who couldn't bear to look. It was also, he learned, she who had nightmares all the following week. From then on Paul's mother would boil a big kettle of water and pour it over the little anthills that the inoffensive insects built in the cracks of the pavement and in the backyard. He couldn't make her see it wasn't the ants' fault, that it was the fault of the bomb-testers.

Worst of all, Paul's mother seemed to be angry with him for forcing her to see *Them!*, as if it had been his intention all along to traumatize her. Their relationship changed. Before, his mother had been anxious that he should not be shocked by seeing anything horrible; she strove to preserve in him an ignorance without which there would be no innocence, shielding him from even imaginary horrors. Now, after the Saturday matinée of *Them!*, Paul sensed that his mother resented him, and later, a little at a time, he accepted her view of him as lost, inured, a hard case.

II.

BRONN once dated a woman obsessed with the movie *Casablanca*. Gloria had a specially made neon Rick's Café Américain sign mounted on the wall of her apartment. In the middle of her living room, under an overhead fan, sat a high-backed wicker chair, in case Sidney Greenstreet showed up with his belly and white suit. A framed poster for the film hung over her bed. Being an intelligent, highly educated woman, Gloria made a show of veiling her adolescent romanticism with irony, but the veil was of gauze.

One evening while she was busy in the kitchen Bronn came across a manila folder on the sideboard and opened it. Inside were paper dolls of old movie actresses, chiefly Joan Crawford.

Bronn had never liked Joan Crawford; in fact, she frightened him. Some years later he saw *Mommy Dearest*, in which a terrifying Faye Dunaway portrays the private life of Joan Crawford from the point of view of her terrified daughter. To Bronn this film was a confirmation of his suspicions rather than a scandalous revelation. Defiant but nonetheless embarrassed, Gloria tried to make light of the paper dolls, claiming that she loved the clothes, in a campy sort of way.

But it was *Casablanca* that Gloria loved best. Bronn also liked the film, of course, but in a detached manner, recognizing in it one of those almost accidental crystallizations of America's idealized self-concept with which Hollywood comes up every decade or so. Tough, tender, semi-criminal yet scrupulously moral, wealthy, courted, provisionally neutral, lethal if aroused. Rick was the bad boy women loved, the bad boy who is not really bad. Bronn understood that Gloria would have liked him to be Rick, or at least Rickish. But he was not like Rick in the least. He was a chemist by profession and, though still in his twenties, was already keen on his career. True, he would someday be a poet but Bronn's poems lay years in the future. Anyway, he had too much self-consciousness to achieve *savoir vivre* of the lofty Rick variety. He wasn't tough or masterful, only neutral. And he knew how grand the canyon was that separated movies like *Casablanca* from actual life.

Bronn was willing to talk about how he should behave in this relationship or, since only indirection would do for Gloria, he was willing to talk with her about *Casablanca*. This meant talking about Rick. Gloria had little interest in the film's other characters except in so far as they allowed Rick to display the many sides of his attractive personality: businessman, lover, democrat, Francophile, thug, gambler, benefactor, jazz lover, humanitarian, integrationist, friend, sacrificer of self.

One evening, when the dinner conversation was flagging, Bronn asked, "What's your favorite line in *Casablanca*?" His own favorite, he said, was "If she can stand it, I can stand it," though he wasn't certain he had gotten the quotation right. Apparently he had, since Gloria would have been quick to correct him otherwise.

"My favorite," she said promptly, "is 'You wore blue, the Germans wore gray.'"

Later Bronn thought about their choices. He observed that Gloria had chosen a superficially romantic, though snappy line, while his choice spoke of suffering. Gloria dwelt on the happy days of new love in springtime Paris, he on the pain and bitterness of dusty North Africa.

Bronn liked that Rick gave up Ilsa. He would have liked it even better if Ilsa hadn't wanted Rick. In fact, he preferred unhappy love stories because, however much he wanted to, he was unable to believe in the other kind.

In this case, for example, it soon became obvious that he and Gloria were a bad match, that they were unable to please each other. When one of his friends asked how the romance was going, Bronn found himself saying that it had about run its course. "I guess one of us is too neurotic," he joked. It was a shame because Gloria was a good companion; she cooked interestingly and told clever jokes. Moreover, he respected the passion with which she approached her vocation, which was unionizing office workers, a thing he could not imagine Joan Crawford ever doing. Crawford was a plutocratic seller of sugar water with the soul of a union buster.

Bronn worked himself up and one Monday night over the phone told Gloria that it was over. He was expecting her to put up some resistance, perhaps even hoping for a fight or a denunciation, but there was nothing of the sort. "I'm not surprised," she said evenly. "I've been feeling it too." Then she thanked him for the good times and said goodbye. Nevertheless, she phoned him a couple days later and suggested that he come over for a final dinner, a sort of farewell banquet. Gloria had her ideas about classiness.

She was dressed in a blue suit with shoulder pads. Her hair was done in an old-fashioned style, and it became her. The situation might have been awkward but, in fact, the table talk flowed affably. She was a perfect hostess, well up to the standard of her movie models.

"I've thought about us," she said calmly over coffee. "It's all right. It just wasn't meant to be."

"I suppose not," said Bronn.

"I believe in fate."

"You do?"

She sipped her coffee. "Um-hm. I like the idea of fate. Really, it's such a relief."

"I suppose. But do you think the universe is that organized?"

Gloria giggled as if he had said something witty. "Probably not, at least not in the fall-of-every-little-sparrow sense, if that's what you mean. I know that. It's all I can do to organize a half dozen purchasing agents. But why suppose fate has to be a form of cosmic hyperorganization?"

"Well, isn't the idea of fate that whatever occurs, especially to human beings, happens according to some plan? It would have to be fantastically complex. Just think of it—the traffic, the planets, schedules for tooth-brushing, political platforms, weather fronts—"

"Not necessarily. You're a scientist. Why shouldn't fate just be the laws of nature? My own idea of fate is a rather ancient one; I mean that it only applies to the really big things in life."

Bronn considered this. "Maybe what you call fate I call chance."

"Well, they could be the same things, except that if what happens by chance is significant enough it's fate . . . You know, 'Of all the gin joints in the world you had to walk into mine . . . .'"

Like anybody else, Bronn occasionally entertained the idea that life could resemble a movie, that life could have shape and form, even a conventional one, a formula. But how could anybody believe this to be more than a daydream? No, he believed fate was either a movie trick or else a defense mechanism. He had no wish to argue with Gloria employing the latter, if that was what was going on.

"I'm just sorry it didn't work out," he said sincerely.

She shrugged her power shoulders. "Oh, like I said, it's just fate."

Bronn had intended to take his leave after dinner but Gloria said that an art theater downtown was running *Casablanca*. Would he go with her for old time's sake? He could hardly refuse and, besides, it really did seem fitting. So they went.

Gloria took his hand when Rick told Sam he could stand hearing "As Time Goes By" if Ilsa could and again when he delivered the line about Ilsa wearing blue and the Nazis gray. At the end, during the climactic airport scene, she even rested her head on his shoulder.

He took her home feeling both perplexed and heavy hearted. When he was about to turn away from the door of her apartment Gloria wiped away a tear, gave him a peck on the cheek, and added bravely, "Who knows, Paul? Maybe this will be the start of a beautiful friendship."

A movie can be at once trauma and *Traum*. Years later, during one of the many long nights when he cursed his bachelorhood, Bronn wondered whether, if Gloria only had loved *Casablanca* less, he might have married her. He had heard that she was wed within a year of their breakup. The groom was an accountant, according to reports. Perhaps Gloria had gotten over looking for Rick or maybe chance had delivered her a bookkeeper worthy of being called her fate. A dream can leave a wound, even a dream someone else has discarded. Had Bronn made a mistake?

III.

FOR a few years in his thirties Bronn took to writing poems. In fact, by the time he was done he had written almost ten score of them and published maybe half. Almost all of these poems were about love in the negative sense.

How and why does a person—an adult, a practicing chemist— suddenly begin writing verses? Had Bronn been interviewed about his poetry, this surely would have been the first question. "The initial motive's seldom aesthetic," he might have answered, if he had deigned to answer in earnest. "First you have to say something, which is not at all the same as having something to say. That is, there's a compulsion to put a feeling down in words, or the words come with the feeling. Later on you begin to care more about how you put things." Poetry, Bronn's at least, was a struggle to balance sincerity and artifice, to arrange the words so that one would redeem rather than undermine the other.

Bronn's work as a chemist was improved by his versifying. In both spheres he became more imaginative in combining elements. His most successful project was finding a way of hardening a new plastic without diminishing its flexibility. This problem absorbed him precisely because of his poetizing, since hardness combined with flexibility was just what he aspired to in his writing. In those years Bronn was emotionally restless, dissatisfied. Nothing durable came of his all too flexible romances, or his friends' sporadic efforts at matchmaking. In a paired-off world he was beginning to feel lonesome and left out. At bottom his poems were only scab-picking and whining.

The movies favored by the women he took out were almost always romantic comedies, date movies, and for these Bronn began to conceive a real disgust. Watching them was like seeing the skin of an automaton peel off to reveal the clockwork and wiring. The engineering of commonplace emotions in these cinematic candy bars was too crude, too regular. Worse yet, Bronn felt the movies as reproaches, as criticism. No doubt many of the women saw all this too but they responded in an opposite fashion. Where Bronn was depressed by the ease with which the couples in the movies overcame obstacles, endured foreshortened, tragicomic reverses, liquidated blocking characters, and found their way to happiness, his dates usually seemed to be buoyed up, given hope. Why shouldn't life imitate such plots, they seemed to be asking him. But this was Bronn's problem; life might imitate art, but it would never model itself on the craft of cheap manipulation. Such films bred fantasies, not aspirations. And the more charming and plausible these fantasies, the more insidious the illusion and the deeper the wounds left behind when life relentlessly failed to measure up.

Bronn now saw himself as a bachelor; that is, he had come to understand his social condition not as a temporary one, as a matter of just not running into the right woman, but what Gloria would call his fate. It is understandable that bachelors prefer to see films with unhappy endings. However, Hollywood, knowing where its corn is buttered, no longer made such films. The public could absorb any level of mass murder, all manner of slashing and dismemberment, but it would not stand for a millionaire declining to wed a good-looking call girl.

All the same, Bronn would not give up the movies or even daydreams, not even if he despised them. And so, like many other people, he tried to turn his hand to writing a screenplay of his own. For a couple months he gave up both poetry and dating to devote his weekends to the work.

Bronn made his hero a physicist/poet in an unnamed, rather abstract country with a generic authoritarian regime. The hero was to be eminent equally as a man of science and of letters, an internationally respected figure deemed an ornament of the republic and thus untouchable. Nevertheless, one morning just after breakfast he is arrested and taken to a house in the country where he is locked in a large bedroom. The regime is convinced that his poems are elaborately coded messages to its opponents plotting in exile. Most of Bronn's script—until he abandoned it as a botch—was made up of the hero's interrogations. He was never able to decide if the interrogator should be male or female, serious or ironic, seductive or sadistic, right or wrong.

The interrogator maintains, or pretends to, that the hero's poems all have hidden meanings, secret messages. The protagonist, provisionally named Philip Bonnard, is at once baffled and defiant.

-What sort of messages?

-You tell me, Dr. Bonnard.

-But there simply aren't any.

-Is that so? We know it isn't a simple matter of ciphers or codes—*s* means *e* or *t* means *a*. There's your imagery. Our experts have found suspicious patterns. And your metrical schemes also appear to be significant. More patterns.

-What patterns?

-Again, you deny—

-I *do* deny. Emphatically.

-Do you mean you don't know what you're doing when you write in an organized manner or that you deny such patterns exist in your poems at all?

-Of course there are patterns but—

-So you agree on that point.

-Look, a long time ago Socrates pointed out that poets don't know what they're doing.

-We all know what Socrates said at *his* trial, Dr. Bonnard.

-Then I'm to be put on trial?

-That depends.

-It's my right.

-Your *right*? How amusing. Look here, Dr. Bonnard, you're a famous physicist, well-known for the fastidiousness, some might even say the elegance, of your work. Are we to suppose that you're less—let's say *deliberate*—when you write poems?

-Why not? Maybe it's just to escape what you call my fastidiousness that I write verses.

-To whom are your poems directed?

-What do you mean?

-I'm asking about your co-conspirators, of course.

-You mean my readers?

-If you like you can call them a *coterie*.

-I have no idea who reads my poems. If it weren't for the occasional piece of fan mail I wouldn't know that anyone reads them at all.

-We know all about the fan mail, as you call it.

-You do?

-Look, you claim to write for no one, for your own diversion. Then why publish, especially in other countries?

-For validation.

-What?

-In order to write more poems. When I publish something I forget about it, but still it's exhilarating, an encouragement, a spur. I like writing.

-Why?

-It's satisfying.

-In what respect?

-It makes me feel powerful.

-I see. So it *is* power you're after.

And so on. Bronn tried to think up various subplots and complications. He tried making Bonnard the uncle of somebody interesting, giving him a worried girlfriend, even making him the spy the government accused him of being. He invented purely visual scenes of escape and pursuit, even a love affair with the interrogator, assuming she were to be female, that would end with her violent death. In the end the thing fell apart in his hands like an old dishrag. He had to admit that his own fantasies were more disgusting, and far less entertaining, than the processed ones being sold in the movie theaters.

Bronn gave up his script and instead wrote a poem which was meant to express the feeling of a truthful movie about love.

THE PURITAN FLUTE

Paradise on slow September Sundays
leaf-smoke with promises of tender change
he at the table composing semi-brilliant
essays she playing her transverse flute
sedately in the corner, in the kitchen.
All the body demanded they gladly gave

gobbling green olives and Cheshire cheese
dreamily rubbing arches, toes and soles
in that ripening otherworldly autumn
of cold rain and November twilight in a
brown room, her scent nestled against his
his breath keeping measure with her flute.

On her birthday he spoke to her in Japanese
strolled reflectively through a pretend garden
selecting the reddest elephant lilies and greenest
shards of jade which she took, twirling her flute
contentedly and exacting more compliments:
you're level-headed and twice as alive as I.
She teased a little roughly: three times, at least.
Oh, it was charming; yet they couldn't concur
on the national debt or the color of a sunset
and this gave her sniffles and misgivings.
He reasoned, there are always difficulties; she
lamented, I'll never see the same world as you—
you could live on Neptune while I'm here;
such middling gaps of ill omen gaped weekly
but worse was the daily abrasion of nubs,
her refusal to speak while he was driving
or laugh when he most needed her to,
his picking at his cuffs, throat-clearing,
taut squint and athletic agnosticism.

Her elsewhere life tumbled with murmurous
infants and minivans, while his played out
on a desert island tolerably fitted with two or
three memories, costly fantasies, and books.
Unspoken feelings run deepest, she whispered one
day laying down the still warm flute, serene in
the face of his sorrow—but exasperation won:

Cut that out or I'll wilt. I will. I'll wilt!
Long into the winter he worried this wound
with an accusing finger, forlornly
chose malleable silence until even
his answering machine refused her calls.
Like six-year-olds denied dangerous toys
the spiteful always insist on their way, she
shrugged to her new friend and together
they went off to join the Sligo excavations.

For him the snow blew over a desert.
Unable to arrange a skiing accident he
bought two terriers who growled at
one another; assuring himself there's
more enterprise in going naked, that life at
last is solitary, dignity won by facing up,
still he yearned for her smell and above all the
puritan flute sounding round his head in that
solemn instant after she had ceased to play.

"The Puritan Flute" was Bronn's final poem.

IV.

IN his forties Bronn gave up not only writing self-exalting
screenplays and self-pitying poems but his search for a
companion. Less and less able to bear the company of even the
unhappily married, Bronn seldom accepted dinner invitations,
and soon received none. He stuck to what he had, chemistry,

books, music, and movies. The VCR freed him from even the minimal social activities of milling about in theater lobbies and sitting in an audience.

One lonely Saturday evening he found himself in the mood for a French film. More than a mood, it was an irresistible craving, as if for *la cuisine française*.

He drove to Video Paradise and probed skeptically through the exiguous section of foreign films. Most were familiar, non-French, or unappealing but at last he came across a film of which he had not heard. The cover told him nothing as it featured only the customary semi-dressed starlet; the précis on the back was wholly unintelligible. The film's title was *Est-Ce Que Les Bâtiments Suffisent?* This seemed to Bronn an odd and curious question, so he rented the film.

He took the tape home, placed it in his VCR, stretched out on the couch. Though he was already sleepy, fatigue did not prevent him from watching every frame, reading every subtitle. Despite its Gallic velocity, the film did not seem eager to discourage a certain drowsiness in its viewers, aiming less at stimulation than at some other, ineffably French condition. *Il ne sait quoi.*

Plain white credits on a flat black background. Euro-jazz. French, Franco-Italian, Franco-German names: Anatole Noisette, Camille von Hardetzen, Georges Gabinetti, Jean-Christophe Tollens, Marie-Alain Joindru, Nathalie Bréant. Mise-en-scène. Cinématographie. Son.

The music stops abruptly, almost a brutal cut. We are in color, *in medias res aut in flagrante delicto*. A man and a woman are making love. Both people are decidedly young. The girl is quite beautiful, a brunette with green eyes, full lips, well-shaped, flexible limbs; the boy is more ordinary, slightly built, with black wiry hair. The unthinking sounds they are uttering (no subtitles as yet) are belied by their somewhat deliberate technique, recalling the overly scripted jazz of the credits. They writhe diagonally across a wide soft French bed. The bed gives up no noises and if there is other furniture in the room it is not visible. The scene goes on for one minute, two, becomes embarrassing, irritating, finally tedious. The director could have any number of motives. At length, just at *le moment juste*, the scene ends.

A wide establishing shot of a provincial town; only the cars in the cobbled streets suggest it is not the seventeenth century but perhaps the 1960s. A small garage. The young man emerges from beneath a blue Citroën. He is wearing blue overalls. An older man, evidently another mechanic, perhaps the owner of the garage, is sitting on an oil drum drinking from a bottle of *vin ordinaire* and talking about the unfaithfulness of his wife. Explaining why he deems it prudent to countenance her behavior, he affects a tone at once avaricious and philosophical, delivering a catalogue of her lovers, taking a hit of wine after each name, then greedily ticking off the benefits accruing to him from each of his wife's liaisons. The young man, disgusted, swears that were *he* married and *his* wife unfaithful, he would not hesitate to kill her, the lover, then himself. The elder man laughs, drinks.

The good-looking young woman is alone in a darkened room. A poster of Sarah Bernhardt is stuck on the wall next to another of the Beatles (yes, it is the 60s). She is reclining on some pillows on the floor in a tank top and bell-bottomed blue jeans. Her long hair is pulled into a French braid; she is listening to a record of Brahms' *Clarinet Quintet*, Opus 115. A little boy comes into the room and greets her perfunctorily, like a brother. From his leather schoolboy's satchel he extracts various objects, all that he has stolen during the week, he says. A fountain pen. A record album. A notebook. Bubble-gum. Cigarettes. A bicycling cap. He is proud of each, but proudest of the last, a red bikini he has stolen for his sister. The sister smiles, rumples his hair affectionately, closes her eyes, returns to Brahms' autumnal world. Chintz curtains billow at the window.

The young man is having supper with his colleague/boss and his voluptuous wife. While the colleague goes to fetch the new field glasses given him by his wife's latest lover, the wife reaches under the table and grabs the young man's thigh. He leaps up, overturning the table. Dishes, a tureen, glasses, the bottle of wine, all crash to the floor. The wife is startled. Her husband returns, laughing and wagging his finger in her direction. "Don't disturb yourself, Cherie. The boy's an idealist."

The older man takes the lad over to the French window, out on a little French balcony, and bids him look through the binoculars and tell everything he sees. The young man sees (as do we) an elderly woman carrying a string bag full of onions and bread. A mugger in an alleyway looks her over, thinks better of it. We see a minor traffic accident, the two drivers gesticulating at one another with comic fury. A bearded street musician plays his violin outside a café. The young man sweeps over the town, searching out the house of his sweetheart. He locates her window. It is dark. He smiles.

Now the action accelerates. The young woman has a fight with her father, a bald man who keeps a small furniture store and suffers from complaints of the liver. In a scene in a small park, she tearfully begs the young man to take her away, out of this insufferable little town. The young man agrees. He steals a blue Citroën. The little brother comes along as well. They decide to drive to the coast, stopping in meadows along the way to eat bread and cheese. They ditch the car in a ravine not far from the Mediterranean. That night the lovers make love on the beach at Cannes while the boy wanders into a fancy hotel where he meets a homosexual writer who catches him trying to lift a crystal ashtray.

That very night the hotel catches fire. The boy is escaping down the stairs (has he been up in the writer's room?) when he hears a dog barking behind a door. The boy is unable to open the door. Flames shoot through the corridor. The young man appears, calling for the boy through the smoke. Together they burst into the dog's room where they find an elderly lady in bed. They save this old woman and her schnauzer as well. The lady turns out to be fabulously wealthy, very kind and generous, a little eccentric. She so closely resembles the old lady in the Babar books that the others call her affectionately Madame Babar, a sobriquet that seems to give her pleasure.

Madame Babar takes the three of them to Paris on the train, first class. During the trip she, the boy, and the schnauzer become intimates, sharing all kinds of little secrets. For example, the boy confesses to her his ambition to become an architect. The schnauzer discloses his fondness for peanuts. For her part, Madame Babar admits she has always wished to have a house built just for her, that she is weary of her family's ancient homes.

Meanwhile, the young pair are befriended by a somewhat older couple who occupy the next compartment. The man is a professional tennis player; the woman owns a hat shop. All five adults get drunk in the saloon and Madame Babar tells the fascinating story of her life to which only the boy pays attention.

They arrive in the capital. The tennis player goes off to the French Open, his wife to her shop. The three vagabonds move into Madame Babar's enormous and elegant two-floor apartment near the Place de la Bastille. The boy is given a room all to himself in which he at once sets to work designing a house for the old lady. The young couple have a room to themselves as well and, as it is a warm May, they wear few clothes. One morning, however, the young woman puts on a miniskirt and goes to look up her friend who owns the hat shop in order to ask for a job; but as she is crossing a street she is struck by a blue Citroën and taken off to a hospital in an ambulance, unconscious.

The boy tears up his plans and begins all over again.

The young man is becoming worried. He paces up and down the apartment, which is magnificently furnished. His sweetheart hasn't returned. Madame Babar suggests he make a phone call. He finds the number of the hat shop, telephones. No, they haven't seen her. He recollects what he had said to his boss at the garage about unfaithfulness. Bursting with anxiety, jealousy, and resolution, he goes into the unfamiliar Paris streets to search for his sweetheart. He looks here and there without any plan and cannot find her. Out of despair, weariness, and the wish to see a friend, he takes the Metro out to Roland Garros Stadium where he watches the man from the train lose a close match to a huge blond Swede.

In the hospital that night an orderly attempts to molest the young woman. Just in time she regains consciousness and screams. The orderly, terrified, puts his hand over her mouth and threatens to cut her throat. She bites his hand, kicks and swears at him until the orderly runs off. With her shapely left leg in a cast, she escapes from the hospital and takes a taxi back to the old lady's apartment. The taxi driver is a nice Russian, a droll character. She admits she has no money but he doesn't mind. He hopes her left leg when it heals will look as lovely as her right one (the miniskirt is gone but in her hospital robe she is still skimpily clad).

A few days later the old lady falls ill. Her three guests and the schnauzer gather around her bed. The boy is inconsolable. His face runs with tears as he holds in his trembling hands the completed plans for Madame Babar's new house. The schnauzer cannot be induced to leave the foot of his mistress's bed. The doctor is not encouraging, muttering about elevated blood pressure. The old lady remarks cheerfully that she is not in the least afraid of dying. Late that night, after the boy has fallen asleep, she asks the young couple if they will make love on her bed while she watches. They are taken aback but agree in order to oblige her. In a scene that recalls, but does not reproduce, the opening shot they do what she has asked. This magic turns the trick. Madame Babar begins to recover.

It is now late in July and plans are laid for the August vacation. They are to go to the old lady's château in Normandy on the ample grounds of which construction has already begun on the new house the boy has designed. The young couple sense it is in this house that she intends to die, but the boy is unaware of this.

The château is lovely and dignified. On a rise near a little

Norman lake the foundation for the new house has already been excavated. The young man determines to write poems with the fountain pen the boy had stolen in the provincial town. Notwithstanding her broken leg, the young woman takes walks in the countryside while her lover composes sonnets. On one of these rambles she runs into a film company. The actresses coo over her unspoiled beauty and the director, a fortyish New Wave type, is enchanted. She invites him to lunch at Madame Babar's château.

Over the meal there is a lengthy conversation concerning the cinema, about which the old lady is surprisingly well informed, even posing a complicated technical question about depth of field. The boy is absent. Madame Babar takes a shine to the director, who is intelligent and devoid of pretension. When he asks if he might use the château as a location for a scene in his film, the old lady concurs with alacrity. "I agree," she says approvingly. "One must always be prepared to improvise."

The boy returns from the construction site where he has been supervising the work and informs everyone that the new house ought to be finished in a week's time. When they all express astonishment he raises a finger and explains that he has employed the latest in prefabricated materials and techniques of modular construction.

The young woman remarks that it is probably time to have her cast removed. The director offers to drive her to Lisieux to have a doctor remove it; the young man naturally insists on accompanying them. The brother says he would like to come as well but his presence on the building site is indispensable. "A moment," says the young woman as they are about to depart. She hobbles up the grand stairway of the château and returns wearing a red bikini under an unbuttoned shirtwaist with yellow stripes. This is the very red bikini her brother had stolen expressly for her. The boy is delighted as are the director, the schnauzer, even Madame Babar. The lover alone frowns. The director fetches his car, a blue Citroën, and the three climb in. As they pull away on the château's circular drive he honks his horn three times and the old lady and the boy wave goodbye. "I should like to see my new house today," Madame Babar says.

The Citroën careens down a narrow Norman road flanked by poplars. The director is clearly driving too fast. Coming around a sharp turn the car collides with a refrigerated truck. Blood and milk spill over the road. The camera pulls in tight on the two liquids running through the gravel, mixing, turning pink.

The old lady and the boy reach the new house. The sun is going down and the workmen have quit for the day. The house is fantastic, with curves, crenellations, two towers, generous curved windows, and unimaginable concrete cantilevers, the kind of thing a highly gifted child might construct with terrifically expensive blocks. The schnauzer leaps around the boy. Madame Babar squeezes the boy's hand. Under the setting sun the white sides of the house turn orange, scarlet, then the same pink we have just seen mixed in the gravel. Finally, the screen turns a blue so dark as to be nearly black.

In a voice-over the boy explains that upon hearing news of the deaths of his sister, her lover, and the film director, the old lady suffered a stroke. Nevertheless, he managed to move her into the new house a week before her peaceful death. She has left him her fortune and the schnauzer.

And so I joined up with the film company. I no longer wished to become an architect. Buildings are not enough. I have learned to make films. People must live as well as inhabit. No, it is not enough to be an architect of spaces in which people will die.

Yes, this was just the kind of film of which Bronn had felt the need, the sort he would have been proud to have written even though it was so thoroughly French: bound by no symmetries, enforcing no overbearing architecture, amply furnished with playful visuals, vivid colors, easy-going lucidity, redemptive randomness, beginning without exposition, swelling to a languorous, watery, haphazard middle, with an abrupt ending followed by a nonchalant moral about the relationship among art and life and death, sensual yet bravely sad, with subtitles. The movie made Bronn feel closer to life or at least that life was a thing it would be good to be closer to. He would really have liked to make the acquaintance of that precocious French boy, the gifted, wounded *metteur-en-scène*; he would have relished talking with the generous old lady as much as sleeping with the lovely young one; he yearned even to read the sonnets of the young man and to see the early films of the director.

So Bronn slid quietly into bed, both satisfied and resigned. With the astonishment of those suddenly aware that they have become middle-aged he wondered how many more movies there could be. A line of verse flickered across his mind, *His house is in the village, though*. Then he fell into a sleep choked with splendid non-architectural dreams, dreams without trauma, sweet dreams.

Kafka's Fountain Pen

THE banquet had climaxed with a surprisingly high-minded speech from the chairman of the town's newly established trade association. It was the sort of speech constructed by heaping one block on top of another. A short man with the watchful face of a guard dog, the chairman took satisfaction in enumerating the business community's recent achievements, including even quite small ones so as to leave no one unmentioned; then, indicating with his forefinger a point directly above his head, he capped the oration off with a rhetorical spire scraping a commercial heaven somewhere up there near the track lighting. When the applause and stein pounding petered out people rose to leave. I was more than ready to do the same. There were statistics back in my hotel room that insisted on being read. I was on the point of bidding farewell to the three men with whom I had shared a table but one of them anticipated me. They were going to stay on for a bit and would be greatly honored by my company. Might I care to join them?

I did not wish to be impolite. In fact, I made it a point to accept almost all such invitations because it was often in informal settings that I picked up my best information.

"Bravo," said Huber, who had done the inviting and was a little tipsy. "After all, we must be hospitable. Distinguished foreign visitor. Assure you. Greatest pleasure."

"Yes indeed. Anyway it's far too early to be going home," added Kehlenbeck. I had noticed he always spoke after Huber.

The third man, Legner, smiled and nodded. "Perhaps I'll stay a little while too."

We adjourned to the hotel's lounge. Huber went directly to the bar and ordered a bottle of brandy. The place was hardly empty but, being a low-ceilinged, spacious room, it seemed so. There were large speakers all over the place, but, it being a Thursday evening, the sound system had been turned off. There was a smell of fried onions and new carpet.

We took a corner booth and sat in a semi-circle, like the people in old photographs of night clubs. The lighting was dim and my companions were half in shadow.

The barman brought over the brandy and four snifters on a silver tray. Huber gave him money, rather ostentatiously, and dismissed him in a lordly fashion. Having established himself as host, he poured for us all.

Huber lifted his glass almost above his head; I was afraid he would spill it. "To the Workers' Paradise," he said with ponderous sarcasm. Kehlenbeck chuckled and, as usual, found something to add. "A good joke, eh professor?" Legner grunted, perhaps in mild amusement. We all drank up.

During the banquet I observed that my messmates had much in common. For instance, each sported a blue suit and had teeth that looked newly minted. All were blond and balding in the way that such men do, prematurely, with the hair on top growing thinner and finer so that it is difficult to make out where their foreheads stop. Kehlenbeck looked to be hardly thirty-five, Huber perhaps in his mid-forties, Legner somewhere in between. But there were differences too. During the banquet, and especially while the speeches were being delivered, Kehlenbeck and Huber found a lot to say to each other and plenty to laugh about. I was uncomfortably reminded of the young men at the rear of my lecture hall, their athletic legs extended or draped over the backs of the seats in front of them, yawning, stifling guffaws. Legner, on the other hand, held himself aloof. Moreover, now that I looked at his face, it struck me as more thoughtful than the others', more adult, as though something serious had happened to him. I had the impression that, unlike Huber or Kehlenbeck, Legner might be interested in more than making money.

In high school back in Indiana I was one of the misfits who elected to take German rather than Spanish or French. It was a consequential choice but not a meaningful one. I was not one of those Nazi-obsessed adolescents deep into negative self-definition, the ones who etch swastikas into school desks and draw tanks in their notebooks. Nor was my family German; I was not digging for Teutonic roots. I simply had a crush on Leda Zucker, the daughter of a Westphalian immigrant, and I found out that she intended to take German. Nothing good came of my efforts with Leda, who developed early and was dating college guys in tenth grade, but I stuck with German. In the fullness of time I produced a doctoral dissertation on certain aspects of the so-called economic miracle of the fifties, particularly ship-building, and turned into a mild-mannered professor in a not-so-ivory tower. When the Berlin Wall came down I applied for a series of grants to study the economic integration of the former GDR. The foundations showered me with dollars, with marks. I made many contacts in Germany and, to my surprise, came to be regarded as a sort of consultant. When pressed I gave my advice with compunction, but I did give it. No one could call me famous; however, in certain commercial circles, particularly in the eastern states, my name was not unknown.

It was my research that brought me to this half-sleepy, half-bustling town. I had heard of the newly formed trade association and wanted to interview the chairman, a successful importer of appliances. As it turned out, he interviewed me. We met in his office from which he could easily keep a sharp eye on his showroom. What he wanted to discuss with me was corruption, though he was too discreet to call it that. The range of his euphemisms for kickbacks, smuggling, and graft was impressive. He seemed to think a measure of underhanded dealing might be indispensable in building a free market. Alluding to my academic specialty he asked in an off-the-record tone if there wasn't "quite a bit done back then that was, let's say, off-the-books?" I advised complete probity, utter transparency, respect for law, and warned of the ruinous consequences of criminal infiltration. Why this was, he said, *selbstverständlich, natürlich.* But I sensed irony in the way he agreed so readily, as if I had been joking, or as though we were being recorded. While the entrepreneurs were certainly among the most liberated of those I met in the East, even they found it hard to rid themselves of the notion that somewhere their dossiers were growing thicker.

Anyway, it was as I was departing, there among pristine slabs of refrigerators and ovens, that the trade chairman invited me to attend his inaugural banquet. "It's our first!" he exclaimed proudly, "a milestone not to be missed." I could see the pleasure it gave him to say, "You shall be my personal guest."

Huber's line was clothing, Kehlenbeck's medical supplies. Legner already operated two Laundromats and had just opened an auto parts store. I heard a good deal about all their businesses over dinner. I asked out of politeness and had only myself to blame. Businessmen, of course, need little prompting to expatiate on what lies nearest their hearts. I heard of triumphs, frustrations, coups, anxieties, visions. On the whole, they were as optimistic as the chairman. As Huber saw it, Europe was bound to flourish and they were in the middle of it. "Thin workers to the East and fat consumers to the West—how can we fail?" Not for the first time I noticed how such people, natural merchants long denied their métier, delighted in the petty details of retail capitalism. Huber, for instance, spoke with positive relish about every turn in his lease negotiations and had even more to say about the hiring of staff. "I interview every one myself. Yes. And do you know, they call me *chief*!" He beamed. As for Kehlenbeck, he adored documents. For my benefit, he narrated minutely his experiences at the town hall when he filed his papers of incorporation and registered his occupancy, listed all the stamps that were affixed to his papers and described the significance of each. Then he began on his trip to Hamburg to sign his first contract. The point was not the journey, but the contract. "I've had it framed," he admitted. Even Legner was comparatively expansive about the new dispensation. "If you work hard and you're clever, then you're rewarded, you expand, you build things up. Last week I called my staff together and announced that they would all be receiving a raise at the end of the month."

Huber hit him on the back. "We've all heard about it. You're quite a hero, Legner."

Legner flushed and looked down into his snifter. "They're loyal," he muttered. "If we rise, we rise together."

The conversation next turned to the raising of capital. Huber spoke disparagingly of bankers.

"Cautious to a fault. Some of them carry prudence positively to the point of constipation," he whined. "You wouldn't believe what a time that miserly Grabmacher gave me over a matter of a few thousand marks."

"It always helps to have connections," Kehlenbeck chimed in, patting the table complacently.

"Ach, you and your father-in-law," grumbled Huber. "Such an old story. Even our distinguished guest must have heard it in America by now! But what about you, Legner? We've never heard how you got your stake."

Legner said nothing.

Huber turned to me. "Can you believe it? He just showed up one day with enough. Straight from Berlin, a real city-slicker." Turning to Legner he asked facetiously, "But you really are an easterner, right Legner? You didn't by any chance jump the wrong way over that wall, did you?"

Legner remained impassive, clearly displeased. "Some joke," he said.

"Yes. Just a joke. You're one of us all right. One of the best at the game." Huber raised his eyebrows and, looking at me, tapped his finger on the side of his nose. "Today Laundromats, tomorrow Mercedes-Benz, eh?"

Kehlenbeck, who sat on my right, leaned over and whispered one word in my ear. "Stasi."

"How's that lovely wife of yours, Kehlenbeck?" Legner asked sharply. "I may only be a bachelor and no expert on such matters, but do you really think it wise to leave her alone so late at night?"

After that the evening came quickly to an end. We parted at the door, Huber and Kehlenbeck stumbling off together while Legner hailed a cab. "Would you like to share?" he asked politely. "Oh, no, thank you," I said. "I prefer to walk. It's just two blocks. It'll clear my head."

Legner paused at the taxi's open door looking as if there were something he wished to say. I waited. Apparently he changed his mind, because he bid me a quick *guten Abend*, and was gone.

• • •

The following day was to be my last in town and I had kept it open with the idea of taking in a few of the local attractions. I slept late. When I came down to the lobby at ten the hotel manager summoned me to the desk and handed me an envelope with my name on it.

Standing as straight as a floor lamp, an object which he closely resembled, the manager made a great show of checking his watch. "Delivered by hand forty-four minutes ago, Herr Professor," he snapped in the regimental tone he affected with guests. It wouldn't have surprised me to hear a pair of heels clicking. I had the impression that since the end of socialism ("We pretend to work; they pretend to pay us") he had reverted to type, set efficiency up as his idol and to it eagerly sacrificed all softness and good humor. Evidently he believed the way to be a good German of the new New Order was to resemble one of the old New Order.

There were half a dozen leather club chairs in the lobby. I chose one, sat down, and opened the envelope.

It was another invitation, but a decidedly eccentric one. Though the embossed address at the top of the stationery identified the author, I looked first at the signature. Legner had covered the whole sheet with his handwriting which was rather spidery and leaned to the left. A handwritten letter was unusual for a businessman but the content was far stranger.

Respected Professor,

"I understand them so well, they were the first acquaintances I had made in the town's small taverns, and to them I owed my first inkling of a ruthless hardness which I was now so conscious of, everywhere on earth, that I was even beginning to feel it in myself."

It is improbable that you will recognize this sentence; however, you may well know its author. He has become my favorite poet, for a poet is what he is, the most visionary and at the same time the most realistic. There is no purer German than that which Franz Kafka wrote. To read him diligently does much to restore our language after three generations of foulness [Unreinheit]. *But it is not exactly of Kafka that I want to speak.*

You may recall that last night I declined to answer a certain question posed by my colleagues. This question obsesses them. Indeed, they may have invited you to join us after the banquet expressly to make an occasion for posing it. They may have reckoned that in the presence of a respected foreigner I would not dare to refuse to answer, that you might just by being there constitute an appeal to conscience.

If so, they were not far off the mark. However, Huber and Kehlenbeck are merely gossips and do not deserve an answer with which they would only try to damage me. I know they think I am concealing a connection to the Stasi, the old State Police. This amuses me because in this country, as you must be aware, it is impossible to throw a hammer or a sickle without hitting somebody with such a connection. For reasons of my own I would like to answer that question; that is, to account for my initial capital, but to you alone. I would regard it as a great favor were you to indulge me in this matter.

I will be at your service at the above address from one o'clock this afternoon until six-thirty.

Many thanks to you for your attention.

Johannes Legner

My first response was annoyance. Why should Legner presume I cared about where he got money to open a wretched Laundromat? My second reaction was caution. I certainly didn't want to become embroiled in some ridiculous quarrel between Legner and his colleagues. I reviewed the conversation of the previous evening in the light of this mutual malice. I recalled Legner's reserve and the way Huber had pressed the question of Legner's capital. I also thought of Kehlenbeck's whispered accusation, which I had taken at the time for some sort of local joke. After all, what Legner said was true; the GDR had been more or less a nation of informants.

I re-read the letter and revised my opinion. It seemed to me that Legner was not actually making any presumption about me but simply asking a favor. Though I disliked the mysterious tone of "for reasons of my own," I was not uninterested. The role of confessor can be inviting, particularly if it is imposed by a man as laconic as Legner appeared to be.

Above all, though, it was the opening of the letter that arrested me, the sentence from Kafka. I had, of course, read some Kafka in my advanced German courses. I found *The Trial* and *Metamorphosis* puzzling, profundities to the bottom of which I could not, or did not want to, dive. This run-on sentence, however, swelled in significance as I re-read it. Who were these "acquaintances" it alluded to? Clearly Legner was implying they were men like Huber and Kehlenbeck, just the sort of people I had been dealing with for years, the buccaneers of the East whose "ruthless hardness" I took for human nature operating freely. I never thought of it as being imposed by the new dispensation, by the pressures of a smug, triumphant capitalism that was in fact spreading "everywhere on earth." This was new ground for me and momentarily my imagination grasped the full force of such a process not in economic but in human terms. Could Legner be saying that he was not guilty however he obtained his capital but rather for making a success with it? If that was how he felt, he could certainly see me as the emblem of the forces that destroyed the utopian illusions of his youth and imposed the dispiriting truth of "ruthless hardness." Kafka was his poet but Legner had come of age in the GDR, had been raised up to the false ideals of which his success would seem a betrayal. Who had explored guilt more intimately than the author of *The Trial*? The night before Legner said it was giving his employees a raise that most pleased him about being their boss. "We rise together." Were those raises an expiation? Did he see himself

as an exploiter of the working class? Was he, like the speaker of
Kafka's sentence, appalled that he had caught the hectic from
people like Huber and Kehlenbeck? Were they, like their association's chairman, enthralled by the crude, self-serving notion
that private greed inevitably leads to general welfare? Did the
ruminative Legner mean to cross-examine me about the blacker
magic of the market?

Well, I said to myself, why not go? It was a fine October
Friday, cloudless sky, crisp air. I would pay my visit to the local
museum, grab a quick sausage and a beer, then stroll over to
Legner's office in the mid-afternoon, if not to oblige him, then
to satisfy my curiosity.

• • •

The office of Johannes Legner was situated in neither of his
prosperous Laundromats nor above his newly opened auto parts
store but on the second floor of an antique building, freshly
stuccoed, four blocks from the central square with its statue of
Luther, clad as an Augustinian monk, vigorously taking his stand.
A modest brass plaque offering nothing but Legner's name was
affixed by the entrance among three more pretentious declara-
tions of commercial occupancy. I walked up a flight of freshly
varnished stairs and opened a door which likewise sported the
same brass plaque with Legner's name on it. He had ordered
two. I entered a reception room with ample space for a couple
of wing chairs, an end-table, two four-drawer filing cabinets,
and a metal desk. A door gave on to an inner office. Legner was
waiting; perhaps he had been pacing. Anyway, he greeted me
with restrained expressions of gratitude, enfolding my hand in
both of his rather than shaking it like a businessman. His face,

every bit as grave as the night before, struck me as more focused and narrower. In the full light of day his blond hair was almost white and I was momentarily reminded of those Nazi posters of long-muscled Aryan fathers and stupidly resolute blue-eyed grenadiers. Indicating the receptionist's desk he announced, "I gave Frieda the afternoon off," as if to assure me of the gravity he accorded our appointment while also making sure I knew that he did indeed have a receptionist.

When I consider that Legner had been waiting for me over an hour, not knowing if I would show up, it is little wonder that he appeared agitated. He needed to make an effort to be polite. He asked if I had eaten. "We could go out, if you like," he said with something like horror.

"No. I ate on the way over. One of your town's excellent sausages."

He nodded once, impatient. "Was I right about your knowing Kafka?"

I shrugged. "I suppose everyone does, in a way. He's become a universal adjective, hasn't he?"

Legner frowned, opened his mouth to reply, then changed his mind. It was clear that my remark disappointed him; maybe it seemed insufficiently reverent. In any case, he turned abruptly. "Please. Let's go into my office." He was already tearing open the door. "It's a little warmer in there."

It was not in the least cold in the receptionist's office. I supposed he wished to confess his secret in a place as sealed off as possible from the outside world, a warm office, snug like a confessional. In retrospect, I think there was another reason he wanted to use his office. Many of us have some room which stands for our selves and this was Legner's.

The outer room was impersonal and businesslike, but the inner was altogether different. Its one large window was bordered by thick drapes of a rich red. If the desk was a reproduction it was quite a good one, a splendid oblong of mahogany, the sort esteemed a century ago for sheer weight and solidity. The rug was a good Shiraz, the chairs of red leather. Against the wall to the right of the door squatted a small oak chest ornamented with carving, with brass fittings and claw legs. Most surprising of all were the bookcases that filled two walls from floor to ceiling, suitable for a lawyer's chambers perhaps, but not an entrepreneur's headquarters. A couple of pictures hung on the open wall by the door, and these I automatically turned to look at. One was a watercolor of the Charles Bridge in Prague, the other a photograph of a man I recognized from the stiff black hair, piercing eyes, and ears like open wings.

"Yes, that's Franz Kafka. I owe him a great deal, you see. Everything. But let's sit down. It's to tell you what I owe to Kafka that I begged you to come."

He sat behind his desk; I took the closest chair. "Before you begin," I said, "there's something I'd like to ask you."

The nervous way Legner played with his hands made me aware that he had planned out how to begin his confession and I almost regretted throwing him off his stride. He picked up a black fountain pen, one of the old-fashioned large-barreled kind, and tapped it lightly, almost tenderly, against his palm.

"In your letter, the sentence from Kafka, what was that about, exactly?"

Legner did not reply at once. He seldom spoke quickly.

He lay the pen down with care, sat up even straighter, leaned forward on his elbows, and was evasive. "If you don't mind, I'll come to that soon."

I smiled. "As you like." If Legner were intent on being mysterious, that was fine by me. After all, it was part of the fun.

"I'll begin, then, by telling you frankly why it's especially to you that I wish to tell my story. Much as I respect it, this has nothing to do with your expertise. It's because you're an American professor and therefore, in a sense, a brother to the one in my story."

Even in foreign parts it is hard to think of oneself simply as a type. So, I was here as an American professor, evidently the second in Legner's life. It felt virtually like a national responsibility.

He leaned back, apparently with relief that I had not interrupted him again, and he looked up as though consulting an invisible text on the ceiling. I was reminded of the chairman pointing to the *Himmel Hoch* of the future. Then he began.

"I grew up in East Berlin. My mother was a nurse and my father worked in a machine shop, both of them thorough proletarians. I did well at school and made it to university where I intended to study literature . . . . You see, I too aspired to become a professor, for a time at least. I learned to stoke the ferocious engine of Marxist criticism, to isolate in each work the class conflicts; I unerringly determined who controlled the means of production. I was sharp at ferreting out the selfish interests of the bourgeoisie in this or that classic, exposing the anti-revolutionary sham of their charity and the sugared illusions of capitalist marriage. I pretended to despise formalism and to distrust any sign of elitist individuality. On my own, of course, I read more widely, when I was able to get books from the West. They weren't so difficult to come by actually, especially in the last years, though they were frightfully expensive. What we students could get hold of we handed round. It was my longing for books that first made me aware of my poverty. Property was disgraceful. Under the old system poverty was common but no disgrace. People were guaranteed employment of a sort, medical care of a sort, and my education was paid for by the State—education also of a sort, since it's really true that you get what you pay for. As you know perfectly well, all that changed overnight. The advertisers moved in as if to mock us. Coca-Cola stuck out its tongue; Sony sang to us like the Lorelei. Suddenly we were poor cousins and everyone resented not being rich, yearned to be rich, envied the rich; above all, the young *expected* to be rich. It seems odd now but the notion of being free without being rich simply didn't occur to many of us.

"I gave up my academic ambitions. I wanted to be a capitalist. Anyone could see there was money to be made. I conceived the idea of setting up a modern Laundromat. After all, not everyone was going to be able to afford those washing machines our new chairman is flogging. I would be supplying a need not just for cleanliness, but also community. People would gather there and perhaps the little that was good about the old system might be preserved. Anyway, for me it would be a start. But no one can be a capitalist without capital. According to my reckoning, I wouldn't need much, but even that little was out of reach. I didn't mind beginning with just enough, but how to get it? That was the question. A loan was unthinkable and I had no resources on which to draw. At this time my father fell ill and on top of that the shop where he worked closed. His legs were bad due to poorly treated diabetes. Between that and the inflation, my mother's pay was barely enough to keep the two of them alive."

Legner paused and began to play with the pen again. He looked me in the eyes, beseechingly yet giving little away. "The essential thing to realize about what happened is that I had no real plan. All I had was desire, but I had plenty of that. What happened was the result of chance, some dubious work, and plain dishonesty. And my desire. Yes, why not? I committed a fraud . . . ." He looked away to the window. Apparently he found his admission embarrassing. No doubt he had meant to come to it more slowly. "You know, Aristotle says that one becomes a flute-player by playing the flute. Just so. One becomes dishonest by being dishonest. The minute before you are upright, a minute later no more." He put down the pen.

"Very well. One day at the university I happened to catch sight of a notice. It advertised an international conference on the German-speaking Prague writers to be held at the Free University over on the Western side. Though of course I knew of this circle, I am ashamed to say that, though I had done some reading, I had studied none of these writers in any depth, not even Kafka or Rilke. It was really just to distract myself from my problems that I decided to attend a session or two. It would be cheap entertainment because, according to the notice, registration fees were waived for students carrying matriculation cards and mine was still current.

"I chose a paper delivered by an American professor. I selected it because I arrived when it was to begin but also for its title, which turned out to be somewhat misleading. *We and Kafka*. To me this suggested a broad discourse, an examination of what Kafka has to say to the current generation. It turned out to be a largely technical lecture on Kafka's use of the first-person plural in several of his late stories. I have to say it was a solid paper, delivered in very respectable German. There was some follow-up discussion by the local panelists about Kafka's last months in the Steglitz and Zehlendorf neighborhoods, which included a reference to certain personal effects supposed to have been left behind when he was removed to the sanitorium in Kierling where he died. I was not much interested. I paid more attention to how well dressed the American professor was, not like an academic at all. He was wearing the most beautiful blue suit I had ever seen and a perfectly white shirt with golden cufflinks that twinkled whenever he reached for a glass of water. In short, I was impressed; I suppose I was envious. This man made me feel not only poor and young but provincial, insignificant. Who knows? My resentment may have played a role in what followed.

"The American's paper closed the afternoon session and when it broke up I followed him, not with any thought in mind but only because I had nothing better to do. He left on foot with his three colleagues from the panel. The weather was fine and they strolled over to the Kurfürstendamm where with much cordial hand-shaking they dispersed. My man went into a shop specializing in fine fountain pens—you know, our superb Mont Blancs and Pelikans .... God knows how the idea came into my head at that moment, how such a complicated, unheard-of thing even occurred to me. But it possessed me all at once. How can I express it? It was like the sudden coming-together of particles in the test tube, a catalytic precipitation, a crystallization."

"And what idea was that?" I asked, brushing some lint from

my trousers.

Legner looked me straight in the eyes, unabashed. "You asked earlier about that sentence from Kafka I put into my letter. It's from his earliest publication, *Meditation*, from a piece called 'Unmasking a Confidence-Trickster.'"

"I see."

Nobody enjoys it when his house-of-cards is knocked flat unless he does it himself. So I had gotten it all wrong. But then I thought, not so fast, perhaps not.

"I waited outside the shop and followed him back to his hotel. All the while details went on taking shape of their own accord, like a kaleidoscope pattern falling in place. My one experience of what true artistic inspiration must be like. Do you understand? I was creating a fiction or rather it was assuming form inside me, though I can hardly claim it was a case of *l'art pour l'art*. It was really fantastic . . . ."

Here Legner seemed to want some response from me, some expression of interest or sympathy, but I offered none. Disappointed, he turned his gaze to the window and went on.

"I spent a difficult night torn between my irresistible idea and a horror of putting it into action. All the while, underneath the moral debate so to speak, my imagination continued working away unrestrained. Inspiration, you see, is amoral. Artists should never be trusted. By morning my mind was made up."

I shifted in my seat and did not bother to conceal it when I looked at my watch.

"Please be patient," Legner begged. "This isn't easy for me."

No doubt your confession isn't easy, I thought, but does it

have to be quite so long?

"I knew the professor's name from the conference notice. In the morning I telephoned his hotel and asked for his room. I hoped to catch him before he went out. As in everything that followed I was diabolically successful. He picked up at once. I began by identifying myself as a graduate student from the East; I even gave my own name. I mentioned that I had attended his lecture the day before. I praised it, of course, but with a certain restraint so as not to injure his respect for me. I then came to the point. I said that I had some things I believed would interest him and that for various personal reasons these things were for sale. He naturally wanted to know what these things were. I went so far as to tell him it was a matter of certain Kafka items and, time being a concern, asked if he could arrange to meet me the following afternoon .... By the way, do you know Kafka's *Trial?*"

"I've read it."

"Then you'll remember the great chapter called 'In the Cathedral' where K. is told the parable 'Before the Law.' An astonishing parable, a rendering of the human condition worthy to set beside Plato's cave, Dostoyevsky's Inquisitor, Camus' Sisyphus, but no less remarkable is the priest's interpretation that follows. K. himself follows this exegesis with perplexity but real attention, since it's a matter that concerns him personally, and he concludes with a stunning verdict. It was this sentence that made me choose a cathedral as the place to meet my professor."

"I've forgotten. What does K. say?"

"He says '*It turns lying into a universal principle.*'"

For a moment I wondered if this verdict might be applied to the great engine of the market too, or at least to the advertising on which it runs. I dismissed the subversive idea as silly overstatement.

"It seems that nothing could follow K's line, but then Kafka adds another that only he could have written." Legner tapped its rhythm out on the desk. "'*K. said that with finality, but it was not his final judgment.*' Wonderful, no?"

I nodded. It really was wonderful and very like Kafka, at least as I remembered his exasperating ambiguity, the way he has of making truth out of giving with one hand and taking with the other. Yes, here on earth even our final judgments are not final. Wonderful too was that Legner seemed to have committed so much of Kafka to memory.

Legner's tone began to change. He was nearly bragging. "There was a second reason why I chose the cathedral, though. In art to have only a single reason is paltry."

"And what was that?"

"Because it's in cathedrals that one finds reliquaries."

Like the character who had unmasked the con-man in Kafka's sentence, I too was getting an inkling.

Legner leaned back in his chair, impervious to interruptions now, evidently relishing the relief of what I had been thinking of as his torment; but he was simultaneously admiring his own cleverness and was eager to draw it out. He did this Teutonically, by philosophizing.

"Relics become holy objects," he mused to the ceiling, "owing strictly to the power of association. A relic may therefore be understood not as a bit of matter that prompts piety but rather the physical manifestation of a psychological phenomenon. A relic embodies holiness in a literally vestigial sense. If we had the living saint before us we could not be certain of recognizing his saintliness. But set before us a suitably ornate reliquary with a hank of hair in it, a shard of bone, and it's a different matter. The Church understands this and so has an elaborate procedure for canonization, a kind of post-mortem *viva voce* complete with devil's advocate. Unauthorized reverence is more threatening to the faith than impiety because impiety, like all purely negative expressions of the ego, has it own way of avenging itself. Veneration, on the other hand, even if misplaced, always tends to self-confirmation. The worship of even an unauthorized relic remains an affirmation of the religious because of faith."

I looked at Legner with surprise. "I'm not sure I follow you."

He held out his palms. "I only mention all this so as to provide a context for what I did. My point is that there are such things as secular relics."

"So long as you can make people believe in them?"

"Precisely. If you were to come across a rickety, splintered, paint-spattered easel in a second-hand shop you'd ignore it; however, if you were convinced in advance that what you were about to see was the very easel on which Rembrandt painted his last self-portrait you would look at the thing quite differently. The spirit of the deceased magically inheres in the objects he used in life. I admit it's quite a primitive principle but there it is. What are the personal effects of the great if not secular relics?"

"So you met my brother professor at the reliquary."

"Fitting, don't you agree? It was just one of the details that came to me in a flash the day before. And yet I had much to prepare beforehand. You may recall that I mentioned a discussion that followed the professor's lecture which touched on certain Kafka items left behind in Berlin. Well, among the books that I had been loaned the year before by one of my old schoolmates was a copy of Ernst Pawel's biography of Kafka. I had skimmed it so the detail must have been buried in my memory. Fortunately, I never got around to returning the book and when I looked up the half-remembered passage it was even better than I had hoped."

A moment before Legner had seemed completely relaxed, even self-absorbed; now he leapt to one of the bookcases. I could see that the whole shelf was filled with books by or about Kafka. He took one down. For my sake, or rather for the sake of his confession's completeness, he had marked his page in advance.

"Listen to this. ' . . . *Dora apparently continued to conceal a number of Kafka manuscripts and letters, while steadfastly denying that she had done so. The sentiment or sentimentality that moved this otherwise recklessly truthful woman to persist in her lie, even in the face of tenacious prodding by Kafka's editors and friends, may somehow be touching, but it led to a tragic loss.'* Dora is Dora Diamant, the young woman the doomed bachelor Kafka wished to marry on his deathbed. I believe she wasn't yet twenty at the time. But here, listen to Pawel. *'Some time in the late 1920s, Dora married a prominent leader of the German Communist Party, with whom she had a child. Days after the Nazi takeover in February 1933, her husband fled abroad, just in time to evade the Gestapo dragnet. The agents, however, raided his home and confiscated every scrap of paper they could lay their hands on, including all the Kafka material.'*"

Legner was now quite agitated. "You see? You see?"

"Oh yes. I see it."

Whether I saw it or not no longer mattered to Legner; he was too excited. He took up Pawel's book again. "*Brod . . . immediately mobilized the Prague poet Camill Hoffmann, at the time cultural attaché at the Czech embassy in Berlin. Hoffmann, himself one of Kafka's friends, did what he could, but was informed by the Gestapo that the mountainous stacks of paper confiscated in those first days of Nazi rule had already reached such monstrous proportions as to defy all rational attempts at locating a specific document. For all we know, those mountains are still there, as indestructible as the secret police itself, being sifted, indexed, and filed in the bowels of some bomb-proof archives beyond the Berlin Wall . . . .*'"

"Indestructible as the secret police," I said ironically. "How about that."

Legner took a deep breath, as though winded from running hard, and laid the paperback down on the desk. "As I said, everything came marvelously together at once."

"You said *diabolically*. But surely you would have needed some proof."

Legner looked down at the floor; I would like to think it was for shame. "I created the proof. Inspiration carries everything before it. In his diary Kafka describes writing his first real story, *The Judgment*. He called the process 'a complete opening out of body and soul' and claims to have accomplished the work at a single sitting, from ten at night through six in the morning. He says he looked at the clock for the last time at two."

"What a Kafka scholar you've become," I observed dryly.

Legner made an ambiguous gesture, a sort of shrug. "I told you. I owe this wonderful Jew everything."

"Why do you call him a Jew?"

"Because he was one. For me, Kafka is the highest type of the Jew, the most alert, the most guilty, the least at home. In my opinion, if Kafka had written only a single page it would be more than enough to explode our stupid anti-Semitism, to refute and condemn it."

I frowned at him. Germans speaking of Jews, even favorably, always make me uncomfortable. I believe I spoke rather impatiently. "So, what was your proof?"

"Like Kafka I wrote at night. During the afternoon I had made the rounds of the junk shops in the Eastern sector. It was easy to find what I needed, a stack of old paper, yellow and brittle, an old bottle of black ink, and a couple of ancient fountain pens, one with which to carry out my forgery, the other to pay for my Laundromat. I didn't have much money left but I also bought a book on Kafka that reproduced some of his manuscript pages. At the end Kafka's tuberculosis attacked his larynx and he was reduced to writing these little conversation slips. Dora would certainly have squirreled some of them away."

Again Legner jumped up and went to his Kafka shelf. This time he retrieved a large paperbound book of photos. He showed me the reproduced manuscript pages and took out a couple pieces of paper that had been folded inside.

"My practice sheets," he said proudly, unfolding the papers and laying them down in front of me alongside the book which he held open with his hand.

I compared Legner's first efforts at forgery to Kafka's handwriting. I had to admit he hadn't done a bad job, but the sentences themselves were more remarkable. *His kindness is a way of showing he can do nothing*, was the first. The second: *Eating and drinking were always painful to me. It is really the allowing life in that is painful.* The third seemed a more personal and graceful plaint: *Now your peonies and I can be thirsty together.* The next two were curt: *Please, a peach next time* and *Mineral water, wine, lemonade, beer.* The last caught a tone of veritable anguish: *Choking, the old woman who stokes the fire.*

"You invented these?" I asked doubtfully.

Legner tapped his finger on the paper. "They sound right, don't they? Kafkaesque? I told you I was inspired. The spirit of Kafka was with me. Why not? It was Kafka who convinced me that for human beings there is no such thing as a world of pure spirit. We are too deeply implicated in the fallen world of matter. Of money. Isn't that the world you study, Professor? When somebody reports seeing a ghost the first thing they're asked is what it looked like. And they always answer, of course: a woman in white, a blue vapor, a wretch tangled in chains."

I whispered, "Relics again." I'm not sure what I meant by it.

"Relics are what the spirits leave us," Legner said reflectively. Then, sitting down, he unexpectedly clapped his hands and once more turned his gaze toward the ceiling.

"To be a confidence trickster requires more than just nerve and perseverance. For example, you yourself have to believe what you're saying while you're saying it. A knack for sophistry is indispensable, particularly when the issue is certainty. People can be every bit as certain of what is untrue as of what is. Certainty by itself proves nothing; in fact, proof without the dispensation toward certainty cannot persuade. We like to suppose it's evidence that induces certainty, but it need not.

Like everything else, certainty must be managed; that is to say, one must strew the path to certainty with certainty. A confidence trickster is a species of theologian: he knows certainty is a matter of faith and that faith is chiefly a question of desire. If he is selling peculiar goods, as I was, he must contrive to be both salesman and scholar. He can afford to look desperate so long as he appears reputable. You'll allow that all this is by no means easy, and yet for me it was, I can't say how."

"Because he was so gullible?"

"Yes, he *was* gullible." Legner seemed more ashamed for the American than himself. "But I never put a foot wrong either. Still, I can't say I felt secure for an instant. How can a confidence trickster feel secure when he's backed up by nothing but his own nerve, no corporate bonds, not even so much as a bank account?"

"You want to make excuses?"

"No. I have no excuse. How could I? . . . In the cathedral I showed him the conversation slips. I could see he was impressed but, naturally, he wasn't convinced, or at least didn't wish to show that he was. He demanded the story as well. The provenance."

"That ought to have been easy—since you were *inspired*," I said facetiously.

"To tell you the truth, I think he would have swallowed anything halfway plausible. Besides, I was holding my greatest inducement in reserve. I told him that my uncle used to work in the records division of the Stasi and that, alerted by me, a graduate student of literature, he had conducted a surreptitious search for the missing Kafka materials. These he had located, lifted, and turned over to me shortly before reunification. Can you imagine? My professor didn't ask even a single question.

And it probably made my story more credible when I told him my uncle had turned up rather little. 'Only these few pieces of note paper,' I said, 'but there's one other thing which I think will interest you more.' 'What?' he said. Sharp, just like that. Demanding to know. It gave him away. I was coy. I played him a little. I asked if he might be interested in buying and, feeling like a virtuoso, even warned him that the price would be rather high. I told him frankly that I needed money quickly. 'Why not sell what you have to the Berlin library, or better still the Czechs?' He actually asked me this. I said, 'The Czechs? Kafka wrote in German, not Czech. They don't deserve it. And as for the Berlin library, well.' I decided to take a chance. There always comes a moment, the supreme one, when a trickster has to form a partnership with his victim. 'Obviously,' I said, 'a public sale would raise difficult questions. No, what I have must go to a private collector.' He considered this, stroking his chin. I had practically told him he would be breaking the law. 'What else do you have?' he asked and I knew I had succeeded. Still, I wanted to give him time to dream of what I might be offering him, though not enough time to think clearly. I made a date to meet him for dinner when I would show him what I called 'my real treasure.'"

I thought of my interview with the chairman. "This is how you see it? Capitalism? The free market? Just a universal con game?"

My question seemed to surprise Legner. He paused then chose to make a joke. "The free market? Why not Marxism? After all, I was offering ownership of the means of production."

This was no funnier than most German jokes.

"It's a harsh world," he resumed, "and it was harsher then.

Kafka understood the world and how it gets inside us with its 'ruthless hardness.' Do you know the last words he wrote in his diary?"

"No."

"'*More than consolation is: You too have weapons.*' I knew precisely how much I would need and that would be my price—no more, no less. I found an old cigar box to put everything in. The fountain pen was green, by the way. Another little joke: Kafka was a vegetarian. My greatest stroke was to have obtained an actual stamped envelope from the records office of the State Police. This was simpler than it sounds. In those days chips of the wall were being sold to tourists, Russian army belts, Vopo helmets, all sorts of communist knick-knacks. I found it on a street corner. It cost me less than one mark. That envelope would be the *bona fide* of my imaginary uncle, a relic around a relic. So everything went into the envelope and the envelope into the box. "

"I blush for my countryman's innocence."

"You shouldn't. It wasn't innocence that overcame him. It was a mixture of feelings. Innocence was the least of them. There was greed, no doubt, but that shouldn't be overestimated. No one believes without first wishing to believe. I counted on his love of Kafka and fountain pens. Of the two, I suspect it was his collector's passion that prevailed. In this he was like Dora Diamant. According to Pawel, Dora loved Kafka dearly but cared nothing for his work. She spoke of it dismissively and with hostility, as of a rival. But Dora would not part from whatever of his she could hold on to. She too lied. Relics, you see, holy objects, the precious physical embodiment of a departed spirit, holiness. What could be more holy than Kafka's last fountain pen? When my professor opened that cigar box, took out the Stasi envelope, and saw that pen inside it was finished. He actually paid me in cash over dessert. He had brought a great deal of it with him. You see?"

"Yes, I see. And why did you want to tell me all this?"

He was almost defiant. "I've said already. Because you're an American professor, like him. Also so you will see how capital is accumulated. And to unburden myself."

It was getting late and the room was now in shadow. The sun sets early in October. I had an appointment in Bonn the next day. I had heard enough. I rose to leave.

He took my arm. "One last thing before you go," he said. I looked at him. His lean face revealed triumph. He took me over to the small chest and opened the top drawer. It was crammed with scores of fountain pens.

Mesopotamia

THREE years have passed since our fountain with its sorrowful main figure ringed by morose angels was officially christened Saint Bathildes' Well. For businessmen like me attendance at the dedication, an unseemly confusion of the religious and the patriotic, was prudent if not mandatory. Still, most of us cannot get into the habit of saying Bathildes' Well and go on calling the center of our city Ludger Square. After all, King Ludger bestrode his noble steed in verdigris dignity on that spot for two centuries. No one is sure what became of the equestrian statue after it was hauled down by the occupying army.

At noon, the hour of the armistice, the children's band paraded the four blocks from Rheinach Stadium to Ludger Square, circled the new fountain, then marched back to the stadium for the speeches. With no more conviction than talent the children pounded out a medley of marches and polkas, all personally approved by the new procurator. Behind them tramped a platoon of border troops. Their dress uniforms were even less clean than usual, and not even the sergeant's had been pressed. It was evident from their difficulty keeping in step that the guards had already begun toasting their nation's victory. Bringing up the rear, spewing noxious exhaust, a single army truck towed a highly polished artillery piece. Only this howitzer looked up to the occasion; it even drew a few cheers from the schoolboys gathered on the sidewalks. In short, this year's Armistice Day commemoration was even less imposing than last year's, just as last year's marked a noticeable falling off from the year before.

I watched the proceedings through the window of Brug's pastry shop which was officially closed for the holiday but unofficially open.

"Not much of a show," said Brug with equal disappointment and contempt.

His wife, a stout woman who always had to have the last word, explained it to him. "That's by design, to convince us things are normal. No longer any need to impress us highlanders, don't you see? Mark my words, in two years there won't be any commemoration at all."

Brug winked as he handed me the popovers I had ordered for my mother, who will not go without them even on Armistice Day.

Squeezed between the Rivers Amar and Scyth, our city, though densely populated, is of no great size. To the west, half a mile beyond the Amar, rise the fir-covered mountains of N., while to the east the plains of H. stretch to the horizon in patches of green and brown that make one think of Scottish tweed. Thus situated our city has always been a natural magnet for merchants and smugglers.

Almost a century ago my great-grandparents, newly married and desirous of a better life than the harsh one afforded by their mountain village, came down to the city. The story of their ferry ride across the Amar in a summer squall was our family's founding legend. Great-grandfather, weary of being a shepherd, determined to set up in the lumber business. His contacts in the hill country assured him of a supply of raw logs, though by no means a large or steady one. With some trouble he managed to establish a small sawmill on the Amar, but transport was his constant anxiety. In those days logs were still brought down by ox-drawn sledge. Foul weather caused constant interruptions in supply. The mill workers drank heavily when there was no work and often went missing when there was. The business survived, but only just. My grandfather fared little better, though he did introduce new product lines, unfinished furniture and planks suitable for floors and panels. The business was transformed when, in my father's time, a group of foreign investors backed a railroad extension. An unusually enlightened government in N. built a proper highway over the mountains and two new bridges over the Amar, one for general traffic and another to accommodate the new railroad. I can still remember the fair held when the iron railway bridge was opened. There were clowns, a Ferris wheel, exotic sweets, even a bareback rider in a short skirt. Everyone cheered when the first engine, somewhat delayed by a rock slide, chugged across at midnight bearing a huge flag. The bridge gleamed like silver in the reflection of fireworks. "Look, son, and remember this day," said my father solemnly as he hoisted me onto his shoulders. "All bridges are good, and this one is going to make your fortune." It was true. My father built up an excellent trade selling planks, boards, and a few finished products to the lowlanders across the Scyth where wood is as scarce as toboggans.

Trade picked up still more when the railway bridge over the Amar was augmented by a similar one over the River Scyth, which constituted the frontier between N. and H. Negotiations went extremely well after the government of H. agreed to pay three-fourths of the cost of the new bridge. Not only did H. wish not to be outdone by N. but the prime minister successfully argued the advantages of increasing trade. These were great days for our city which flourished as never before. The population rose so rapidly that apartment buildings of five and six stories had to be thrown up to accommodate all the newcomers. Many of these were citizens of H. In the general euphoria of prosperity there was no objection to this; in fact, the lowlanders were welcomed. "More hands to the wheel," was the general sentiment. Besides, the population of our city had always been an unusually mixed one and almost everyone could speak both languages.

My father hired a score of the lowlanders who came over the Scyth looking for work, both skilled and unskilled. Among the former was a master cabinet-maker, Grune by name, a man of few words and remarkably strict habits. Father placed him in our new furniture factory. Everything had to be done a certain way, otherwise he would become dispirited or fly into a rage. On these latter occasions he was never known to strike even an apprentice, but the walls might be smashed and his work-bench was liable to sustain a gouge; once he even clove it in two with an axe. If so much as a chisel were not hanging from its proper hook he might simply go home. Despite his moodiness Grune was by far the most competent and hard-working of the employees in the factory. No doubt the others feared him but they also looked up to Grune. In fact, I often heard my father remark that whenever Grune left the floor things went straight downhill. "It's as if he took the rhythm of work away with him," he would say.

"There's nothing for it," said Father over dinner one night, as if he had been turning the matter over for some time but could not decide without food. "Grune will have to be made foreman."

My mother, who took a keen interest in business matters and

would sometimes press her views, looked at Father sharply. "You aren't worried that the others will be angry?"

Father was surprised. "Why should they be angry?"

Far from lowering her gaze Mother glared at him. "Because he's from H., of course. They're liable to resent him. A lowlander in charge."

Father laughed. "I never heard such nonsense. Why should they care where he's from?"

To my father, a businessman through and through, frontiers meant only the ridiculous inconvenience of excises and inspections. That the Scyth should be regarded any differently from the Amar seemed to him absurd. For such obstacles as borders and tariffs he could find no sound reason, only the greed of politicians and customs officials.

These were good times for our city, unexampled times. Lives seemed to float pleasantly from weekend to weekend. Time was marked by new purchases, graduations, weddings, visits, vacations, peaceful deaths. If there was ill will between the newcomers and the older residents, as my mother anticipated, few signs were to be seen. In fact, marriages between the two groups, while neither common nor universally approved, were becoming almost frequent, a half-dozen or so a year. On this too my parents took opposing views. Not only did Father see nothing the matter in these unions, he positively rejoiced over them.

"It's hardly surprising," he said across the well laid table, "that young people growing up beside one another should fall in love." He looked tenderly at my mother, as if to propitiate her. "That's what happened to me, as you know better than anyone, my dear."

But Mother was not so easily mollified. "Hard-headed businessman! No, you're a dreamer, a dreamer. You suppose that because everyone buys and sells nothing else matters to them."

Father shrugged. "Well," he said reflectively, "what should matter more? Look, when they put the railroad through both governments agreed to use the same gauge. For two peoples to be tied together, not only by iron, but by love—this is a wonderful thing. Yes, a wonderful thing."

All my mother would say to this was that she hoped he was right but that he might consider that railroads could carry more than iron and lumber.

My parents made no effort to conceal such disagreements from me, though it never occurred to them to ask for my opinion. Pessimism can be a form of restlessness, and Mother's conviction about those halcyon days was that they could not last. I understood her anxiety as just one more manifestation of her overall lack of repose. As was natural, I inclined to my father's position. Not only was I too young for pessimism, but Father was my chief authority on the world and how it worked. Besides, I had made a few friends among the lowlanders. While I shared my mother's restlessness, mine was the restiveness of adolescence; I was eager to travel to H., especially to its capital, which my new friends claimed put our own city into the shade. And so, the summer of my eighteenth year, I begged my father to send me to the capital of H. to finalize a contract with an old customer of ours named Trow, a furniture retailer.

"I can handle the negotiations as well as anyone," I pleaded. "I promise to follow your instructions to the letter."

Father did not take much convincing. In fact, he seemed

pleased by my eagerness and looked me up and down as if only just noticing how much I had grown. "Why not?" he said, already warming to the idea. "All right, I suppose you might as well get your feet wet. Besides, Trow is a good man, an honest dealer, hardly likely to take advantage." This way of putting things did not delight me, but it suited my purpose and I kept quiet.

Because I had seen so little of the world the capital really did impress me. Under the power of suggestion and only eighteen, I thought it an exotic pleasure park, though in fact there is little remarkable about the place. It was not the capital that shone but myself, proud to be on my own and charged with an important responsibility. My self-satisfaction was further exalted when Trow, far from trying to intimidate me in our negotiations, made no fuss at all about the contract but a rather big one over me. He was no taller than I but a good deal larger and stronger. He laughed for no reason and sported an imposing edition of the short, wiry beards common among the lowland men. Trow appeared to be a man enjoying his prime, so full of vitality that the love of life seemed to animate all his gestures. Such a nature was rarely to be found among the inhabitants of N. where a reserved and introspective character may be due to generations of solitary pastoral life in the sparsely populated high country. Trow was in every way an outgoing, affectionate, and generous man. He liked to touch and was quick to embrace, as he did me at our first meeting. He would not hear of my eating at a restaurant. Nothing would do but that I should take my dinners with his family. On the spot he instructed one of his salesclerks to take the afternoon off in order to show me around the capital. This clerk, happy to have the time off, was both deferential and thorough. He showed me the municipal library, the new opera house, the public gardens and arboretum, two galleries, several apartment blocks, his favorite tavern, the disreputable district where all the vices of the metropolis were concentrated, and the seat of government, which was constructed on the Roman model, complete with fluted pillars. All the architecture struck me as refreshing; all the people looked fascinating; every novel face and form appeared to me charming. I was at the age when seeing beauty is particularly easy.

I went to dinner that night and was introduced to Trow's family. He had two daughters and I instantly fell in love with both of them. Trudi, however, was three years older than I, had a tendency to mock me, and was already engaged to a cavalry officer. Anna, on the other hand, was a year younger than I and did not make fun of my accent. Though just as shy as myself, Anna found ways to make it clear that she was intrigued by me and guessed that I was interested in her. How she managed this is still a mystery to me but things proceeded with amazing speed. We knew there would be only a short time together and so, when I returned the second night, the eve of my departure, Anna and I agreed to write to each other. We were alone in the garden for only two or three minutes. She gave me a kiss and I kissed her back.

With the kiss from Anna still tingling on my cheek and the signed contract in my pocket, I arrived home in a state of complete bliss.

Father was there to meet me at the station. "Well, and what did you think of Trow's daughters?" That was the first thing he asked. He did not even mention the contract until we were back at the office. He shook my hand when I turned it over to him, as if I were already his partner.

My courtship of Anna lasted two years. We corresponded constantly and of course I took every opportunity to go to H. Father found it necessary for me to go at least once every month and, during the summer, he even instructed me to stay a whole week. Mother was almost horrified but, as Father put it, "The boy must learn the business at both ends." And when Mother asked why he never sent me into the lumber camps up in the mountains, Father just shrugged. "Later," he said.

Having witnessed my parents' disputes I was keenly aware that bringing Mother around to the idea of my marrying a girl from H., even if she were the daughter of one of our best customers, was a fool's wish. But if grudging acceptance could not be hoped for, I was quite prepared to settle for resignation. As for Father, when I disclosed my intentions to him he was not in the least surprised, though I could see he wanted me to think he was. In fact, he was thrilled, seeing in the union an advantageous prospect for the business. He slapped me on the back.

"All bridges are good," he said. "Remember?"

"Mother?" I asked in the shorthand of families.

"My job," he answered resolutely and clapped me on the back a second time.

Anna had an easier time of it with her parents; but then, as Mother acidly observed, "Anna is not an only child, only a second daughter."

We had, in a sense, two weddings. The regular ceremony was

organized on a grand scale by Trow, very nearly as majestic as the wedding of Trudi and her cavalryman. The cathedral was decked with carnations and full of guests; an entire restaurant was rented for the wedding feast and bottles of champagne were popping open well into the night. Anna and I spent the night in the bridal suite of the Crystal, the same hotel where visiting heads of state lay themselves down after consuming formal banquets and negotiating treaties. Two days later a more sober reception took place in our own city, in the large ballroom called Shepherds' Hall. Quite a few guests came to both events, including, of course, Trudi and her dashing husband, who was already a captain.

Father and Trow were, of course, already on splendid terms and this somewhat allayed my worries about Mother, who had in no way come around. In the event, though, she behaved almost perfectly. In H. she was an agreeable if subdued guest, in N. a gracious and dignified hostess. At the reception Father stood up, clanged a knife against his glass and called for silence. Everybody cheered when he then announced I was to become a full partner.

Anna and I settled down in a good apartment in one of the solid old four-square buildings with walls of yellow stucco that are still to be found in the vicinity of Ludger Square. The furniture was the gift of my father-in-law; even Mother was affected by the mahogany sleigh bed and an antique armoire with carvings of hunting scenes.

In family no less than in professional life I took my father as my model. Like him, I wished to be easygoing and optimistic, quick to forgive, free of unnecessary worries and poisonous grudges. As for Anna, she proved herself a good wife from the first. Like Mother, she too interested herself in the business, but she was far more agreeable, even, to begin with, rather submissive. Anna made clear her wish to please me in all things and in this she certainly succeeded. Her adjustment to our city was an easy one, for she already knew many of the lowlanders who had settled here and I introduced her to my friends, who liked her. It was not long before Anna, organizing everything like a general planning a campaign, gave her first dinner party. It was a splendid success.

Before long our son, Alexander, was born and two years later our daughter, Rosalba. For five years life ran as smoothly as the trains across the Amar and the Scyth. With the aid of my father-in-law our business in H. grew rapidly and my only worry was getting enough logs to keep up with the demand. I placed Grune in charge of all finished goods, answering only to me and Father, and he amply justified my confidence. Seeing how well I was doing, Father left the business more and more in my hands and, after the children came, Mother began to warm a little to Anna.

Then one evening in March I arrived home to find Anna sitting by the window looking upset.

"What is it, my dear?" I asked. "Anything wrong with the children?"

She held out a letter. It was from Trudi. A few months earlier a new government had taken over in H. Well informed businessmen like myself were aware that the new prime minister was fond of nationalistic harangues but no one took these seriously. According to Trudi's letter, it appeared the government was going to introduce conscription. My brother-in-law, now a colonel of cavalry, had already been ordered to take his brigade somewhere. Trudi could not say where as it was forbidden to tell his destination.

Within the week our own government had fallen and was replaced by one as addicted to patriotic speechifying as the one in H.

The suddenness with which conditions had altered made my head spin. The initial response in our city was simply disbelief. People spoke of the growing crisis as anything but a crisis. Businessmen nodded knowingly, reassuring one another that their worldly wisdom knew how to regard these fanciful political games and what sensible economic interests would dampen the hotheads. It seemed impossible that the excellent relations between N. and H. should be interrupted if only because there was, as my father insisted, "no sound reason" for them to do so. The city was determined to ignore the ridiculous quacking coming from H. and the hardly less ludicrous echo emanating from our own capital over the mountains. But the mood changed overnight when the mayor announced that conscription would begin the following Monday when all men between the ages of eighteen and thirty were to come to the Town Hall to be registered. Suddenly the lowlanders among us were regarded with suspicion. Many put their families on trains and sent them across the Scyth. A few men were dismissed from their jobs.

"What is it, Grune?" I asked when the blunt fellow showed up at my office on Friday morning.

He did not beat about the bush. "Do you want me to go?"

"Certainly not, Grune."

"You're sure?"

"Yes. What has all this nonsense to do with us?" Then, feeling certain of the answer, I added, "You don't *want* to go, do you?"

Grune looked at me gravely and rubbed his strong forearm. "I may," he said.

I was thunderstruck.

On Saturday I visited my parents. To my father the crisis was no more comprehensible than to me. As for Mother, she found grimly rewarding the satisfaction of long held expectations. Her whole bearing said "Didn't I tell you so?"

The most disturbing change was in my wife. When I mentioned my conversation with Grune, complained about the closing of the frontier and the ill will beginning to infect my employees, I expected sympathy. I was surprised when instead Anna declared, "You know, you might be needing me and my family more than ever."

The conscription never took place. At dawn on Monday morning the troops of N., brought to the banks of the Scyth on trains, crossed the river, then marched rapidly through the city and vanished into the mountains beyond, leaving a large garrison to protect their supply lines. We awoke to find ourselves occupied. All business came to a halt. The lowlanders poured into the streets to celebrate while the rest of us, shocked, stayed indoors. Ignoring my objections Anna took the children to see our brother-in-law, who had been placed in command of the garrison. I felt perplexed and alone.

At least the war was brief. There were a few skirmishes in the highlands, negotiations were initiated, and a settlement proclaimed—all within two weeks. The treaty had but a single significant provision. The border between N. and H. was henceforth to be fixed at the River Amar rather than the Scyth. In other words, our city had been ceded to H.

Why did the war break out? What were its causes and what was its purpose? What runaway train of thought had been sent barreling down the line in H. to be met in the government offices of N.? Had the lowlanders who had settled in our city, so quick to celebrate, always dreamed of such a turn of events; might some even have plotted to bring it about? Had the people of H., all those who claimed that their capital cast our city in the shade, have regarded us with envy? Was our city the prize for which the war was fought or merely a token of a minor victory, a way out of madness?

The victorious army of H. withdrew through the city, watched apprehensively by the population, cheered by the lowlanders. The garrison stayed on. Down came the equestrian statue of Ludger. There was some minor looting, two rapes. The culprits in the latter cases were arrested at once and prosecuted by my brother-in-law, after all an upright man. Since official documents were already printed in both languages, the one that used to appear second now came first. We were issued new passports and had to buy different postage stamps. The currency changed. Things settled down.

The occupying garrison was reduced in size within months of the armistice. Our mayor was replaced by an official appointed

in H. who was given the imposing but misleading title of procurator. He interfered little in the city's affairs which have been
conducted in a businesslike fashion by the old elected council.
Some lowlanders have assumed positions of more substance
and influence in the city but these are chiefly the most energetic and intelligent of those who arrived before the war. They
are not undeserving of their elevation and there is only a little
grumbling.

Five years are long enough to get used to anything. One
might say with justification that what changes there have been
are superficial. And yet I have come to feel the opposite is true,
that what is the same is only superficial.

So, what has changed?

Many insist nothing has. Frohl the iron dealer, for instance,
likes to joke that the border posts have merely been shifted from
the banks of one river to those of another. "So now the tariffs
go to N. and the bribes to H. instead of the other way around.
The pigeons shit on a dead saint instead of a dead king. What
do such things matter? Oh, and the money's blue instead of red;
all the same people want it just as badly."

We still get enough logs from the mountains of N., though
they cost more. On the other hand, we no longer have to pay
excise on our finished goods. Last year the children began
school, where they will be taught the glorious history of H.
Anna announced that she intended to take in hand one side of
the business, the finished goods. She works directly with Grune
and I have to admit they have built things up. My authority
has been diminished not only at work but within the family as

well. As is only natural, my children want to be good citizens of H. They sometimes tease me about my accent; thanks to their mother they never quite developed one of their own.

I cannot say we are oppressed. Even at the beginning the thumb of the new state rested on us almost weightlessly, as my brother-in-law privately assured me it would. True, Lander, the accountant at the cement works, was arrested on the first commemoration of Armistice Day. Out of absent-mindedness, he insisted, rather than patriotism, he had hung out the wrong flag. But Lander was released after paying a small fine. This too became a joke for folk like Frohl. Perhaps we are not a people given to patriotism. My mother would certainly agree.

On the day after the armistice was announced, when Anna was visiting her brother-in-law and I was feeling lonesome, I went to see my father. We were sitting in his study. Mother had just marched out of the room in a huff. Father had been saying to me, "It's as if they abandoned us, almost without a fight. I can't understand it. Weren't we good citizens? Didn't we feel the joys and sorrows of the nation?" Mother answered him angrily, striking the air with her arm, including me in her denunciation. "The two of you—a pair of sentimentalists. Don't you realize we never fought for ourselves?" She slammed the door on us, perhaps as much out of frustrated aggression as anger. Father sat ashen-faced and said nothing, as if he had been slapped. Then he looked over at me. "You know, for a time—perhaps for a long time—we will be neither the one thing nor the other."

Father no longer comes to the office at all. He has retired and, to tell the truth, I can see that he has become a little childish of late. Mother protects him, sometimes with ferocity. Last

Sunday, when the children were annoying him in the garden, she chased them away, calling them "devilish lowlanders." Not surprisingly, her relations with Anna have become more frigid than ever and this is difficult for me. I am caught between the two women; and, though I love them both, I somehow feel little allegiance to either.

Now that our city has become part of H. I no longer relish crossing the Scyth or journeying to the capital city that once delighted me. In fact, I find that I now look forward to my business trips across the Amar. It is a pleasure to go up into the pure air of the mountains among the tall firs and to look on the high pastures speckled with goats.

Two Poets

———————————

1.

SHORTLY after midday, swerving to avoid three children, a recklessly overloaded truck rolled on its side, spewing a shipment of Malaysian refrigerators and steel sinks across the recently finished Presidential Highway. The sight of new refrigerators, irresistible in that sultry, fetid city, drew people from the shanties beyond the rows of dusty palms on either side of the road. The police had to disperse the mob with threats substantiated by a few skyward bursts of machine gun fire. The upshot was that the arrival of the world-renowned poet Luz de Lanavalli was not followed by the intended procession up the six-lane Presidential Highway from the airport to the Presidential Palace. The unfortunate truck driver, hauled off to police headquarters, was beaten into unconsciousness.

Lanavalli had accepted the dubious invitation to deliver the opening address of the First International Conference on Cultural Rights chiefly because of the wish to see one of the few countries he had never visited. Moreover, he intended to make the junket into the first leg of an extended honeymoon, for Luz was a newlywed. Less than a week earlier in the Cathedral of Notre Dame de Paris, he, a widower near seventy, had married Min-Sun Paik, age forty-five, translator of his many books into the Japanese and Korean languages.

When he was informed of the traffic accident by the suave,

not-quite-obsequious Chief of Protocol, the poet said he deeply regretted to hear of it. Yet he profited by the contretemps, since the limousine inched through the teeming streets of the capital, past decaying colonial buildings that reminded him of certain British authors he had loved in his youth, quite contrary to his political convictions, through squares crammed with market stalls that leaped with color and wafted astounding aromas through the open window of the Cadillac, whose air-conditioning was putative. People made way and gaped. Some waved. Lanavalli waved back and felt elated. "What do you think? I could almost be the Pope!" he quipped to his bride.

Min-Sun seldom spoke. Indeed, the poet's friends had speculated that it must have been the woman's taciturnity that won the heart of their ebullient Luz, her wordless serenity which they readily ascribed to Asian submissiveness. To them, she appeared a silent vessel into which all Luz's volubility could be poured, a sort of sexual complementarity. That she adored him went without saying.

The Chief of Protocol did not trouble himself to act as a tour guide. Though he did not like to show it, he was perturbed by the change in plans and confined himself to answering the poet's many questions with a brevity that turned increasingly acerbic.

"What is the population of the city?"

"Twice what it ought to be, Señor Lanavalli."

"Do people lose their tribal affiliations in all this hectic urbanization or do they tend to settle together into neighborhoods, like birds of a feather? Are they able to keep up their traditional ways here? Do they ever yearn for home, for village life?"

"Tribalism is a thing of the past in our country."

"I see. And were many ex-tribespeople displaced by the building of the new airport, which looks exactly like every other airport, and that rather grandiose highway?"

At this tendentiousness the Protocol Chief, who could boast of one degree from Oxford and another from Berkeley and frequently did, merely shrugged. He was anxious that the accident scene should be cleared by tea-time when two Airbuses full of worthies were scheduled to deplane.

"The sunlight here has real weight. Just look at that, Min-Sun! The way those three fellows are bending under the sun as if it were a load of bananas. '*See how noontime desiccates the scene / how one substantial shaft of light / drops like a yellow guillotine.*' Remember, my dear?"

The Chief of Protocol did not recognize that Luz was merely quoting a translation of himself and had chosen English for his benefit. He did not care for the mention of a guillotine.

"What is the title of your address, sir?" he asked, to change the subject.

"I've completely forgotten. What is it, Min-Sun?"

In her long white dress and smooth black hair, Min-Sun did not move a muscle or waste a word as she replied, "Cultures and the Conquest of Hopelessness."

2.

OLVIDADO Andrieu laid down his book, gazed out over his hazy garden, and wondered that he was still alive. His existence was a tuneless noise, one vacant, stupidly prolonged harmony. Time did not advance because he looked forward to nothing, and it did not move backwards because he lacked the self-deception of nostalgia. He lived in a country plagued by strange infections, swarming with frightful parasites, above a city that exuded a permanent miasma as if it were conceived by some myopic Impressionist, and yet his health was perfect.

And if I had married? Andrieu asked himself, as he often did when overcome by a mixture of self-disgust and longing. He recalled his cousin Sandor back in Chicago. Sandor had been like him in his unwillingness to socialize. But Sandor's wife Molly would "drag" him, as they both put it, to parties. She would invite people in, plan group outings in Lincoln Park. And, strange to say, Sandor was always the life of the party, always admitted afterwards that he had had a fine time. Nevertheless, this did not prevent Sandor from instantly recoiling into his congenital anti-sociability, like a badger retreating to his snug burrow, leading to yet another "dragging" scene the following Friday. Andrieu had also been invited to some of Molly's gatherings but, for him, just because he lacked a Molly of his own, they only honed the edge of his loneliness. "Solitude," he once wrote, "is best endured alone."

Andrieu's paternal grandparents had managed to emigrate to the Americas right in the middle of the First World War. Their son Istvan, later Esteban, married Elena Olvidado y Herminas, third daughter of the army captain who, for a negligible bribe, had done them a kindness upon their arrival, stamping papers of doubtful authenticity. When they wed Esteban did not love Elena, who was not exactly pretty, nor did Elena love Esteban, who was not exactly gallant; however, as sometimes happens, their marriage was a success, and more of one the longer it lasted. They came to esteem one another, first as business partners, and later as people with good hearts and congenial intellects. Respect grew into affection and affection flowered into the deepest love almost without their noticing it. It was their only son, born in 1926, who was most keenly aware of what was going on between them. For most children, the best of their parents' conjugal relations are fixed before their arrival. Things can only stay the same, a foundation to be taken for granted, or deteriorate into bitterness, separation, divorce. Young Olvidado, however, with precocious sensitivity, felt himself to be the odd-man-out in his parents' blossoming love affair, and he was jealous of them both. Perhaps this is why Olvidado remained a bachelor, and generally celibate, looking on the paired-off world around him with alternating scorn and envy.

Thanks to his parents' reverence for all things of the mind or an unconscious wish to be rid of his sulky presence, young Olvidado received a first-rate education at two of the best boarding schools in his country after which he was sent, at considerable expense, to the University of Chicago, where some Andrieu relatives had settled after the War.

When he returned to his homeland, Andrieu took up the profession of diplomat, thanks to the help of his maternal grandfather who, in the meantime, had risen to a high position in the military government. He also began to publish poetry, essays, and reviews.

Forty years later people look back on those years as a sort of small-scale Renaissance. From this vantage-point Lanavalli and Andrieu appear to be both its leaders and antipodes, marking out the two horizons of a new literary prospect. Lanavalli was accessible, popular, profligate with words and astonishing images, a man of articulate appetites and intemperate sympathies, while Andrieu wrote practically as if he did not live in the material world. Difficult and abstract, recherché and reticent, Andrieu's work nevertheless attracted its enthusiasts and even imitators, not only at home but also abroad where his peculiarly cerebral brand of idealism was taken for universality.

Andrieu's diplomatic career was fairly successful while it lasted, even though his shyness and formality were against him. At the age of thirty-nine, he was made ambassador to one of the newly decolonialized nations. The place struck him, according to an early dispatch, as "savage without nobility and corrupt without sophistication." Indeed, with his background, it was not easy for him to accustom himself to so gaudy a display of indifference on the part of the life force as this tropical backwater presented. After only a year he was offered the job of cultural attaché in Washington, the government wishing to turn his growing literary reputation in the United States to account. The three years he spent by the Potomac were his most productive period. He turned out a book a year.

Who would have predicted that when a coup brought an abrupt end to his diplomatic career he would elect not to stay in Washington, to go home, to Europe, or even back to Chicago, but to bury himself in that semi-civilized country so near the Equator? True, the money left him by his parents would go further there, but that was not his reason, nor would it account for why he simultaneously renounced writing, or at least publication.

When Prospero gave up his magic he left his island for the political and social whirl of Milan. When Olvidado Andrieu surrendered his gift, he embraced a companionless insularity, an existence without a Miranda and almost completely without an Ariel. While neither his good-natured housekeeper nor his dignified gardener qualified as Calibans, they preserved a distance between themselves and the strange foreigner. In the best maintained of the villas in the low hills above the capital he kept no pets and entertained no guests. He read much and, when there was electricity, listened to his radio or, more often, to music on his phonograph. He never traveled.

3.

LANAVALLI was not surprised that Min-Sun did not complain about the heat or the intermittent plumbing or anything else. This, indeed, was one of her leading traits and, for him, great charms, this lack of a bleating ego. Stoicism is a philosophy, he had argued in a recent essay on the cross-pollination of cultures, Asiatic in origin. Its founder Zeno was not a Greek but the offspring of those bumblebees of Antiquity, the Phoenicians. As for himself, he was not only an unregenerate

Western dualist, but a lyric poet who had begun by emphatically bellowing in the first person and had never ceased doing so. Owing to his sensitivity and penchant for letting the world chew on its fruits he had, as he knew, a tendency to whine. He hated doing it, "playing at Jeremiah" as he said self-mockingly, but could not help himself.

"After all," he said to Min-Sun and her unbreakable smile when he had wound up his screed about the shower and the toilet, "you married one delicate seismograph. All right, so what's next? Have we got time for a stroll?"

"No, Luz. You must get dressed. The itinerary insists the banquet is black tie. See, it's even in italics. *Black tie*. Then you give your address. Then there is a reception and everyone congratulates you."

"Black tie? Such pretensions!"

"To mimic Europe, to appropriate it, measure up to it."

"But why always the Europe of a century ago? Anyway, did you even pack the costume?"

Min-Sun went to the closet and fetched the poet's tuxedo which she carefully laid on the bed. Then she got out the violet dress he had bought for her in Paris and draped it beside the tuxedo.

The poet chuckled at the sight. "Behold our carapaces, my dear, our disguises, the heartless shells of Luz and Min-Sun on the bed, but without desire."

"Desire is important," replied Min-Sun pensively.

Lanavalli's speech was delivered in a gymnasium into which tables, chairs, and various colorful hangings had been conveyed.

The sound system had not been properly checked. Evidently someone had supposed the more loudspeakers the better. The result was that his words began to eat each other up when they were only half spoken. Not that most of the delegates were concentrating on his views. Thanks to a chef the President had flown in especially from Rome, the food had been first-rate and as Luz spoke most of the lesser luminaries, already stuffed to repletion, were struggling to do justice to the French cognac and Spanish port. The poet's most attentive listener was Min-Sun.

"To make a system of hopelessness may be an individual undertaking, may even be an individual's fate, yet it can never be the task of an entire community, nor can the group sympathize with such a life. The task of the community, or rather those of its members who are charged by nature, education, and circumstance with the great task of sustaining it, is precisely the opposite; that is, to construct a system around this hopelessness as a spider weaves her web around air, so that when the job is completed one sees only the web and not the air. And these networks, each of which has its own beauty, must include certain elements in their designs. Even should the web of a culture, a living, vibrant culture, prove untrue to the conclusions of the scientists, offer offense to the imperatives of the economists, appear naive to the cynicism of the historians, and, yes, even should it violate the strictures of the moral absolutists—still these elements will remain true to the eternal needs of humanity, the phantasmagoria of stirrings and yearnings, thoughts and emotions, made necessary by the remarkable capacity of our species' crania. All cultures must give hope, which is to say they must devise a future. All cultures must also form a meaning from existence, which means they must organize the past. There is no single way to achieve hope and meaning. In fact, there is no man, no culture. There are billions of human beings; there are myriads of cultures."

As her husband was winding up this peroration Min-Sun smiled in a way that might as easily have been sad as serene. She was seated in a place of honor. On her left sat the President of the Republic, a ponderous crafty man in a specially designed white and purple dress uniform that made him resemble a turnip. Throughout the dinner he had addressed her with an urbanity that verged on the comical as well as offering the table at large some astute, if brutal, obiter dicta. The President fancied that he was famous for his table-talk. He had been informed about the recent wedding and proved as much by launching the banquet with a carefully composed toast to "the happy couple who, in their marriage, incarnate the very theme of our conference." When Luz began his speech, the President leaned over to Min-Sun and asked if she happened to know what the last sentence might be. She did not hesitate to tell him. Consequently, the President was the first to leap to his feet and burst into applause, the remainder of the assemblage following suit by only the slightest of pauses.

Limited to the most select of the conferees, the reception took place in a drawing room of the Presidential Palace decked out, just as Luz had predicted, like a Victorian bordello. Dignitaries lined up to shake hands with the poet and thus with the President, who never left his side.

"In the bad old days," he jocularly explained, "one could not become a chief without bagging a lion. You, Señor, are my lion. The whole nation is grateful for your presence."

"The whole nation, Your Excellency, is not here. Besides, I doubt that the industrious and law-abiding citizens of this country, yourself excepted of course, know a word of my work."

The President made a deprecating gesture. "It is pointless to argue with such becoming if unwarranted humility; but you must remember, sir, the literacy of fame. All people everywhere know that the great Luz de Lanavalli is their friend and their champion. Besides, we have been reminding them of it for at least a fortnight."

Luz had a good laugh at that.

"Also," the President went on, "there is at least one inhabitant, in addition to myself of course, who knows your work well."

"Would that be your chief of protocol?"

The President shook his head. "Mere veneer, highly polished but quite shallow. I assure you, a bowling ball. No, I was referring to Olvidado Andrieu, your fellow poet and I believe your compatriot. Surely you two know one another?"

"Andrieu?"

"Oh dear. Is he as forgotten as all that? Didn't you know that we have had the honor of his presence for something over two decades?"

"I supposed he must be dead," said Luz rather coldly. "We may have met once. I'm not sure."

"Ah," laughed the President, turning to Min-Sun. "My people have a proverb that appears to be apropos. Two lions, two territories."

Min-Sun asked the President if he ever saw Andrieu.

"Alas, though Señor Olvidado Andrieu pays his taxes promptly he sees no one. The fellow is a recluse, an anchorite. But surely he will see you! No, you cannot think of leaving without paying the old boy a visit."

"Anchorites do not generally receive visitors," observed Luz.

Min-Sun smiled and softly disagreed. "I believe Saint Anthony received devils."

4.

NEWS of Luz de Lanavalli's visit with his new wife—yet another pairing!—had not escaped Olvidado's notice and it upset him. Just as disturbing was that he could not put his finger on the reason. After a life of unstinting, even reckless introspection, one ought at least to know oneself. That old Greek injunction was a mockery. One can know horticulture or the oil business, but who knows himself?

Andrieu did not consider himself a good poet on the ground that a poet is a person who writes poems, as a good poet is one who composes good poems. Lanavalli had written quite a few of these and apparently not in spite of but by giving rein to his *joie de vivre*. Olvidado examined himself for envy and found a full store. Nevertheless he did not give it much weight. In his view envy is not willed so much as a social reflex. If the doctor strikes a man's knee and as a result gets kicked, is he justified in accusing the man by saying, "You kicked me"? True in a way, of course; yet the yoking together of subject and object by a verb freighted with moral intent is misleading. To covet another's career or his happy family is absurd since it means wishing to remain oneself while inhabiting the happier existence of another. But one's life, like one's face, is too much the result of what one is.

Andrieu had received an invitation to the conference, and to the banquet as well. He was sent invitations to all the self-promoting circuses the President loved to mount. He was even pleased by the courtesy, but he never attended. Whatever professional knack he might once have had for society—and it never amounted to much—was long gone. He had never ceased to be the sophomore who, whether from pride or spite, felt out of place at Molly's parties; even in old age he was still the little boy exiled from that ever jollier banquet that was his parents' love.

Though he had renounced the writing of verse and any thought of publication, there was still a little of the old Ariel-magic in Olvidado. It took a form he had admired since he first read about Einstein, the thought-experiment. He had been drawn to the phrase because it seemed to him to cover the whole terrain of imaginative acts, those of novelists and painters no less than physicists. The impersonality of the form appealed to him also because he had a distaste for self-expression and thus believed in his own detachment. Some thought-experiments are meant to *prove*, others simply to *see*, to see what will happen. His were of the latter sort. The childish magic of *once upon a time* yielded naturally to the apparently more adult sorcery of *what if* and *suppose that*. Andrieu's thought-experiments, like the verses and essays of his youth, were rigidly constrained and formal. Three pages were the utmost he would permit himself.

The morning after the banquet and Lanavalli's speech, which he had listened to on the radio, Olvidado sat on his patio under the shade of palm fronds to look over the little piece he had scribbled down the night before. Irritation had inspired him. He was aware that his minuscule thought-experiments were merely ragged remnants of a once-promising career, the sort of consolation that made loneliness more poignant, like listening to Mahler. But to him loneliness was the ground of writing's being and nothing was overcome by it, certainly not hopelessness. On the contrary. Culture is play, writing distraction; but in so far as either reveals the truth of things then, no matter what dinner speakers might say to soothe postprandial or postcolonial dyspepsia, this truth is solitude, despair, courage. As Olvidado conceived it, Luz's fantastic webs of culture merely limn the nothingness between their tenuous filaments.

5.

HOW different is translating a poet from marrying him? In both instances nothing is going to happen without a spark that either sputters or ignites. Should things go well one discovers by stages coincidences of taste and feels sympathy with a unique apprehension of the world. Next comes invasion, preoccupation, an investing of one's citadel by thoughts and images amounting almost to a personality. Thus the politics of one's psyche are transformed until finally there grows up true intimacy, an understanding beyond modesty, sometimes even beyond words. In the end, one is pleased even by underwear carelessly tossed beside the bed, a damp toothbrush, the touchingly meaningless groans of sleep.

Min-Sun Paik felt her vocation was fated, ordained at birth. Her mother had been among the girls forced into sexual slavery by the Imperial Japanese Army, one of the so-called "comfort ladies." Min-Sun had been one consequence of that policy. Another was her mother's ostracism after the war. A third was poverty. The almost immediate catastrophe of the Korean conflict devastated yet saved her. When her mother died of typhus in 1951, Min-Sun was taken in by an orphanage supported by an American foundation. School was all her love and she was very bright, the top of her class in all subjects. She won a scholarship to the university where she concentrated in languages, all of which came easily to her. Min-Sun approached each new tongue as a puzzle but gradually, as she mastered its rules, the game gave way to a deeper fluency of the heart. It was at the university that she got her first taste of translating poetry. A certain professor of Spanish, intimidated by Min-Sun's gifts and prejudiced by her semi-Korean background, sought to test her limits. With her humiliation as his goal, he set her the cruel task of translating "The Cemetery at Viña del Mar," one of the longest, bleakest, and most abstruse poems of Olvidado Andrieu.

Immediately after graduation Min-Sun and a girlfriend moved to Japan. While her friend searched high and low for a restaurant job, Min-Sun found work at once with a small publishing house. She overcame the objections to her being non-Japanese by offering the company a completed translation of a 500-page Argentine potboiler. She had even initiated a correspondence to secure the Japanese rights. True, the director refused to put her on regular salary. She was offered only a tiny stipend as a retainer and would be paid for completed assignments. Min-Sun was not greedy, not even particularly materialistic; but she was tired of hand-me-downs and bad food. She liked that the size of her income was in her own hands.

Despite her parentage and the bias it provoked the American missionaries had raised her to marry, not to be self-reliant; yet the memory of what her mother had suffered and of the utter hopelessness in which she died made Min-Sun wary of men. She also distrusted life. In twenty years of successful independence she had resisted the attentions of more than a few suitors. Two weeks before she married Luz she confessed, to his great astonishment, that she was a virgin. That is why he went to the considerable trouble of arranging for the ceremony to be performed in Notre Dame. He called his divorces annulments and claimed that Min-Sun was a Catholic. He thought it ought to be enough for the Pope that his bride was a virgin and that she had agreed to marry him.

Min-Sun's life had not been without a kind of sexuality. In fact, the secret of her excellence as a translator was that she poured her passion into conjugating not bodies but verbs, into making tenderly her own the texts of exotic writers—above all the poets. When she translated "The Cemetery at Viña del Mar" she believed she had discovered at once a confirmation of the solitary sorrow of life and an answer to it as well.

If she were to marry, whom could she wed, then, but a poet? She loved the verses of Luz de Lanavalli long before she met the man. To her, his poems suggested a gaily bedecked pachyderm charging through life. Their romance really began, not when they were introduced at the publisher's office, but the moment she read the opening lines of "Against Discouragement":

> You know it's mere vanity, this wishing
> to be told you've been a swan all along,
> needing a license to breathe someone else's
> air; yet the want of a nod or some smudged
> stamp has left you stateless, a refugee
> tiptoeing across a shattered globe,
> forlorn and feckless and unshod.
> I can see you, conquistador of deserts,
> wandering your room, charting each square
> and minim of its narrowness . . . .

He might have written it expressly for her. Yes, yes, I understand, little girl, he seemed to murmur, but chin up.

All the male poets who were introduced to Min-Sun, and not a few of the female ones, fell in love with their translator. If they were at all indirect she took no notice, and if they were aggressive she acted as if they must be joking. How could anyone love her when she was not lovable? How could she risk even the vulnerability of being loved? How could she betray hopelessness with hope, escape her solitude even with a writer? Besides, it was their poems she cared for; it was the message that charmed, not the messenger.

Things were different with Luz chiefly due to his persistence, or more exactly his need. He was a famously energetic old man. His first two marriages had ended messily, the last with his wife's death; and though he was welcome in almost any country on the planet he told her he considered himself an exile. He simply could not live alone. "I'm not cut out to be a bachelor," he complained. "My country is Woman. My country, Min-Sun, not my colony. My national anthem is the feminine pronoun." Luz was gentle with her, even patient, exquisitely tender, but also unrelenting. When compelled to leave Tokyo for two weeks he wrote her fourteen sonnets, one a day, each more beautiful, importunate, and implacable than the last until, on his return, she relented; she finally believed him. Almost before Min-Sun knew what was happening it was adieu to the small apartment in the quiet district of Tokyo and off to the Rive Droit, to Luz's coterie of admirers who all made much of her. There were restaurants and picnics, parties every night. Everyone she met had done something distinguished, even the drunkards. By the day of her wedding she was exhausted.

Back in their hotel room, after Luz had gotten out of his tuxedo and had finished in the bathroom, Min-Sun, standing by the window, reminded him about Olvidado Andrieu.

Luz scrutinized his bride indulgently but also with some surprise. She had never asked him for anything before. He ran his hand over his bald head. "Should I be jealous already?"

"Don't be ridiculous. Our flight doesn't leave until two. We have the whole morning."

"Did you ever meet him?"

"No, of course not."

"Do you like his work?"

"I admire it, yes."

"Thank you for choosing your words with such delicacy, as usual. A poet's ego is just a big wineglass. Well, that Andrieu's a cold customer, a mackerel who for some absurd reason has sunk himself deep in the torrid zone. Apparently it hasn't warmed him up much."

"Can we visit him anyway?"

"What makes you think he'd see us?"

Min-Sun crossed her arms over her chest. "Saint Anthony."

"Oh yes, the first monk, the one with the devils."

Min-Sun shrugged. "He didn't invite them. Let's just go, like devils. If he turns us away then we leave."

Luz stretched out on the bed. Though displeased he was, after all, freshly married. "Anything to oblige you, my dear, even deviltry. But now I have a question for you too."

"Yes?"

"How badly are you missing that virginity of yours?"

Min-Sun shrank back against the window and blushed.

6.

WHERE it was caught in the upper foliage the morning light looked pale green, but it became muddied as it glanced off the showy purple bracts of the bougainvillea vines. Yellow and blue insects hurled themselves at the screens. The white paper showed bravely against the oiled walnut of the table.

Olvidado was making ready to revise the thought-experiment

he had written down before going to bed the night before when his attention was caught by the pull-up shade, one of those imitation rattan things made of vinyl. Suddenly incensed at its hideousness, its vile color, he tried to tear the shade from its brackets and partially succeeded. It was at that moment he heard the crunch of gravel in his drive.

It was obvious who it must be. What had he said in that review so many years ago? He had called Luz de Lanavalli a little boy with a big diamond.

No housekeeper, no gardener. Should they knock at his door—and how long had it been since anyone had done that?— he would either have to pretend not to be home or let them in.

The knock came. Olvidado laid down his pen, threw a furious glance at the torn shade, experienced a *frisson* of childish panic, then went to the door.

The two poets looked at each other, blinked, and felt their age.

"Good Lord, Andrieu. We all thought you were dead."

Olvidado cracked a feeble joke. "Perhaps I am."

Luz turned. "My wife, Min-Sun Paik, also my translator."

"Not in that order, I hope."

Min-Sun stood in the doorway with her usual stillness and looked steadily at the thin old man. When she spoke she dumb-founded both poets.

"The first poem I ever translated was one of yours, Señor Andrieu."

Olvidado was startled by her words but touched by her voice which was soft, shy. He managed to ask which one.

"'The Cemetery at Viña del Mar.'"

Luz scowled. To him, this was a terribly significant detail of his bride's life and he resented not having known of it. It was nearly as though she had confessed to not being a virgin after all.

"We can only stay a little while," he said hurriedly, as if Olvidado meant to detain them.

"Why have you come at all?"

Luz did not wish to say that it was because Min-Sun had asked to see him and so he lied with what would sound to her like graciousness. "To prove to you that you are not entirely forgotten."

"And should that please me?" said Olvidado as he gestured for them to follow him through the house and out to the porch. He had forgotten all about the torn shade.

"Fame is the spur," Luz quoted jocularly, aware of how hollow this old tag sounded.

"Would you care for something to drink?"

"Nothing for me. We've just breakfasted."

Min-Sun shook her head.

As they walked onto the screened porch Olvidado looked up at the shade. So accustomed had be become to living within himself he was amazed by how humiliated he felt that these people would notice it.

"I congratulate you on your career," he said hurriedly to Luz then turned to Min-Sun, "and on your translator," he added with creaky gallantry. The woman's impregnable smile troubled him. Was it merely vacant or did she mean something by it?

"And what of *your* career, Andrieu? Why have you buried yourself out here?"

Olvidado just shrugged. After all, how could he explain himself? Why should he?

They all sat down in high-backed cane chairs. Now that there was a table between them, a table with a fountain pen and some paper, it could have been forty years earlier.

Luz leaned forward. "Let me indulge a hypothesis then," he said. "For you, I believe, writing begins and ends in solitude, even to the point of solipsism, an attitude essentially adolescent in origin. I suppose that for you writing started out as a way of creating a house inside your house, so to say an inviolable chapel with entry forbidden everyone else—the uninterested parents, those dull thugs at school, the idiocy of the newspapers, our politics, the common people. In a space apart from everyone you began to write, separated even from your readers, if you ever imagined such creatures. That poem about the cemetery for instance, with all the fancy allusions, might as well be hermetically sealed, and now its author is. Right?"

Again Olvidado shrugged. "And for you? How did writing start for you?"

"Well, as for me, it was nothing like that. I'm no intellectual. To me writing is simply a way of shouting at more people for a longer time. Writing exists on a continuum that runs from *The Iliad* to the rudest gesture of a Buenos Aires cab driver."

Olvidado raised an eyebrow. "Then you actually meant what you said last night about hopelessness?"

"Every word."

"This is how success speaks to failure. I congratulate you, Señora. Your husband has all the world's cultures to support him. His taste for life admits no frontiers." Olvidado made it sound like a reproach. "He is one of those who live on the plains where the air is plentiful and thick with voices and, as he prettily puts it, even gestures. For him life is a joy, even its bad days which he makes stylish, even its stupid politics which he makes colorful, simply because he's at home among people. He's always the life of the party, isn't he?"

Luz gave a contemptuous little laugh.

Min-Sun, who had not ceased looking at Olvidado, who deeply felt but did not wish to show her kinship with him, lowered her eyes.

"I suppose that a poet must live more richly than others or he must be as dead as he can."

"Ah," said Olvidado.

For the second time his bride had astonished Luz. He had already delivered the speech he had worked up during the drive and somehow Min-Sun had crushed it to powder with her disjunction. Then he smiled. After all, she was his; she had chosen the open air of the plains on which he lived, not the exalted but stifling silences of Andrieu's sterile mountaintops.

As for Olvidado, he now made a sucking sound and unconsciously placed his hand over the paper lying on the table.

"Ah ha! What's that?" asked Luz with affected good humor. "Don't tell me you've been writing all this time. Ah, that's even better. Hidden treasures!"

Olvidado ignored Luz and looked only at Min-Sun, who

had impressed him. Then he picked up the paper on which he had written so quickly the night before. Without offering any explanation, he read it to them.

"Ten centuries ago, during the first years of the Sung dynasty, two youthful poets who happened to see some of each other's poems began a correspondence over a dispute concerning prosodic technique. Owing to various circumstances, their administrative careers kept them at different ends of the Empire. Still, the correspondence continued; it blossomed, comprehending more and more topics. At the close of every letter each declared how he yearned to see the other. In the fullness of time both poets, despite the difference in their styles, became famous. Word of their letters began to get around. It somehow pleased people that the two poets should be friends, that each, as people imagined, should enjoy the benefit of the other's ideas and, even though they were separated, find in the other a worthy and sustaining companion.

"Then one day deep in the Forbidden City the Empress was told the story of the two poets and their correspondence which by then had been going on for nearly forty years. The story delighted and moved her. With the thoughtlessness of the powerful she resolved to do a good deed. She gave orders that the two old men, without being told the reason why, be ordered to appear on a certain day in her presence. She longed to hear the wonderful things they would say to each other.

"The day arrived. The Empress, full of anticipation, sat herself on her throne in Peking surrounded by eunuchs and ladies-in-waiting. Scribes were placed in each corner of the room so not one precious word would be missed. On the Empress's command the two poets were admitted simultaneously but through opposite doors. Both kowtowed to the Empress. Then she introduced them.

"Still kneeling, the two old men could not bear to look at one another. Each was embarrassed. Neither had anything to say, nor did either guess that for forty years the other had pulled all sorts of strings just to keep from having to meet him."

Olvidado laid down the paper almost triumphantly. Luz frowned. "So this, I suppose, is how failure seeks to vanquish success?" But he felt his irony fall flat and, annoyed, made a move to rise when Min-Sun grabbed his hand and stopped him. Then she, who had translated the words of both poets and in whom the two had unconsciously and even unwillingly met, reached out and took Olvidado's hand.

"If I had been that Empress I would have told those old men that they had grown so foolish that they did not even know what they meant to one another." Laying down their hands she continued with a vehemence that shocked the two poets. "And do you know what I would have done then? I would have ordered them locked up together for three days in the tiniest cell in my palace."

With that, Min-Sun got to her feet, left the porch and, with the muted firmness typical of all her movements, closed the door behind her.

EIRENE

*O*SWALD *humming as he fussed with his train, I dusting my doll house: that's how I remember those brief and interminable afternoons, each hour like an icicle melting in sunlight crazy with motes. We were little then but made littler to squeeze into the miniature world that filled both the living room and our imaginations, a Lilliputian haven of houses and trains. So long as we played with these toys the great world hardly existed for us, didn't need to, couldn't get in. How punctilious we were, Oswald's Lionel streamliner running on a strict schedule past my tidy Victorian mansion. You must know the way childhood memories draw themselves out like taffy, multiply themselves so that what may have lasted only weeks seems to have gone on for centuries. Escaping imposes the bittersweet duty to look back and I do, with compunction for Oswald and my mother who will never escape, and even for my father who did it so soon. But escaping is not right; it feels wrong to slip out the door when what you really wish for is to set a long table and invite everybody in, to entertain them out of your own supplies until, sated and pacified at last, they exchange pledges and vows.*

1.

L IKE a conductor hushing the crowd by spectacularly doing nothing, he waited for us to quiet down. "All right, people. People? Thank you. And thanks for showing up. It's good to see so many of you. Okay, let's begin. We'll get to the readings in a few minutes. First, I've got a short questionnaire I need you to fill in."

There were groans, companionable ones, from everybody but me.

Our director was a scruffy twenty-something with a voice probably higher than he'd have preferred and certainly shriller. He called us "people." Perhaps this was a theatrical convention, a neutral term, or maybe he thought it established him as our leader—chief of our little tribe. He wore a corduroy sport jacket, a painfully starched white Oxford shirt, and blue jeans—in my estimation, a costume calculated to suggest that he was both bohemian and keen on discipline.

Aristophanes' masterpiece is *Lysistrata*. We all had paperback copies of it in our laps.

"Call me Paul," he said to no one in particular as he moved briskly around the room, handing out his questionnaires. He might easily have had us pass them around but he appeared to like control, the personal clutch. When he worked his way back to me I could see he was giving everybody a fixed, up-close glance, meant to be penetrating or domineering. When he handed the questionnaire to me his face froze in an appraising frown and for an instant I felt like Medusa.

"Name." I decided to write mine as the registrar did, in reverse. *Strahlend, Catherine.* I thought it would distinguish me; yet, on the page *Strahlend, Catherine* looked stiff, a bit regimental or first-day-of-school, so I added a nickname in brackets, *Cat.* This was an impromptu inspiration. I had never had a nickname— let alone one as cool as Cat. It flattered my feline aspirations: to move gracefully, keep my own counsel, to purr or scratch as circumstances required. Cat. I felt less nervous already.

Though I had my coterie of friends in the dorm I wasn't satisfied. Among the reasons I was trying out for this play the chief was to enjoy the camaraderie. People who pretend together, I figured, who slog toward a common artistic goal, surely must form a special bond. I didn't aspire so high as the lead; the Chorus would do for me. Still, this wish to be a joiner didn't prevent me from sitting off to the side of the classroom, or putting my feet up on the seat in front like a teenager at the movies. Why was this? Hauteur? Defense against rejection? I didn't know anybody there and wasn't sure how to behave. So I sat alone and gave myself a nickname.

Strahlend, Catherine was good, *Cat Strahlend* better, but *Strahlend, Catherine [Cat]* best. It was all new to me, the theater biz, but at least I'd read the play three times.

Next we were asked to rate our choices in order of preference: "Acting...Lighting...Management...Scenery/Props." Management? I looked around the room. None of these people was going to put management anything but last.

Sing? (yes/no), Dance? (yes/no). In for a penny, I thought, and circled yes, yes.

List your experience in reverse chronological order. The director had left a lot of space for me to leave empty.

At the bottom: Females: willing to appear onstage in a bikini? (yes/no).

I assumed all these eager drama queens would circle yes. I didn't dare say no to anything, not with all that vacant space in the middle of the page.

2.

MY father ran away from home when I was five and Oswald seven. It was another six years—my whole life again—before I nailed down for sure why he'd left, though by then it wasn't much of a mystery. Mother's official story was credible only so long as you believed in it, which I didn't do for long. Poor Oswald believes it to this day and, for all I know, his believing has convinced Mother to believe it too. Acknowledging the truth that those you love refuse to is isolating; it makes you responsible since you have no choice but to abet their delusion or smash it. In the end, I yearned to move on.

It was early on a Sunday morning in April, after the last and most terrible of many nights, a night with two loud voices. Oswald woke Mother up. He wanted his breakfast. Mother looked funny; she came downstairs in her nightgown, which was unprecedented, and made us sit on the couch in the living room. The spring morning gushed through the big window and splashed over the Persian carpet. Oswald trembled beside me and I took his hand.

Mother was grinning unnaturally, and her feet were bare. I couldn't take my eyes off those vulnerable unprotected feet. She broke into an embarrassed grin and when she was finally on the point of saying something she stopped, as if she too had noticed her bare feet. "Oh, just a minute, darlings. Just wait here, will you?" She rushed upstairs. Mother was a careful dresser. She seemed to regard the occasion as one requiring that she be clothed and shod. Oswald and I were still in our pajamas. Mother knew that he couldn't sit still for two minutes.

I took my big brother's hand. He stamped his feet; with his free hand he rubbed his eyes. "Where's *Daddy*?" he whined. "Where's *breakfast*?"

I moved my hand to his thigh and rubbed it. "Shush," I said.

"I'm *hungry*."

"Just wait," I said. "We'll eat soon."

In her best blue suit and matching pumps Mother came down the stairs; she'd put on powder and lipstick, too. She looked exactly the way she did when we went to Mee-Maw's funeral.

"Did somebody die, Mommy?" I asked.

Oswald began to wail.

"No, sweetheart, nobody's died," she said, sitting down in the armchair that faced the television, Daddy's chair. Oswald began whooping, gulping air. Mother crossed her legs impatiently. "Oswald," she said sharply. "Stop crying. Now."

Oswald didn't stop crying. I tried rubbing his back.

Mother uncrossed her legs and leaned toward us. "Now, I need you both to listen to me. All right? Daddy's had to go away." And then she told us her story, the story. Nowadays, I think she made it up on the spot, just the way I extemporized my nickname. First, she explained what an *orphan* was and how sad and terrible it was to be an *orphan*. Could we imagine how sad? And then she said our father had to go and take care of a whole house full of these poor orphans, because they had no fathers or mothers of their own and surely we could spare him just for a while, since we had *her* and *she* loved us more than anything in the whole wide world.

"*Hate* orphans," hissed Oswald, rubbing at his tears and bouncing furiously on the couch.

"Where's this house where all the orphans live?" I asked.

"Far away, I'm afraid, darling. *So* far away that Daddy may not be able to visit us, for a while. Maybe a long while."

"*How* far away?" I insisted.

"Oh, very, *very* far. In another *country*. On the other side of the *ocean*."

"The *ocean*?" screeched Oswald.

Oswald always had peculiarities, tics. Starting on that Sunday these grew worse, became more domineering, as if they were parasites that had moved into the place vacated by Father. He can't bear the feel of wool against his skin and the sight of even a hint of fat on a piece of meat sends him rushing to the bathroom, heaving. Left shoe on before right, left trouser leg before right, buttons from bottom to top, never top to bottom. Can't stand any kind of hat on his head, fights having his nails cut. First the milk, then the corn flakes, then the sugar, and just the right amount or else.

My method for calming my brother's tantrums was this: the louder and jerkier he got the more calmly I spoke to him, eventually dialing down to a whisper, all the while rubbing his hand, his arm, finally his back. Mother could never manage it. The minute he started up she'd yell for me.

Two weeks after Daddy left to take care of the putative orphans a couple big boxes arrived. One was addressed to *Master Oswald*

Strahlend and the other to *Miss Catherine Strahlend.* They were sitting plump in the middle of the living room when we got home from school, huge brown rectangles that took up nearly the whole floor. Oswald and I were beside ourselves with excitement.

Mother was preternaturally calm and spoke in a whisper as she handed me the scissors. "They must be from your father.... F. A. O. Schwartz," she hissed bitterly. "It's the most expensive toy store in the world."

So I got my doll house, Oswald his trains. Maybe children delight in small things not just because they themselves are small but because they're bigger than their doll houses and electric trains. They can deploy homes, tracks, families, depots and towns just as they choose, little worlds over which they loom like caring parents, wrathful gods. Little boys adore the Tyrannosaurus because it's so huge and aggressive and can rip apart anything in its path. They equate size with power. Oswald relished lording it over little things, but his power was not of the stomping, masticating kind. He and I were both in harmony with our F. A. O. Schwartz toys and with each other because we wanted order, calm, regularity—and to be reminded of our father. Arranging my doll house, saving up for a tiny wooden table, making a bed out of a tobacco tin and discarded felt, setting the old lady with the bun of white hair on her rocking chair, drawing a little picture and gluing it to a wall, picking violets and dandelions to stuff into the tiny window boxes—these activities comforted me the way Oswald's rubbing his finger along the silky border of his blanket soothed him. Father's toys put us in a trance, dissolved time, gave us a temporary yet repeatable power at the center of our powerlessness. The difference was that Oswald never grew out of it, never dreamed, like me, of turning out rather than in or of seeking power in the wide world. I wanted to be bigger but I believe Oswald, if he could, would have chosen to be smaller, to take up residence in his perfect plastic microcosmos with its little farm and depot and milk cans. One day he gave a name to his little railroad town. He announced it was named "Pleasantville." What else? He was the Mussolini of his hamlet, for the trains always ran on time. He could declare it day or night, summer or winter. His will was at once arbitrary and precise; it could be Christmas one day, July Fourth the next. Everybody in Pleasantville, he assured me, was happy all the time—a whole populace that was visible only to him. I asked him if my doll house was also in Pleasantville, since the tracks ran by it. Uncharacteristically, he answered at once.

"*Just* outside," he said with something like an apology.

Unlike other Lionel-loving boys my brother wanted no collisions, no speeding trains jumping the tracks, and, when such accidents happened, he blamed himself like a god surprised by the indeterminacy of his creation, a god with too much compassion. Like all utopias, our miniature worlds were serene, dull, and compensatory.

How can I describe Mother? *Hysterical* is politically regressive. *Highly-strung* is half a century out of date. *Fragile* might do, but it's rather open-ended. A sufferer from nerves, the vapors, megrims, intermittent instability, inclined toward sudden tears, self-pity, fits of suffocating sentimentality. You get the idea. Father's jumping ship wasn't exactly therapeutic. Aunt Teresa came for a short stay and that was a help to Mother, a relief. She just turned things over to her sister for a time. I liked Aunt Teresa because she was a ruthless organizer, like me, doing for our deranged household what I did for my doll house. She set things up, shook Mother back on her feet, worked out a budget, a schedule of chores and then, on the grounds that she had three children of her own and a needy husband, left. We adjusted, of course, which is what you call it when the abnormal becomes normal.

In those early days, fooling with my F. A. O. Schwartz doll house, I used sometimes to fantasize, almost always about my father returning from his exotic orphanage, itself a fantasy. After he came back, the youngest once again, I would be the apple of my family's six eyes. They would beam at me, take pride in my astonishing accomplishments—the platinum record, the Olympic medals. For my Sweet Sixteen, Father would take me on a grand tour of Europe. There would be no disappointments, no missed trains, never any recriminations, nothing but sweet concord clear across the Old World: a Henry James tour but with short, declarative sentences and a happy ending. While we were off enjoying the pleasures of Rome, Paris, Vienna, and London, Oswald would have become normal, even popular. While I was off with Father, he'd be with Mother up at our L. L. Bean summer house in Maine. In August, he'd invite a dozen of his friends to stay, all good-looking, courteous boys exactly two years older than me. What a jolly time they'd have, sunbathing, sailing, and playing lawn games, killing time waiting for me. Then, on Labor Day, we'd all be united and there would be a huge clambake under a full moon and a towering bonfire. The boys would sing folk songs and motets and, like their singing, everything, including my mother and father, would resolve into one imperturbable harmony.

3.

HIGH-SCHOOL dalliances turn out to be real escapes only if they're also catastrophic, in which case they're anything but escapes. In fact, from what I observed, the girls who pinned their hopes on boys pulsing with hormonal bravado only found fires to replace frying pans. They got aborted or had babies; became embittered or broken-hearted or annulled or sent away. In retrospect I'd have preferred an all-girls school with plaid skirts, knee socks, a high fence.

I found I was curious about boys. They were different from my brother and I wanted to know how different. I also wasn't above wanting to belong, even to be popular, at moments anyway. I enjoyed being clumsily flattered and contemplated with satisfaction becoming the subject of envious gossip. I approached and avoided, I avoided and was approached, anxious all the while that no boy should leave a scar or even make a dent. The moment one of them was less than kind to Oswald—who would have slavishly doted on them all had I permitted it—I gave them up, sent them away. So, I was thought to be cool, verging on icy. This reputation suited me.

One boy told me I was the prettiest girl in school and for a few weeks I believed him. I was slim and looked taller than I was. It's a social asset not to be taller than most of the pool of boys. My eyes were large; my breasts were small, but my legs were good. My hair looked okay either up or down and I deployed it one way or the other depending on how I felt: *up* signified serious, intellectual, busy; *down* was supposed to mean glamorous, seductive, indifferent, and melancholy. I became the kind of girl other girls didn't like yet with whom they preferred to be on good terms. I was aware that boys liked how I looked, but I didn't set much store by my appearance or obsess over it. Prettiness I thought of as an incidental advantage, like being good at algebra, only better.

So I had an easy time of it in high school, in so far as such a thing's possible. The alienation I felt was practically a choice. I led a double life, of course: that of a pretty girl with good grades and that of my mother's shrink and housemaid, my brother's keeper and playmate. I was the youngest person in the house but the only adult.

Life at home was so demanding, the responsibility so serious, that all the schoolhouse pairing-off sometimes seemed just frivolity. My relations with girls were more fraught than those with boys and provided more of my sentimental education. Starting in elementary school, I had a series of best friends. It was through these girls that I came to know myself. There was an episode, to give an instance, that proved to me that it wasn't only my duty but my nature to displace contention with harmony. Two friends fell out over a boy named Paul Belfiglio, a gorgeous lacrosse jock and classic two-timer. They stopped speaking to each other but had plenty to say to everybody else. The escalation could be measured by epithets: from *back-stabber* to *slut* to *bitch* and on up from there. And, mind you, these were *nice* girls. Meanwhile, Belfiglio continued seeing both, actually *using* their jealousy to work his way around the bases. "Why not? *Cheryl* let me." "Come on, Cheryl. Alana *loved* it when I did that." The jerk's conceit swelled up like a mandrill's butt. I knew all this because I was a confidante to both Cheryl and Alana. Finally, like dust in my doll house or Oswald's untucked shirttails, I could stand it no more. I invited both for a run through the park one Saturday morning. Cheryl turned up first. She was glad to see me until Alana turned up. They glared. I made a speech.

"Look," I said, "Paul's an asshole. Either of you is worth twenty of him. *Fifty*. He's obviously playing you against each other. God, he even *brags* about it. Did you know that? What do you think you're doing, murdering each other's reputations? I'm sick of it. You want my opinion, you should both dump him—bang! You should do it *together*. Then you should kiss and make up...and, and let him *see* you doing it. Okay? Think it over while we run. Come on. Five miles."

In the cause of peace and order I could be a bully. Like Lysistrata.

In high school I was liberated from the task of defending my brother which I'd done fiercely in middle school, actually earning some respect for it. But in ninth grade Oswald, after a short, unequal battle between Mother and the authorities, was assigned to a vocational school. I agreed with the experts. Oswald turned out to be pretty good with computers, not at writing code, of course, but repairing glitches, keeping a system up and running. It wasn't so different from the care with which he maintained his railroad and Pleasantville: good with things, bad with people. With girls, Oswald wouldn't even try. I once asked him if he'd like me to fix him up. "No!" he yowled. He was panicked. I backed off, not a little relieved, and stayed backed off.

My own experience of high school was of a just-tolerable waiting-room, Purgatorio rather than Inferno. College I imagined as Paradise. My dreams shuddered into life the moment I opened my father's letter with the enormous check in it, a check that was, as he said, "just for starters." He pledged himself to pay whatever the four years would cost, adding sweetly that it wouldn't break his heart if I could swing some serious financial aid. So I applied to four expensive schools, got into all of them, too.

I spent that summer at home working at Walgreen's and preparing Mother and Oswald for my coming defection. They were so dismayed at the prospect, both of them alternately clutching and resentful, that I came to relish my hours at the drugstore as a paid respite. I loved my mother and brother and accused myself of treason for leaving them—above all, for *longing* to leave—but, *Life called.* I told myself they'd be all right, turning it into a financial calculation, as if that were the point. Mother was a part-time receptionist for two dentists, the same job she'd talked her way into a couple months after Father took off. She loved working there, thought of herself as indispensable to her dentists, calling herself "the pin in the pinwheel." I knew she also got checks from Father. To be fair, he never stinted on the price of freedom. As for Oswald, at the start of his third decade he astonished us by landing a job and then holding on to it. My brother was probably the world's only minimum-wage IT guy. On the recommendation of one of his teachers, he'd been taken on by a three-branch local bank that had just been snapped up by a much bigger one. The big bank wanted to upgrade and Oswald was a cheap frill, diligent to the point of zealotry, willing to work any hours they wanted; he'd have swept the floors too, if they asked. He'd take the bus straight home to his Lionels and the veggie burgers he'd adopted as his staple diet. That summer he'd come through the door calling my name.

No ivory tower, no mere escape, College was to me the one place where reality was seriously thought about. So far as I could see the so-called real world ran on advertising and public relations, or tried its hardest to do so. Anyway, the point wasn't just to get to some other place or to have something I lacked but to *be* someplace and *become* something. I was the most eager of freshmen, one who'd feared that she might never get to be one. College loomed above me not as some post-adolescent warehouse; it was the possibility of liberation, the place where the books I loved were loved by others, the chance to actualize the finest word I learned in my first philosophy course, my *entelechy*. I was that kind of college student; I was the sort who can get excited even by Aristotle. My father may have absconded but he didn't abandon. He sent money which, in my circumstances, wasn't such a poor substitute for love—and maybe it wasn't a substitute at all. A doll house and then college…not such a bad deal. When the president ended her welcoming address by saying "Let the adventure begin," I didn't laugh like the girl next to me; I murmured *amen*.

The Boyfriend. That's what I called him: first to myself, then my friends, finally to his face. *The Boyfriend*…the sobriquet exalted him, as if there were only one in the world, but also reduced him to a single function. *The Boyfriend*…a phrase that, it now seems to me, denied the intimacy it seemed to proclaim. *The* Boyfriend and yet only The *Boyfriend*. It must have sounded as if I begrudged whatever affection I felt for him.

We met in October in the hallway of my dorm. We both liked what we saw. He was dressed to take somebody to a party; I was coming out of the bathroom, wrapped in a towel. The Boyfriend was handsome, well built, and moderately bright. He was a sophomore majoring in business and pretended he was taking me *under his wing, showing me the ropes*—he actually used these phrases. I suppose I was a mystery to him. According to a book I read, male sexuality is all mixed up with aggression; their urge to penetrate begins as curiosity; the biblical verb "to know" is ambiguous yet precise. Maybe the Boyfriend thought he could figure me out by getting into my pants. To be honest, The Boyfriend was pretty ordinary. Part of his charm, in fact, was to make me feel I was the one thing in his life that wasn't. To me, his normality was exotic, as my eccentricity probably was to him; it was the mutual fascination of the rabbit and the snake. For a time I hoped that being the Boyfriend's girlfriend would make me indistinguishable too. I put it to him, "I want to go unnoticed, but at the same time I want to be extraordinary."

After I went out for the play in February I told the Boyfriend that he should start calling me Cat.

4.

A FTER we handed in our forms the director blitzed us through a set of readings, our auditions. He sat in the first row, called out our names from the forms, held up a sheet of paper. On each sheet he'd typed a speech from the play which we had to stand at the front of the classroom and deliver. He appeared to scrawl savage notes on each form before saying *Thankyounext*, but I couldn't see his face until it was my turn. An inscrutable countenance it was, cold as the stuff caked on the top of the freezer compartment. *ThankyounextCatherineStrahlend.*

To me he assigned a bit of the heroine's ferociously level-headed speech explaining to the red-faced Commissioner how wool-working is the archetype for sound politics:

> First, you take raw fleece
> and you wash the beshittedness off it:
> just so you should first lay the city out
> on a washboard and beat out the rotters
> and pluck out the sharpers like burrs, and when
> you find tight knots of schemers and plotters
> who are out for key offices, card them loose,
> but best tear off their heads in addition.

I didn't feel I'd done at all well with the speech—hadn't been sufficiently furious or mocking—but when I got the call-back a week later I couldn't prevent myself from thinking I must be up for the lead.

Blind hope, of course. It took the director a quarter of an hour to deal out the parts, to announce the identities of *his* Kalonike and Lampito, *his* Cinesias and Spartan herald, all the members of *his* two choruses and who'd lead each. Finally everybody in the room had a role but me, Ms. Humiliated. Must have been some error, I figured, that call-back. If only there'd been a door at the back, I'd have made a dash for it.

"And last but *any*thing but least, our Harmony," said the director with a lascivious grin. "That'll be you...you..." With an excess of drama he glanced down at my form, "Catherine Strahlend. That's Cat, right? *Cat?*"

Meow. Craftier than I, none of the other females had agreed to appear next-to-nude for five minutes in the final episode. It wasn't modesty, I realized. It was because Harmony had no lines, that hers was the one role in the history of classic Western drama in which a young woman is absolutely objectified, trans-mogrified into an eroticized map. I felt I'd been kicked in the midriff. Ouf! And yet the instant he said *Cat* I knew I'd go through with it, wear that nano-bikini and the cheesy beauty-contest sash with *Harmony* spelled out on it—that I'd be just a piece sublimated into Peace.

I not only read Aristophanes' play five times but, with no lines to memorize, actually thought about it.

You know how it goes. By the end, the women's sex strike has worked so well that the horny warriors of Athens and Sparta are just dying to end the Peloponnesian War. They want to screw more than to kill; they're yearning to be husbands again, to get down and dirty: *I'd like to strip and get to plowing right away.* The Athenian's so befuddled by lust he doesn't even know he's punning, doesn't connect his drive to deposit his seed to how desperately ravaged Attica is in need of planting, of husbandmen. Harmony's brief scene, that virtuoso riff of double-entendres, epitomizes the entire play.

The women suffer too, of course, also feel deprived; in fact, sexual frustration is their chief motive for going on strike, giving up what they want to get more of it. Aristophanes is too smart a comedian to include any sentimental or lofty anti-war talk. The women want men and the men are off fighting and getting killed. The women only go to *war* with the men because they want to go to *bed* with them; the men make peace because they want to have at it with the women. To Aristophanes as to Freud Eros is in the driver's seat. The play leaves you suspecting that the only reason Lysistrata prevails is because the women hold out fifteen minutes longer than the men. Aristophanes is instructive; he shows us that the war between the sexes can be perpetual only because it has an infinite number of truces. Luckily.

On my last reading I had a thought that was almost deep: that the democrats who invented drama erected it on the most durable foundation, that of biology: as sex is to comedy tragedy is to death.

So what is Harmony's role? It is to be the incarnation of comic Eros, all curves, plenty of skin, a dumb land ripe for a plow and the best alternative to the murderous phalanx.

So at the end Lysistrata presses the negotiations with the Big Tease. This is literally where I come in, viz. *A naked maid appears from inside.* Lysistrata directs me to conduct the tumid ambassadors to her in order that she can dictate terms. *If he won't give his hand, then lead him by the prick.*

The men can't tear their eyes off me—*What an unutterably lovely ass*—so that the diplomatic negotiations turn into ogling, a butchering of my body: *Now first suppose you cede to us that bristling tip of land, Echinos, behind which the gulf of Malia recedes, and those long walls, the legs on which Megara reaches to the sea....*

The scene's mercifully short, at least. My job's to absorb all that war-making testosterone and empire-building passion and make sure they think with their pricks. A dirty joke? The ultimate in Aristophanic daring? Mere wisdom? The play didn't end the Peloponnesian War, of course. In fact, the war got worse. Still, it's a play with a message nobody in the one-drachma seats could miss. Make love, not war.

And what of the maid, of Harmony? She's Aristophanes' theme made flesh, though just a topographical slut, a mere doll. She's nobody's girl and everybody's. Eirene's a doll without a house.

5.

THE play was to go up in April; we rehearsed through March. The campus enjoyed an early and perfect spring, daffodils and azaleas, quads like cricket pitches; but for me it was a time of troubles and changes. I carried on with my coursework as I used to play with my doll house, by excluding everything else. I could manage this for up to three hours at a time. I saw my friends, ate salads in the Food Court, sipped coffee as I walked to class, attended rehearsals, phoned home. You wouldn't guess anything was wrong.

What changes, what troubles? First, the Boyfriend. I broke up with him and wouldn't, couldn't tell him why. He was flummoxed, clueless. I simply raised my hand and pointed implacably to the door, bore a flaming sword and expelled him from my garden. At first he was almost teary but quickly became angry, which was much preferable, and accused me of freezing him out, said it was as if I'd hung up on him. Well, until he stopped calling, I did that too.

To my surprise, I told Professor Lieberman, my World Lit teacher, all about it. I didn't intend to but by then there wasn't much I didn't tell him, of whose abundant office hours I took extravagant advantage.

"You look a little blue."

"I broke up with the Boyfriend."

"The Boyfriend?"

"That's what I call him—*called* him."

"I see. And you're what? Devastated? Relieved about it?"

"Yes and no."

He nodded. I sat in the chair he kept beside his desk. I liked that he didn't put his desk between himself and the students who came to see him.

He waited. He was good at that, in class too. He'd ask a leading question (*If Hamlet's father was king and he's dead then why isn't Hamlet king?*) and could tolerate the ensuing silence longer than any teacher I'd ever come across so that, exasperated by his patience, somebody *had* to say something.

"We were in this store. The cashier was slow making change— you know, had trouble figuring it out. The Boyfriend turns to me and smirks. 'What a retard,' he says, just like that. *Retard.* That's what jerks used to call my brother."

Lieberman picked up his pen and fiddled with it. "Couldn't

get by it, then?"

"No. That's just it. I couldn't. But, I mean, I've got to ask myself whether, if it weren't for my brother, if I'd have objected so much? On the other hand, I don't want to be the kind of person who's indifferent to casual abuse of the weak. Was I seeing the truth about the Boyfriend or misjudging him by a snapshot?"

"What do you think?"

"I think it doesn't matter because it's just as you say; I can't get past it. When I think of his voice it's all I hear. *Retard.*"

Professor Lieberman wistfully looked up toward the window. "Like a thunderhead at the end of one of these nice spring days."

"Pardon me?"

"Blots everything out."

This simile somehow raised my spirits. Professor Lieberman could always make me feel better, even when I didn't need to. So I smiled at him.

"Well, I don't suppose you came to see me about…about the *Boyfriend*, did you?"

"Nope. I came about Aristotle, actually."

"Aristotle? He's not on our reading list, not even the *Poetics.*"

"Actually, I wanted to ask you about something that happened in my Ethics class."

My special relationship with Professor Lieberman began on the first day of class when I reluctantly answered a question he asked.

Introduction to World Literature I. The sheer poundage of that title seemed to squash my aspiration to read everything.

But instead of starting with ponderous words, he'd led off with a little exercise. He gave us each a copy of "The Lady of Shallott," told us to read it and write down three statements describing it. Then he asked some of us to read what we'd written. I can recall the response of a smart aleck who, in an adenoidal tenor, read out of his notebook: "1) it rhymes and rhymes and rhymes and a lot of these rhymes are the same, 2) it's way too long, 3) 'The Lady of Shallott' is exactly the sort of poem people have in mind when they say they hate poetry." Professor Lieberman did his best to transmute this lead into pedagogical gold without denying that the lead was really lead, which I liked. Then he called on me. I connected the poem to *Idylls of the King*, commented on the Victorian enthusiasm for medievalism, and wound up by categorizing the poem as a literary ballad that was probably written in emulation of Keats' "La Belle Dame Sans Merci." This made me a much worse wise-ass than the poetry-phobe; nevertheless, Professor Lieberman beamed on me.

"Okay," I said. "My ethics professor lectured on Aristotle's idea of practical virtue, that Goldilocks, not-too-much, not-too-little idea—not a very inspiring notion of virtue, by the way. Well, anyway, it was an okay lecture; he gave clever examples and really nailed it down."

"And so?"

"Well, after he finished he asked if there were any questions— you know, the way teachers do when they don't want any. But I had one. I asked why we shouldn't ever join the teenagers in the Camaros to the left or the blue-hairs in their Buicks to the right. That's not how I put it, of course. I wanted to know *why* Aristotle said that the proper course in life lay between a vice of excess and one of deficiency. The professor looked at me as if I were an imbecile and gave me a condescending answer. 'Aristotle *said* it, young lady, because he thought it was *true*.' Oooh, *young lady*. The class laughed at me, of course, but I raised my hand again and this time he sighed and said 'What now?' I apologized and said I must have expressed myself poorly. 'What I wanted to know was *why* Aristotle thought it was true.' 'I've no idea what you mean,' he said and dismissed the class."

"A river without fish, a forest without trees, a school without questions."

"What?"

"Just an old saying. Did you feel humiliated?"

"Well, annoyed, I suppose. There's something the matter with that course. *You'd* never talk about playwrights or poets the way *he* talks about philosophers. You'd explain about *them*, not just what they wrote. You've taught me that poems are written by people who live particular lives at certain times, that the best works transcend their origins but they're still rooted in them. Right? So, there's no disembodied, spotless, a-historical, cerulean blue heaven where the writers sit around and write. But that's exactly how he talks about philosophers."

"Quite a speech! So you've brought your annoyance to me instead of your philosophy professor."

I laughed. "I guess. Anyhow, what do you think? Am I missing something?"

"Well, here's what I think about Aristotle. I think he was born middle-aged, middle-class, middle-of-the-road. I think Aristotle's right about so much because Plato was so much more brilliantly wrong. I think a doctor's son from Butte, Montana isn't going to look at the world the same way a Manhattan kid with a trust-fund does. I think Plato never got over knowing Socrates and Aristotle never met anybody remotely like him. But then philosophy's not my field."

"I wish you *did* teach philosophy."

"And I wish you'd talk back to your philosophy professor the way you do to me."

"Touché," I giggled.

I loved that Professor Lieberman had a soft spot for me. I could see he found me smart—smart and pretty. It was a joy that his course ran for two semesters, that there was an Intro to World Lit II. In fact, I'd grown so fond of the man that I wondered if I might be turning him into a surrogate father. Everything that's trite isn't untrue.

Once, I impulsively asked why he taught a freshman survey course when—as I'd learned—most professors of his rank and reputation couldn't be caught sight of by an underclassman except with high-powered binoculars. "Wouldn't you rather spend time with English majors and your grad students? Isn't this, well, slumming?"

He raised an eyebrow. "Slumming? Look, Cat, let me put it this way. This is something to be kept just between you and me, please. You never know what freshmen might become while with graduate students I'm afraid it's only too clear. Anyway, I happen to like young people and think it a privilege to be around them. Maybe if I'd ever resolved the problems of adolescence I wouldn't feel that way."

"Well," I said, "we like you too—maybe because we sense that you like us back. I don't think young people liked Aristotle very much."

"No, I doubt it. He's too much like a wise uncle who's always right. Young people like Socrates. Aristotle's the anti-Socrates."

"And he's always *defining* everything to death and, besides, his science is so wrong."

"But he's nonetheless a real scientist."

"What do you mean?"

"Scientists will dump their prejudices as soon as they're pointed out to them. Give Aristotle a good physics textbook and another on biology and I'm sure he'd change his mind. I think he'd be grateful."

"Whereas people in the humanities…?"

Professor Lieberman laughed and got to his feet. "Time's up. Off to class."

At the door I had a wicked inspiration, an exhibitionist's impulse. "One last thing, Professor. I'm going to be in the Drama Club's production of *Lysistrata* at the end of the month. If I get you a ticket, think you could come?"

Okay, no more Boyfriend. Not so bad, but April had much worse in store. One Monday night Mother phoned in hysterics (sorry, it's the only word) to say that my brother had been accused by a female teller of an improper assault.

"Improper assault? You mean *sexual*?"

"Yes," she blubbered. "They fired him, Catherine."

"Can I talk to him?"

"It's useless. He won't speak. He just plays with his trains."

I hesitated, heart beating wildly. "Police?"

"Thank God, no. But he's been *fired*."

6.

I couldn't get home until late Friday night. Just as Mother said, Oswald was shut down. I fell into bed. At ten the next morning Mother woke me to say she was going to the mall with a friend; she needed a break, blessed me for giving it to her, and left.

Downstairs, Oswald was in his pajamas, as if he were still eight years old, already at his trains. I noticed how much Pleasantville had expanded, new houses, tiny pines, a bridge. I grabbed a cup of coffee and, when I came back into the living room, crouched on the floor near Oswald. He ignored me. I began to clean out my doll house, which was thick with dust. Best go easy, I thought, best take your time. I didn't ask him anything at first, only remarked on the changes in Pleasantville, admired his new boxcar. Nada, impregnable zilch. After an hour of this I was fed up; I grabbed him by the shoulders and demanded to know what happened.

Oswald looked at the floor indifferently. "I was fired," he said tonelessly.

I got in his face. "No. What happened with that *teller*?"

He shrugged.

"Did you—did you touch her?"

Oswald shrugged off my interrogator's embrace, plucked the streamliner off the tracks and threw it at the wall. It made a terrible noise and left a dent. I was scared and pulled away, but then I took my poor brother in my arms.

When Mother came home Oswald was napping. My doll house was dust-free and I had a chicken roasting in the oven, a real bourgeois dinner. I'd forgotten the agreeable if short-lived satisfaction of good housekeeping.

Mother asked where Oswald was then, after I'd explained he was asleep, began talking fast: "What do we do? Did you get anything out of him? At least they're not filing any charges. I was terrified that—"

I patted her back. "Calm down. Look, you'll keep him home for a while and then, next month, I'll be home and we'll find him another job."

She sniffed. "Around *here*?"

"We'll try."

She started to cry. This exasperated me and I asked a question calculated to make her stop. "Did you tell Father?"

"Tell your father? That's a laugh," she said and then, to prove it, actually forced a noise that was vaguely like a laugh.

"Mom, is there enough money?" I asked quietly.

She rubbed her eyes and nose with the back of her hand. "Yes. Just."

I was back at school on Monday. On Tuesday I wrote a ten-page paper on John Donne. Wednesday was dress rehearsal; we opened on Friday.

I didn't even get to pick out the bikini. We had a wardrobe mistress, forsooth, a Juicy Fruit-chewing, improbably coiffed sophomore named Danielle who invented names for colors (angry-barracuda teal, three-day-old saffron), could discourse at length on textures, and told me with unshakable certainty that she'd be starting out in fashion journalism before moving on to designing her own line of ready-to-wear designer clothing. Except in a nightmare, Danielle said, she wouldn't dream of appearing onstage in a bikini (*Look at these hips!*) but relished the idea of putting one on me. "You're almost model-skinny," she said while measuring my chest. "Dynamite pee-wee boobs, Cat," she crowed, though they were, truth to tell, larger than hers.

"Doubt I'll be able to score a *flesh*-colored bikini, even online. Too bad, really. Hm...," she mused, "...we *could* go with paint-the-town pink or—I know—Commie-Manifesto red. That's it! I mean you're *so* consumptive-poet pale, it'll be irresistible, like blood on Ivory Soap."

So my costume, the little there was of it, was red and my sash was white with red letters and my skin—lots of it—was "mommy-dearest pearl." The director, who interested himself a bit too much in these details at the dress rehearsal—insisted on seeing me with my hair up and then he wanted it down again. He opted for down because, he said in his most masculine voice, "With it up you make me think of those ladies that parade around the ring between rounds."

I endured all this calmly, submitted to being an object for the director, Danielle, the crew, for the Spartans and Athenians. As I learned from Epictetus, Stoicism is the noblest recourse of the unhappy slave.

On the Wednesday before opening night Professor Lieberman sent me an email. "Thanks for the ticket." I'd shoved it under his office door. I could hardly hand it to him after class, not with everybody watching; in fact, I shouldn't have given it to him at all. He went on professorially:

Have you read Plato's *Symposium*? I ask because you're taking a philosophy course and, anyway, you seem to have read everything. I ask because the play is *Lysistrata* and so I was wondering if you know the speech Aristophanes makes at the drinking-party. I think you'll see the connection:

Mankind, judging by their neglect of him, have never at all understood the power of Love. For if they had understood him, they would have built noble temples and altars in his honor; but this is not done, and most certainly ought to be done: since of all the gods he is the best friend of men, the helper and healer of the ills which are the great impediment to the happiness of the race.

Whatever part you play, Cat, I'm sure you'll do a fine job. Break a leg.

Prof L

Backstage in Rheinach Hall is a long corridor with four exiguous rooms off it. A few minutes before the play started I took refuge in one of these rooms, away from the hubbub and flirting. I had a white terrycloth robe around me—"Baskin-Robbins vanilla," according to Danielle—and half-listened to the excited bustle in the hallway. The director and stage manager were behaving like a panic-stricken shepherd and his dog, issuing their commands in stentorian whispers. It was functional chaos.

At the end of the corridor was a wide door that opened on to a concrete loading platform. During the big teasing scene between Cinesias and Myrrhina, I put on my sneakers and slipped out into the spring night.

Oswald, Mother, Father, the Boyfriend, Professor Lieberman—my mind ran on them. Eros the helper and healer. I reviewed with detached amusement the director's decrees. "Remember, Cat, you're a wind-up doll," he said, "so, wide eyes, dumb smile, please. You take the guys by their hands, very gently, and move them center-stage. Then I want you to stand still on your mark, full-frontal. *Absolutely* still. A *statue*. Got it?"

Should I ignore his orders? Should I rebel and grip the men by their biceps, covering up their strength, yank them across the stage, shove them up against one another? Could I really just stand still, like some life-sized kewpie doll?

It was still warm and not yet fully dark. The air was sweet with the smell of dirt and flowers. I could see the quarter moon and what must have been the evening star—Venus which, like me, isn't really a star.

Yank. Shove. Help. Heal. I didn't want to stand still. I wanted to dance around them all, Spartans and Athenians, oblivious to lustful eyes, greedy words. I wanted to glide in my nakedness through choruses of crones and geezers, following the measures of a peaceful sarabande only I could hear.

TEN-MINUTE NOVEL

WARREN

S HE had not gone to bed with him, consoled or inquired after him, eaten with him, reproached, upbraided or mocked him in seventeen days. Before their last time together there had been a hiatus of a week and a half. And he knew she was free too, free over the three-day weekend, on Wednesday afternoons when they were both off as usual, and last Thursday night when her husband, fifteen years too old for her, had been out of town; and so when he asked *why* and there was a viscous silence he'd broken it by blurting *I've had enough* and that it was *obviously over* and in that moment their whole romance or affair or whatever it was had turned into a downhill slide, a shift of semantic stress from "Nothing is better than *this*" to "*Nothing* is better than this." She hadn't even bothered to remark on how long it had taken him to catch on.

So he'd been the one to end it. Technically. The words had bubbled out before the thought, without any consideration at all, which was a new experience for him, a careful and deliberate man, afraid of bars and drug addiction and even pornography, as, indeed, was the whole unprecedented thing. It had been adultery and young love at once, with a married colleague from the nonprofit where they both labored in the odor of secular sanctity. People who work for human rights organizations make a lot of assumptions about each other that speed up conversations. The affair really began when over their salads one day he had lightly asked her who her best friend was and she'd blushed and said she guessed *he* was. It was a stunner. Sure, she'd told him a few things about herself and, as for him, he'd divulged more than he intended because it was a pleasure having a confidante—but her *best* friend obviously ought to have been her husband or her college roommate and if they weren't, if *he* were her best friend, then something had been going on of which he had been oblivious. "You know how you look when you see me?" she purred later, in his bed. "You just light up. I swear I saw your knees buckle." She giggled. "*Twice.*"

It was true. He remembered the knee-buckling and how it had perplexed him—a brain tumor, vertigo, hypoglycemia? Once you assume nothing can happen because she's married and a colleague, well then the body proceeds all uncensored.

Warren opened the window of his one-bedroom apartment and looked at the night which seemed to him a shroud full of bullet holes. He would forever remember this as the weather when his life changed, when the hope of her showing up at his door with a valise in her hand and a plea on her face ended in five seconds of the thickest nothingness, the substance of nothing. Is nothing *ever* better than something?

He put on his running shoes, grabbed up his wallet and keys, threw a hooded sweatshirt over his shoulder, headed for the door, then the stairway. Getting out must be a kind of tropism, an instinct lodged deep in the reptilian brain. He needed to get out.

BURCU

BURCU hated driving out to where Konstantinos lived with his good-looking wife and two nice-smelling children. He considered the suburbs more American in the worst sense than the city, for they were indulgent, lazy, boring, denatured, bland, rich but not so prosperous as they tried to appear with their hedges and green street signs. To his friend Nikos he once described his brother's neighborhood as full of trees that belonged and grass that didn't. He had been acerbic. "Everything is too nice, you know? And the houses, they all look like pumped-up body builders."

Burcu coped with his envy by exaggerating it, especially to the children. "This is your room?" he'd said to his niece as if it was beyond belief. "All this space to yourself? Amazing! Uncle Burcu lives in a shoebox, and not a big shoebox either but the kind *baby* shoes come in." In the kitchen he feigned awe. "What's this thing?" he asked his nephew. "What? A machine that just washes dishes—and it's called, what?" The boy had howled with laughter and his sister-in-law smiled tightly. Her smile was as clenched as her husband's fist. The kids laughed when he told them his diet consisted exclusively of sardines and saltines, which he often got mixed up. As he stroked the family terrier he told them tales about his own pet, which he said was an ant. "That's how lonesome your Uncle Burcu is," he'd moaned. "He made a pet of an ant. Well, it's all he can afford. But this is no ordinary ant; she can do tricks. For a crumb she does up to three somersaults—that's the record—not easy with all those extra legs." What was the ant's name? "I call her Athena, because she's a girl ant, and very wise. Hardworking, too." He told how she had built a house under his bed with thirty-seven tiny rooms so she would always be prepared in case relatives showed up. Athena was prudent as well and saved up spare crumbs in a matchbox, again for guests. "What's a matchbox?" asked his nephew because no one in the suburbs smoked, at least not where children could see them. "Aunt Athena!" his niece would cry as soon as Burcu came through the door while Konstantinos squirmed in his leather slippers. "Tell us another story about Aunt Athena." Aunt/Ant, they thought that was just hilarious. His sister-in-law always smirked and coyly asked him if he were seeing anybody special and when would they get to meet her and Burcu would force himself to grin and say that he was content to play the field, not being quite ready to settle down.

It was not a pretty dance, but all of this humiliation he endured to get Konstantinos alone and ask him for money. His brother would frown and cross his arms. Even as a child he would make that face, cross his arms just as stubbornly, and say, "I am the ant, Burcu, and *you*, you are the grasshopper." Perhaps that was the origin of his pet, Athena, with her full larder and big house full of tiny rooms for siblings and cousins who never arrived.

When they were at last alone on the big wooden deck with its gas grill, flowery umbrella, and the concrete planters with petunias spilling out of them Konstantinos said just two words. *No more.* How my big brother loves being a success, thought Burcu, buying a whole lamb every Easter, hiring and firing, writing checks to private schools, yelling at his suppliers. *No more.* Then he said it again, this time in Greek.

Burcu lit up a Marlboro the second he was in his used-up Toyota, which was stuffed with trash and stank. He drove back on the almost empty highway, over the bridge, into the city streets, paying no attention to the blinking light on the dashboard just to spite all the world's prudent ants. Then there was clunking and smoke and finally the car juddered to a stop. Burcu hammered his feckless grasshopper's fist against the dead steering wheel and got out swearing in good demotic Greek. No more.

HERB

TWENTY-SEVEN years at Donnelly Manufacturing Company cranking out copier cases, refrigerator shelves, wing struts, specialty fasteners, interlocking ducts, God-knows-what-all. When business got hot six years ago he'd volunteered to work nights for the extra pay, so Peg did too, at the hospital. For a time they had lived in a kind of photographic negative but found it had advantages or at least got used to it. They'd been able to put some money by and thank God for that, though it probably wasn't nearly enough, a lot of it going to help Harriet with her tuition and then the wedding. And so on.

What are the odds of getting laid off the same week you become a grandfather? Come to that, what are the odds of *anything*?

So for three days he'd been a grandfather and for five unemployed but he still couldn't sleep at night when Peg was on the night shift and he should have been and so he'd watched TV and downed beers which made him feel stupider and fatter.

At night the apartment had the feel of a funeral parlor. The minutes went slowly and, though they'd said they might, Donnelly didn't call which wasn't surprising, given the way home sales were tanking, the shuttered stores all over the place. And so on.

Peg worried about him. He liked that she worried. He encouraged it. He also liked it when she tried to cheer him up. "Business'll pick up soon, you'll see," she chirped. The nursing racket was going great guns at least. She came home at dawn exhausted and told him what had gone on in the ward when she was dying to fall into bed. She probably thought it would perk him up to realize that at least *he* didn't have a brain tumor, bacteria eating his flesh, or half his guts cut out before it spread.

Harriet and Bob lived under an hour away. They'd named the baby Harold. Herbert, Harriet, Harold. Everybody would call him Harry, or maybe Hal. Boys went for one-syllable nicknames on the ball fields, on the basketball court. He'd always been Herb. "I love fresh herbs," Peg had whispered in his ear the first time he put his arm around her in the movies. The baby was healthy, thank God, and Harriet took to mothering as if she'd been at it all her life. If he didn't find a job he might turn into their babysitter. Hal and Gramps at the beach, the ballgame, going fishing, working on a science project, telling each other riddles. *Okay. What color is an orange, Hal?* If a little brother or sister came along he might be back on the night shift. He pictured Harriet and Bob at dinner parties, restaurants, in theaters as he turned into one of those *au pairs*.

He should be feeling grateful, ought to be counting his blessings. He should pour a heaping dollop of resignation into the shaker and call the cocktail contentment.

Daytime felt too bright and busy. Yet he knew the night no better, not really. He was used to being in the shop making things, trying not to lose a finger. His hands were still complete only now they were empty. He missed George and Sal. Hell, he even missed sour Mrs. Hilsop. The hobbies he'd always complained he hadn't enough time for bored him now because he had too much. The *idea* of hobbies bored him.

The corduroy-covered couch, the absurd lamp with a half-topless Diana carrying a bow and followed by whippets, which had been Peg's mother's, the worn track down the middle of the Belgian-Persian runner, the dust caked into the kitchen corners, none of which he'd noticed for years, he now couldn't stop seeing. He began remembering things like standing up and spelling *mosquitoes* wrong in third grade and his cousin breaking his leg when he jumped off the garage roof and Patches, the dog they'd had to put down when she began dragging her hind-quarters like a busted hook-and-ladder. Never anything good, even when he tried.

So he began to take walks. He didn't tell Peg because—seeing what came into the Emergency Room—she'd have scolded him saying that the city was unsafe at night, that it was, as she liked to say, "a war zone." She'd given him suggestions because she never criticized without offering alternatives. "Why don't you make something for the baby," she'd say. Make what?

"Damn it," he said aloud and turned off the television, put some folding money in his pocket, and headed for the park.

KARL/RODION

THE Raskolniki were gathered in the musty basement of Chuck/Mitya's grandmother's apartment building, smoking, ragging on each other, but chiefly weighing the merits of *Les Caves du Vatican* against those of *Les Faux-Monnayeurs*. Everyone agreed that Lafcadio flat-out buried Bernard Profitendieu and so they favored the former. Karl/Rodion had given them their head up till then, keeping his *obiter dicta* dry. He expected not servility but deference and generally got it. So they all raised their heads and listened when he declared, "*The Counterfeiters* may not be the better book, but it's certainly the greater achievement."

"And what the fuck does *that* mean?" asked the ever-combative Fred/Ivan.

"The way I see it," Karl/Rodion explained a little menacingly, "an achievement has an objective element to it—how long it took to accomplish, its magnitude and complexity, its influence, stuff like that. On the other hand, whether one book's better than another—that's purely subjective. Somebody just likes one more, which usually means he likes being inside of it."

"Bullshitter," Antonio/Versilov laughed admiringly.

"Shit, Bernard, Lafcadio—they're all gay anyway," groused macho Julio/Stavrogin.

"Not at all," said Karl/Rodion coolly. "Neither one, actually. Just the author."

"What about that Olivier dude?"

"Okay, I'll give you Molinier."

"So what's *that* tell you?"

"Hey, what happened to that cell we boosted last night?"

"My sister. Gave it to my sister."

"Gave it? *Gave* it?"

"What? You gotta problem?"

The conversation broke down into dialogues to which he paid no attention. Karl/Rodion's mind was on Miki with her long black hair, exotic eyes, slightly bowed, very white legs, and that Yoko Ono accent. She had transferred into his linear algebra class three weeks ago—apparently, she already knew calculus. He tried to figure out what he liked so much about Miki, what made her irresistible to him who liked so much to resist. He decided it was that she was the most self-contained sane person he'd ever met. It was as if under that dignified seriousness lay depths of chocolate sweetness. He was compelled to delve into them. Eros had him by the short hairs, again.

He would give her something nice, an expensive present. He'd have to guess what she'd like, a sweater or a necklace, maybe one of those German fountain pens. Then he'd leave it for her somewhere with an unsigned note, wait a day or two and ask her about the sweater or the necklace or the pen and she'd catch on and he'd ask her to go dancing with him. Something like that. It would mean shopping.

The Raskolniki were a gang but also, as Karl/Rodion repeatedly had to remind them, a *coterie*. His ninth-grade English teacher, Mr. Ardekian, who was so raw and enthusiastic he wanted everybody to call him Larry, singled Karl out because he'd broken his rule and spoken up in class. The discussion that day had been so numbingly stupid he was provoked into saying something sharp about the Dickinson poem that begins, "After great pain, a formal feeling comes." Ardekian accosted him on his way out of the room and, all lit up, began larding on the positive reinforcement. With due sullenness Karl made clear to Larry that he hadn't the least interest in Dickinson's poetry, had only spoken out of exasperation, and had no plan to do it again.

Two days later Ardekian slipped him an oblong package wrapped up in brown paper and tied with twine. He handed it off to Karl surreptitiously, in the hallway, without saying a word, as if it were a stash. Under the paper was the Penguin edition of *Crime and Punishment*.

Karl chose his posse over the next year and a half. His requirements were strict but few: high intelligence, good criminal instincts, and a level of alienation falling just short of outright socio-pathology. All boys. To get in a candidate had to read that Penguin edition of Dostoyevsky's novel in a week then pass a test. Most finished in less than four days and all but one passed the exam.

Karl/Rodion figured that to obtain what he wanted for Miki it might help to have some cash. Cash is always useful. He had been mugging people—women mostly—for a couple of years; it was safer than shoplifting, what with those damned cameras all over the place. Mugging was quick and easy, especially after he'd gotten that old .22 from Jasper. You didn't even need bullets.

W B H K/R

THE branches of the ancient maples on the west side of Rheinach Park obscured the street lights so that the broad sidewalk by the wrought-iron fence was in darkness. Herbert's routine took him as far as the park entrance, where he would turn back. It was in this recessed entrance that Karl/Rodion waited impatiently, considering what would make the perfect gift for Miki and composing the elegantly mysterious note he wouldn't sign. A quiet night. No single women had walked by as yet; he reckoned an old man would do. His right hand was in his jacket pocket gripping the little pistol. It's rusty, he thought, but so much more *chic* than an axe.

Herbert was just preparing to turn around when the thin boy in the leather jacket leapt in front of him, nose inches from his face. "Okay, turn it over," whispered the boy with stunning nonchalance; it was as if he assumed they had both been through this transaction scores of times and knew the drill. There wasn't even any "or else."

Herbert felt fury bubbling up like heartburn, like magma, and he calculated his chances. The boy looked almost frail but could be hopped-up on anything, probably was. He knew that he shouldn't resist but there it was. He said, "No." Enough had been taken from him. Hal's grandfather was no coward. "No way," he repeated. "Get lost, dickhead."

Just as Karl/Rodion, irritated by this lack of cooperation, was taking out the pistol, Warren came jogging around the corner twenty yards to the east and, simultaneously, Burcu's overheated Toyota pulled to the curb a dozen feet away. Warren accelerated as the car door was slammed and Burcu stomped out yelling what sounded to Warren, Herb, and Karl/Rodion like gibberish.

This sudden increase in the local population distracted Karl/Rodion in the middle of extracting the pistol. He hesitated. For an instant he thought of running into the park but then he saw that Warren was coming at him full tilt. Burcu caught sight of him too and let out a roar heavy with testosterone. Herbert shouted "Gun!" as if he were a cop—which he might have been, off duty, heading home. Swiveling his head, Karl/Rodion pointed the gun upward, counting on just showing it, and that's when the old man made a grab for his arm. He tried to step backwards but by then Warren had delivered a chop-block to his knees, as Burcu loomed up behind the grappling Herbert, bellowing like the bull closing in on Europa.

Now Karl/Rodion was on the pavement and all three men were hitting and kicking him. The gun fell; Burcu snatched it up and hit him hard on his left temple with its butt. There was an eruption of incandescence and he wanted to protest that this was out of all proportion but there was blood in his mouth and he'd lost his wind from a kick in the stomach. The kicking and punching went on and on, each man's violence egging on the others, granting them permission. The last thing he heard was their crazy panting and no words at all.

Urbs Fabula Sine Argumentum Est

———————————

HER mattress was queen-sized and covered by a European feather bed then a comforter that billowed like the sea in a French watercolor. To this exotic bedding she had added a couple bolsters and ten pillows. An expensive reading lamp stood beside the bed, the kind that can be bent to any angle. Her headboard was a long bookshelf mounted on cinderblocks, four pieces of pine stained to look like cherry wood. He learned to be careful about the corners.

Her hair was dyed jet black but not so short as to be a rejection of femininity. Both of them had pierced ears, favored black leather jackets, and had taken retail jobs intended not to lead to careers. He worked at Ace Hardware; she, at the Gap. Neither wanted what their peers did, not washer/dryers, not even tattoos. They were artists. They had recognized each other as such almost instantly.

They met on the subway. He had been staring at her as she read a heavy black book. He looked later and discovered it was called *Buddenbrooks*. He raised his camera furtively and shot. He thought she hadn't noticed. She leapt to her feet, stepped across the car, and demanded to know why he had just taken her picture. Didn't he appreciate that this was an invasion of her personal space, of privacy, that this is what the Fascists did, the death squads? Flustered and a little frightened, he pulled his portfolio out of his shoulder bag and held it out to her.

So far as he was concerned the great oblong of fluffiness

that took up half her apartment was Omphalos, the navel of the universe. He liked making love to her. For her part, she said, she could take or leave the screwing. It might be good for their work but it might just as likely be bad; they would have to see. The important thing, she stressed, was not to confuse physical intimacy with intimacy of any other sort. *Intimacy is a dangerous delusion devised by nature for our undoing.* According to her, the truth of life, at least under present conditions, was alienation and to that truth she meant to cleave. She laid down certain rules. Nothing oral, no toys, no bondage. Once either of them had achieved orgasm she would be free to ask him to leave, but on no account could he stay later than 3 a.m. She added that she disliked pillow-talk and so would wear her I-Pod during sexual intercourse; however, this was not mandatory for him. He agreed to try it, though.

She wasn't finished even then. She told him that people get into trouble by thinking sex can overcome their essential solitude. They weren't hunter-gatherers, were they, cave-dwellers? They were urbanites who could claim no extended kinship group or tribe. These existed only in childhood, if then, and time had quickly abraded them away. City life could dissolve even the strongest clan in three generations, she said, even crime families.

He saw nothing to be gained by arguing with her. She had obviously thought things through much more deeply than he. It was easier to defer. He was an artist of the intuitive sort while she was a real intellectual. His work depended on a lack of premeditation, was a matter of the instant, the gut. Not for nothing were early cameras called reflexes. For her, though, everything had to be deliberate, complicated, heavy with implication and theory. It was tiresome but admirable, too. *I'm the product of traditions I long to step out of and demolish*. She could say things like that. In college he had read as little as he could get away with. Apparently, she couldn't get enough and had asked all her professors for reading lists. She was still working her way through them.

The first time they made love she chose the *Abschied* section of Mahler's *Das Lied von der Erde*. He had programmed some old Nirvana tracks, also, for fun, a couple by Beau Soleil. He had loved *The Big Easy*. In his opinion, listening to separate music in bed was weird but he was willing to try it. He asked to hear the Mahler but couldn't make head or tail of it. Everything was so slow and long and in German. She asked him what he thought. He told her it sounded to him like death and she nodded her approval. *Chinese death*, she said. Sometimes the wires became tangled or an ear piece fell out, but he improved with practice.

That first night together she talked as if starved for talking. She laid out her theory of egoism, that the city turned people into pool balls; they merely collided against one another, caroming here and there, making deals and dates, transactions and babies. She grabbed a book from the headboard and read a marked passage. She suggested that it might serve as an epigraph for their project. *For the savage people in many places of America, except the government of small families, the concord whereof dependeth on natural lust, have no government at all....* To his objection that the author probably meant the Indians, she replied that this didn't matter in the least, that Hobbes had achieved an anticipatory insight. Many thinkers had been *psychological* egoists; Hobbes was the first *ethical* one. He understood that people should pursue whatever they personally wanted at any given moment, that this was the only purpose of life, the famous *pursuit of happiness*. In America, she said, sociology was just the study of the vestigial remains of crumbling associations. Families disintegrated, being no more than merely provisional organizations founded on temporary sexual infatuation and curable economic dependence. Political life was incoherent. In the end, we were all alone. An American city was a swarm of individuals racing around horizontal and vertical grids, a vast novel crammed with characters but lacking a coherent plot. Even its crimes were haphazard. Beginnings could be middles and middles ends. Significance was arbitrary and purely factitious. This is what art needed to express.

To all her lecturing he listened patiently though with fluctuating attention. What really mattered to him was the accessibility of her body and that she loved his photographs. Her words were hard but her bed was soft.

The first of his pictures that she selected was blurred because the car, a blue or black sedan, was moving. Still, he had managed to focus fairly well on the driver's profile. The man appeared intent yet somehow oblivious, concentrating but on the wrong thing. He had the air of a successful professional, except that he wasn't wearing a tie. His gray hair was closely cropped. A persuasive, plausible man, his features inspired confidence, like a bank executive or a heart surgeon.

Three days later, with a smirk, she presented him with what she called her "initial report."

Only two months after he retired, his wife, with whom he had planned to travel around the world, was diagnosed. He discovered the lump himself, a fact which troubled him. In an act of casual tenderness he had found out the hard kernel of death. He was sixty-four, a man who had always been at ease with money though never particularly excited by it. Events moved rapidly and in one direction, the way water spirals down a drain. His daughter and son-in-law flew in from Seattle. Though each day was endless the weeks flew by. The morphine carried her far away and then she was gone. There was a period when people were solicitous. He tried to be gracious but he didn't really care for it. He still had the urge to travel but at the same time there was nowhere he felt like seeing. In the public library he found a selection of books-on-tape. He had never listened to one, had rather despised the idea of a book on tape. Nevertheless, he rented three: a popular travel book about Provence (he might want to go there), a biography of Douglas MacArthur (perhaps he should know more), and, out of a sudden access of sentimentality, a detective novel by one of those Englishwomen his wife used to read. The next day it snowed. This prompted him to make a reservation at an inn in Vermont near where he'd been to camp as a boy. He packed a bag, fetched his car from the garage, and headed north. The travelogue and the biography, while unobjectionable, were not pleasing to listen to on the road. There was no rhythm, nothing to dance to, so to speak. Apparently journeys needed plots. He inserted the detective story and found himself so enthralled that he was scarcely aware of driving. He was actually displeased to find himself at his destination with two cassettes left. Being in Vermont aroused no nostalgia and did not relieve his feelings. What he longed for was to get back on the road and listen to the rest of the detective novel. The story was set in the Cotswolds among hyphenated villages, Bourton-on-the-Water, Stow-on-the-Wold. Even more than the wish to find out whodunit, though, he was captivated by the detective, with his good, busy wife and his staunch sense of duty. His job was to shore up the moral order by finding who was guilty and who was innocent. He liked the detective's old-fashioned manners and methods, his code which was so deeply rooted that it didn't need to be mentioned, his complicated relations with his difficult, grown-up daughters, with his loyal sergeant and his bothersome superintendent. He liked the man's quirks, such as his fondness for fountain pens, and admired his penetration. So he cut short his stay and eagerly got back in his car. Later, he tried reading detective novels but didn't enjoy them that way. He bought a tape recorder and tried listening to one at home, but that proved even less satisfactory. The magic, he realized, works only in the car, in the insulated, moving space where you are free to fart and fantasize and that propels you unaccompanied through the world, dreaming and untouched.

He told her he was delighted and said that now he really grasped her idea. I'm completely worn out, she said. He offered to give her a massage. He listened to U-2 as he kneaded and rubbed his hands over her flesh. She rolled over lazily with pleasure, like a piece of driftwood in her ocean of a bed, listening to Rachmaninoff's *Moments Musicaux*.

Dreaming and untouched, she sighed as she fell asleep.

We need to organize ourselves. Limits are indispensable. For example, let's say you take half a dozen pictures every day from five to six o'clock. Once I choose, I get two days to write the text. This first one is exactly 525 words. That will be my absolute limit. We can fit it on one legal-sized sheet, under your picture.

He was excited. We'll make flyers, he said, and put them up around the city late at night.

Unsigned, of course. It will be a mystery.

He proposed they could eventually collect them, make a book of them. She was dubious but he liked his idea. People will talk about the flyers; the newspapers will have articles, maybe even reprint them. He rubbed her thigh. Some of my subjects may come forward.

That could mess things up, she said frowning. A *pinacotheca*.

What? A pine tree?

Pinacotheca. Latin for picture gallery.

It could be the title. Okay then, we'll see, then? It was enough that she hadn't completely rejected the book idea.

She asked to see the new pictures.

Lines of disapproval scored the face from the narrow nose to the turned down upper lip. Around his eyes rage gathered, an ascetic aspect. A beard would have softened the rather mean mouth but he was closely shaven. Black suit and raincoat, clerical collar, large ears, high forehead—forty, at most forty-five. A church almost cringed behind him.

He might have been waiting for a cab. He was impatient. Perhaps one had just passed by.

Look how furious he is, she said. Splenetic. Who'd confess

their sins to him? Go away. I have to write about him.

He feels himself ever more at odds not only with his Church but all churches, synagogues, mosques, and temples. His vocation is just as strong as when he had felt its first tingling in his teens. Stronger. He was educated to serve, his mind honed by medieval scholasticism and baroque apologetics. He had researched the Albigenses, written a celebrated paper on the Arian heresy. He had read the existential theologians, often with irritation, but sometimes with ardor. There were ferociously heterodox pages of Kierkegaard he loved, especially when the Dane argued that faith is an unreasonable passion that makes one into an untranslatable language. The *Unscientific Postscript*. For a year he had been enthusiastic about but then rejected Teilhard de Chardin with contempt. His superiors patted his head, passed around his papers, recommended him with only the slightest misgivings. His realm was intellectual; he had never had a parish of his own. His first book had made a stir, though it was too often dismissed with the evasive word *contrarian*. He had achieved the editorship of a respected theological journal, had spoken at conferences the world over, held honorary degrees from the Universities of Leiden, Tübingen, even Notre Dame. But all the while his anger had been waxing, his patience waning. He had become a full moon of wrath. And now he had delivered his philippic, a screed. He was out on the street, naked as Kierkegaard mocked by the urchins of Copenhagen. He had attacked both ecumenism and fundamentalism. The former he had denounced as nothing but a gathering of the pitiful remnants of a failed business, the latter as willfully brainless counter-revolution, what Nietzsche called *little bigots*. Both, he had declared, were futile reactions to the shrinking of the supernatural, its dissipation into abstraction and empty forms. The ecumenists sought to propitiate science, which ignored them and in which they secretly believed, by blurring all their doctrinal distinctions in a concord so cloudy that it amounted to a fog barely concealing panic and self-interest. They talked like social workers and shrinks, not evangelists. The fundamentalists did not make the mistake of accommodation but were nostalgic for the days when Muslim missionaries could convince natives that the explosion of Krakatoa was a divine commandment to murder Dutchmen. Faith, he had said, joins us to a God we cannot understand, not to each other, whom we understand only too well. As he looked over those well-fed professional actors, all he could think of was, *Here are the lukewarm whom God spits out.* As he considered the self-righteous haircuts of the rollers and tongue-speakers, he was reminded of Mark Twain's account of the type: *good Christians in the worst sense.* Nothing, he had said, is more absurd than a congregation. Religion has become bingo on the one hand, demagoguery on the other. Now, out on the street, he comforts himself with thoughts of Rabbi Ishmael, told by a Heavenly voice that he could be spared martyrdom if he wishes; however the world would then lapse back into chaos.

When his parents called each Sunday, he gave short answers to their questions, sometimes told them a joke. It was an art to reassure while disclosing nothing; it had taken him years to perfect it. They were keen to find out about what they called his social life. He had always been a peculiar, lonely kid; they didn't understand him and had settled on a strategy of quiet concern tempered by generous support. Every conversation ended with the same question, *Do you need anything?*

Need is a deep question, he thought. Needs aren't wants, aren't desires. Needs aren't optional. Needs are the software that comes with the hardware.

What do you need? he asked her one night in bed after she had taken off her earphones.

She shrugged. The basics. Sustenance, shelter, freedom. A few appliances. Heat in winter. A credit card. My body to function. Music.

Two college girls came into the Gap. One of them was holding the flyer she had just torn from the pole outside. She watched them read it. *He looks just like your dad*, one of them teased. *Not even a little bit*, protested the other indignantly. *My dad's like totally bald. But he takes a lot of trips, doesn't he? You're such a bitch. My mom's not even dead yet.*

It was a chilly night. He was tired from unloading stock and she had come down with a cold. Stay away, she warned. Just show me some pictures.

Just, one of her favorite words. She discarded a dozen. I don't like any of these, tearing another tissue from the box on her lap. Her nose already looked like raw meat.

Why not, Rudolph?

They're not right. Not truthful.

What do you mean? I caught them at the wrong moment?

Well, yes, I suppose that's part of it. For me your pictures work when I look and suddenly I just know the subject, when the person's revealed—I don't mean in general—but to me, just me. What I'm trying to say is the truth isn't in your pictures but in how I see them. That's true for the whole *pinacotheca*, by the way. Five hundred words aren't worth half a picture, you know, if they're the right ones.

So it's all about you? *You're* the artist?

You too, everybody. The brain isn't just film; it's an editor. Your pictures are my *donnée*; I have to do something with them. Despite the cold she was getting wound up.

Look, she said, human relations emerge from non-relations and then vice versa. Empedocles' *Eros* and *Eris*, love and strife. The universe runs by gravity and entropy. Everything comes together and everything falls apart at the same time. Only the atoms survive. I don't know, maybe not even them. By nature everybody's related and we're all isolated. We're all somebody's child yet zipped up in these bags of skin.

So you see my pictures as just a bunch of separate skin-bags? I can understand that, but how can you see them as related too?

Easy. For example, they could all be carrying the same deadly virus or casualties of the same terrorist bomb or victims of the same serial killer. Or, if you go in for what passes for a happy ending, they could all be guests at the same wedding.

That's not unity. That's just accident.

In my opinion, unity's always an accident. Didn't we meet by accident? Weren't we born by accident? Planned parenthood, there's a laugh. People concentrate on the thin scum of choice and forget the ocean underneath. Then along come the intellectuals brandishing their skeleton keys and holler there are no accidents, that it's all economic determinism or libido or what-not.

I think my pictures are unified by me. What holds all these people together is that I happened to take their pictures. I think the city does have a plot, lots of stories. Stories of how people need each other.

You can see it that way if you like. People build up dependencies but the more stable everything looks the more precarious it is. Just take the cops out of your sentimental city for two days and what do you think's going to happen?

Maybe the pictures are wrong. I mean misleading. Maybe it's wrong to take only individuals and I should start shooting people in groups.

That would be even more misleading. In my opinion.

You really believe what you write is true? Truer than the pictures?

She sneezed and shook her head impatiently. Neither more nor less, she said, wiping her nose. Your pictures are really marvelous. Really. I mean it. I couldn't do without them. For me they're the catalyst that crystallizes things. I never wrote like this before. They're true together—your pictures and my writing—apart, not so much.

Until he met her he had felt incomplete, yet, even here in her apartment, he didn't feel entirely whole either.

Look, it's in the mind, in the solitary mind that things really happen. That's where the truth gets made, so it's both relative and absolute. Everyone's absolutely convinced but of different things. She sneezed three times then moaned.

Poor baby, he said, and took out the last picture. He had snapped the woman on the subway, just as he had her. Mousy, in a beret, knees tight together, a tote bag on her lap. Wisps of hair, thick glasses, tweed skirt, sensible shoes, nothing attractive about her. Had he thought her repellent or simply sad? One more bruised pool ball, another bitter pill? Curiosity and love both try to penetrate. Was photographing her an aggressive act, a violation?

Oh yes, she said with a rheumy drawl. I want *her*.

B.A. Smith College, M.L.S., Simmons. Childhood by L. L. Bean out of John Cheever. Summer place in Pemaquid, Old Greenwich day school, a silver-plated drinks table. Her brother aspired to be just like their father, leaving her to pick up the dropped Oedipus Complex. She had not always been asexual. Experiments with both boys and girls commenced at twelve, out of duty more than curiosity and *sans finesse*. At Smith three lovers, one each year excepting the fumbling first. An English major with a public allegiance to the Romantics and a private one to Gene Derwood and Mina Loy. She was thought pretty then, even interesting, in her way. *Waspish pedigree, waist, and wit*, someone said of her. Between semesters, a bleak January in the great house that looked perfect from any distance. Brother scheming to ski and fornicate, Mother using too much toilet paper, Father's face too red too early. Secret phone calls after midnight. *Oh, horrible beyond words. If only you were here.* The summer escape to Europe, thanking God and grandfather for ill-gotten old money. Loved libraries the way perverts do schoolyards, ghouls cemeteries. So, *faute de mieux*, she chose her voca-

tion. *Just until you get married, naturally*, Father said offhand-
edly, perhaps even without irony. Labored for a couple years in
a university library and nothing changed except that she became
plainer every day. Then she fell in love with a girl who had pre-
Raphaelite hair. It ended quickly and badly. She was hurt. Work
was salvation. More than proficient, she attained professional
sprezzatura. Desperate to get away from Boston she applied
for an important job at a famous private library. What with the
recommendations and her looking like the collective unconscious'
archetype of an archivist the trustees snapped her up. It was
in this temple that she came on the complete papers of Edith
Moorhouse Salazar (1895-1957), donated but uncatalogued.
EMS, unjustly forgotten author of scores of poems, a couple of
plays, three novels, correspondent of the clever, bedfellow of the
celebrated, had eloped with an Argentine diplomat's son during
the Spanish Flu epidemic, returned seven years later with two
children and a trunkload of mss., just in time for the hysterical
crescendo of the Jazz Age. All her free time went to cataloguing
EMS' papers, editing her correspondence, and writing the first
critical biography. Her favorite poem is *Pinacotheca*, set in the
Prado Museum. *Toldeo spreads herself beneath the storm / like
Danaë's still golden, fly-blown corpse.* Father early dead of a heart
attack, Mother mindless of everything but her resentment in an
high-priced *salle d'attente*, brother guzzling away his days and
trust fund in Santa Monica. She gives a lot to the Opera, the
Philharmonic, UNICEF, eats simply and takes the subway. She
is alone and not happy yet infinitely nobler than Edith Moorhouse Salazar or the pompous academics who sneer at and rely
on her. Bad poetry, she believes, hides from life; good poetry, just
the opposite. She takes up as little space as possible. Her one

indulgence is the two-bedroom apartment in a decent building off Park Avenue, magnificently furnished. She has an eye, has crammed the place with fastidiously chosen first-rate paintings she will someday leave to the Museum of Modern Art. She has a horror of being noticed, let alone photographed.

Oh, I like TV, he said. I just don't like watching it.

In college I knew this girl. She'd been a serious ice skater, you know, the Olympics? Started when she was about three, never got to the top but her childhood was devoted to it—practicing, competing, endless traveling. Apparently she took plenty of cocaine but never saw any television. She was like some Greek who'd never heard of Zeus or Athena, couldn't catch a single allusion, totally clueless. It left her detached.

Maybe we all watched too much back then. Overdosed on sit-coms and cartoons. They weren't all that funny.

How do you get your news? For me, it's radio.

Mostly TV, I guess. Though I can't stand all those laxative ads.

Radio's better than TV. Sometimes after you leave I listen to news on the radio, NPR, BBC. Bedtime stories like the Grimms', only worse. Today Hansel and Gretel, Snow White and Briar Rose were all buried in a mudslide. The rigged election in the Black Forest was pronounced free and fair. The musicians of Bremen were squatting in the warehouse that burned to the ground. Child soldiers on drugs cut off Goldilocks' hands and raped Little Red Riding Hood's grandmother.

TV was supposed to kill radio. Funny how people think the new is always going to make the old obsolete, although I guess it often does. Buggy whips and clipper ships.

Rose hips and collagen lips.

He pointed to his digital camera on the table across the room. People still use film. I love black and white. Hell, people still *paint* pictures, I mean portraits.

The new reveals if there's something unique about the old, anything irreplaceable.

There are some shows I tape, he admitted.

Really? Like which?

I like the ones set in small, imaginary towns.

The global village. These days even the art of belonging's second-hand.

Hey, is this Edna Moorhouse Salazar real or what?

She is as far as I'm concerned. What? You didn't try Googling her, did you?

He knew better than to answer. He lay back and changed the subject. What is it you like best about my pictures?

Their silence. The little cages they trap people in. Their imperfection.

He nudged his nose into her hair and took a deep breath.

Time to go, she said. *Show his eyes, and grieve his heart; come like shadows, so depart.*

Stealthily at dusk the hunter steps through the forest of the city. Snap.

The man he shot was slumped in a doorway. His clothes—

suit, topcoat—expensive and filthy. His face resembled soldiers' from the Second World War, unshaven, lean, eyes focused on the far side of the universe. Strung out, still young but ravaged. He had no doubt been handsome once, perhaps like Señor Salazar when he had swept Edna Moorhouse off her feet and out of the northern hemisphere.

Hey, fuck, don't take my picture.

Chill, man. Cameras don't steal your soul.

Everything can. Anyway, isn't that what you want?

She said nothing when she saw the picture, just drew in her breath and held it up to her eyes, went over to the reading lamp, studied it some more.

He felt uneasy. Chelsea, around five-thirty, five-forty, he said. You can almost tell from the light. He needed her to say something. I take it you like that one?

She nodded.

What do you say we order pizza?

I still don't feel well. No appetite.

What? You want me to take off, then?

She's still clutching the picture. I need to sleep, to write. Write and sleep.

Look at this Puerto Rican girl. She has this wonderful hair.

Leave it. Okay?

No answer on her phone, her cell, to his e-mails. Silence

when he knocked on her door at eight o'clock. *Are you in there? Are you all right?* The next day he took a long lunch break and went to the Gap. *Sorry. Not here. She called in sick today.* He was really worried. Then, as he was leaving, he saw the new flyer taped to the pole outside. The ruined homeless guy with the thousand-mile stare.

Like Dylan, like Fitzgerald, he was born in Minnesota but meant to leave it. Comprehensive ambition impelled his bountiful adolescence, seasoned his appetites which were at once commonplace and impossible. Want, desire, and need fermented to a promiscuous brew of juvenile exhilaration. He yearned to gobble the country entire, garner galaxies of experience, perforate his generation with a billion pinpoints of insight. His enthusiasms lacked discretion; he loosed his libido on species, books, epochs, on string quartets, cornices, ferns, clapboards, railroad depots. He was passingly passionate about DNA and the national debt, Dada and Napoleon, Dickens and Napier. Children followed him though he was a child himself, fated never to achieve unequivocal adulthood. He was his own church of natural religion, a locomotive of skepticism, juggler of concepts, trickster of delights, conjurer of beauties. He sang in a choir, debated, cooked, criticized, celebrated, spent whole nights in the backyard peering through an eight-inch telescope. He wished to know everything but never knew what to do. College brought him East. Gatsby in a pea coat, Raskolnikov with a guitar. He was Endymion, gorgeous goddess-meat. They met in a required class, calculus. Though proud of her practiced invulnerability, icy and lunar, she fell for him on sight, threw herself at him, couldn't bear not being with him for more than half an hour.

Thus, using a certain calculus, she courted, bewitched, seduced, enchained. *Let's get married*, she whispered, shrewdly choosing her moment. That nobody approved gratified her, not suspecting he might not either. After graduation they moved into urban squalor that she joyously labored to make picturesque, bohemian. They took crappy jobs and contemplated their assault on the aeries of culture. She applied for grants to write poems while he began his first novel the opening sentence of which was *Let's go faster*. He made friends who played frat-boy drinking games, others who smoked too much, began to oversleep, lost his job, wore out a thesaurus-worth of synonyms for depressed. Once there was an old man who, informed by an eloping couple that they planned to live on love, ruthlessly replied, *Love and nothing else is soon nothing else*. By the time she finally threw him out, changed locks and filed papers, she couldn't stand his reek, his pubic hairs in the tub, his bare feet, whiskers and whining. What kind of bad joke is it when the happy ending comes first? At the last he cursed her and dove into the savage, pool-ball city. She snubbed her friends, ignored her family yet was surprised when the city abruptly emptied out. *Even thou, who dost thy millions boast / A village less than Islington wilt grow, / A solitude almost.* She gave up writing verses and grants to write more of them and, out of spite, took a job at the Gap. She became an eight-ball. One day this geek took her picture on the subway. He snapped lots of pictures, one person at a time, each divorced from all the others. Just like this one. She saw the truth in these pictures, these separations. Then she understood. This is the truth.

THE WITHDRAWAL OF WAWANU

1.

I would like to imagine it for you, but that is the task of a poet. You shall yourself have to supply the smells, impossible to convey: the ferment of bacteria devouring fallen leaves and the corpses of insects on the forest floor, the mixed aromas of a cook fire and damp thatch, drying fish and humid flesh, black hair fragrant and stiffened with mud and urine. You will need to conjure up tiny sounds like those made by scuttling ants, or day-moths flapping their huge weightless wings, or the lurch of armored stag beetles as large as your foot. Feel free to imagine the loud noises too, such as the alarming wails of monkeys and the soft shush of tons of shifting fronds. Try to hear the noise of people as they await something breathlessly, the shifting of feet, the quickened pulses, the stifling of gas and the protests of babies held too tightly. All these sounds are dulled by sodden air and form a sort of acoustic scrim for the scene I am asking you to picture, like the green and black of the forest itself.

It is noon and hot. Under the canopy the light is dusky, but there is a clearing by the river, forty or fifty square feet on which falls a pillar of sunlight. The length of the clearing is marked out by two great darkwood trees, prized by cabinet makers; the width by the village's huts and the river. Imagine you are watching from a canoe on the river. From that distance the tree trunks look smooth, but if you were to touch them they would feel like sandpaper. Two young men are bound to these trees; their left arms are tied to the trunks at the biceps by thick vines dampened then pulled tight. At the rear of this clearing, in front of the huts, you would see four or five score people. The two bound men are naked and sweating; they eye each other fiercely, flex their muscles, take deep breaths, puffing out their chests and exhaling slowly so as to steady their nerves. Each is hefting a four-foot stick in his right hand. You may recall what a real poet said: that there is a Providence that shapes our ends, no matter how we rough-hew them. The sticks are sharply pointed.

Apart from the crowd, upstage from the Chorus so to speak, are two figures. One, a young woman, stands a couple of yards in front of the rest with her eyes cast down, arms crossed over maidenly breasts. Her face is not easy to read. You might not guess at the repressed anxiety because her bearing is one of dignified submission. The second figure is a man somewhat older than the two tied to the trees, a lanky fellow dressed in a skirt made of leaves and some sort of furry, feathery headdress. He is equi-distant from the bound men and holds two long rattles made of vertebrae strung on painted sticks. These he holds stretched out in front of him as he looks from one man to the other, exactly like a basketball referee preparing to toss up a jump ball. He raises the rattles deliberately. The two men are torn. Both would like to watch the fellow in the skirt for the sign but neither can risk taking his eyes off the other.

2.

IT has been over a decade since the Arapoi people were decimated and dispersed and their land taken. The Wawanu no longer exist as a tribe. Of course, it is possible that deep in the forest a band may still endure, but if so their way of life is not the old one. The Arapoi were a river people; most of their protein came from fish they speared. Nowadays the fish are netted and the river belongs to the loggers, as the land does to farmers and ranchers. I should not omit also the tourists from the north, such as yours truly, there in part to alleviate the general slashing and burning.

The Arapoi were never a united people and relations among the tribes could be complicated. For example, the Arunama-Arapoi were at once the bitterest enemies of the Wawanu-Arapoi and their closest allies. How could this be?

When nature came up with sexual reproduction as a way of speeding evolution on its way, the world was imbued not only with love but by a new sort of antagonism. What is jocularly called the battle of the sexes is not only a genuine war, but a perpetual one. Nature is wise and has ordained that a perpetual war entails an infinite number of truces. One might think that it is during these intermittent armistices that nature has her way; but in fact she may achieve her ends equally well by war, so closely allied are love and aggression, and so amoral is she. Whether Venus insinuates herself into Mars's bed or Mars throws her down on the ground, biologically speaking the result is the same. What I mean is that the apprehension of differences is the origin of love no less than war. Difference breeds fear, and fear hatred; but difference also fosters curiosity, and what is curiosity but the first stirring of love, the tenderest of aggressions? Difference can eventuate in anything from a caress to vivisection.

Now I admit I am speculating on sketchy data, a capital error for a good scientist (though not, I think, for a great one). But I am no more a scientist than a poet, so please do not form the impression that I am propounding anything like a scientific hypothesis. This paper is merely meant to be the occasion for your own imaginings, or for you to imagine by my side, as if we were roped together to explore a cave.

The Arunama and Wawanu lived near one another and, in most respects, their cultures were identical. The Arunama, however, worshipped the goddess from whom they derived their name, while the Wawanu were eponyms and devotees of the male god Wawanu. If you are alert you may already be guessing at the consequences.

According to Arapoi theology, Wawanu and Arunama became consorts. As the first male and female one might say their relationship was ineluctable, though it was not a case of no sooner said than done. Both tribes believed it was through this divine union that the Arapoi came to exist. As the word *Arapoi* means human beings, it follows that non-Arapoi, with whom neither tribe had much contact up to the time I am describing, are not human. I am told the closest equivalent for the Arapoi word for non-Arapoi is *demons*. How they believed the demons came into existence I am not sure. But back to sexual theology.

When Arunama and Wawanu first encountered one another they fought for twenty-eight days. They battled with insults, insects, snakes, sarcasm, trees, mud, fire, arrows, spears—curiosity being also the urge to penetrate. At last they came to grips and as they rolled and wrestled their bodies gouged a furrow in the earth. Blood from the menstruating Arunama filled it. Sweat from the straining Wawanu filled it. The great turbid river became the enduring monument of a titanic stalemate. Terrified by the sight of his fair opponent's blood, Wawanu clambered up into an ebony tree while, repelled by the stench of her muscular enemy's sweat, Arunama tore off into the bush. They did not wish to see each other again for a long time, yet of course neither could think of anything else and, in the end, nature took her course and yearning set in. The sky rang with their moans, imitated to this day by the howler monkeys. Finally overcome by longing they rushed together, Wawanu bounding across the river in one lustful leap; and by the shore they fell panting on each other's bodies and coupled. A happy ending? Yes indeed, but such happiness is as much an interruption as an ending.

Until the Arapoi were born Wawanu and Arunama lived contentedly with each other, fashioning canoes, spearing fish, weaving leaves, twining vines into ropes, fermenting alcohol, inventing culture and dreaming measureless dreams. But when their offspring grew old enough to show affection, Arunama and Wawanu began to compete for their favor, spoiling them with all kinds of gifts. The gods grew ever more jealous of one another and began to quarrel bitterly, then to fight. When matters grew intolerable they separated, each taking half the Arapoi. They swore eternal enmity, without considering the aforementioned infinite number of truces.

The Wawanu and Arunama tribes were enemies from this time, born to feud, and would kill one another on sight to please their respective parent-gods. As the generations marched on, though, their original enmity became conventional and, so to speak, stylized. The tribes generally engaged in ritual warfare rather than the real thing, though not without periodic night raids and the occasional massacre.

A perpetual war indeed demands an infinite number of truces and the battle of the sexes winds up in bed. Because of, also despite, their enmity, a curious tradition arose in both tribes about marriage. The Wawanu came to favor spouses from among the Arunama and vice versa. Depending on your view of wedlock, you might think of these nuptials as truces or just a continuation of war by other means. For the Wawanu to steal a female from the Arunama was, after all, to win a convert for their god, reuniting daughter with father. For the Arunama to abscond with a Wawanu woman was to please their goddess and show the ex-Wawanu prisoner that her theological bread was buttered on the matriarchal side. The same principle applied to males who, though captured less frequently, could also be taken in either battle or love and so marry, either willingly or by compulsion, into the enemy camp.

It was an intriguing system, a check on inbreeding, but not an exclusive one. Wawanu might also wed Wawanu and Arunama Arunama and both could also mate with Arapoi from other bands, though it goes without saying that *demons* were strictly off limits. Still, there was a kind of premium on marriages between Wawanu and Arunama owing to the glamour of the alien and the allure of hostility. Such weddings instigated the wildest rejoicing, brought the highest prestige, occasioned the most lavish feasts, procured the most opulent gifts.

3.

THE shaman snaps his arms above his head and the bones clatter. The young woman who is standing apart from the others, the one with the high breasts who was still Arunama because no wedding had yet taken place, cries out as the bound men, missing the balance of their left arms, draw back their right ones and, aiming down the shafts of their spears, let fly. The spears slip through the air so quickly and the distance is so short that the whole business is over even before the bones have ceased rattling, before the woman's cry is stifled by horror.

Rarapuno and Kunxilo and the maiden Malajola: the geometry of this story is more ancient than Euclid's.

The previous morning a band of six young men returned to the Wawanu village with Malajola, claiming to have captured her in a night raid on the Arunama. Kunxilo's eyes narrowed when Rarapuna claimed her for his bride, saying that it was he who had caught her as she tried to flee into the river. "No," said Kunxilo, flinging down his bow and quiver. "She is mine. I captured her when she tried to run into the bush like Arunama." "You lie," said Rarapuna and clenched his fist. Kunxilo smiled sarcastically. "We shall see who lies," he said and called out for Xanxaniplo. Rarapuna glanced reassuringly toward Malajola who gripped her shoulders and kept silent, like a real captive, and cast her lowered eyes furtively at Rarapuna.

Xanxaniplo came out of his hut rubbing his eyes and yawning; but, groggy as he was, he needed only one look at the two men and the unfamiliar woman to know what was up. The shaman looked Malajola up and down but did not ask her anything. He could see that she would have liked to speak but the girl was not yet Wawanu. The law was clear, and before she could say anything Xanxaniplo called his wife to take her away.

A great deal of river had run by since he had last needed to invoke the god's sure-fire method of resolving such disputes and he did not want to do so now. He tried interrogation first.

"I captured her in the river," proclaimed Rarapuna.

"I caught her by the ankle in the bush," insisted Kunxilo.

The brother of Rarapuna agreed about the river, while the brother of Kunxilo was just as sure about the ankle and the bush. Family honor. The other men said that it was dark and they were busy themselves with fighting and could not tell who had the rights of the matter.

Next he attempted to negotiate. Taking each man aside he asked him what he would be willing to give up to buy the other off.

"I will gladly give him an arrow in his lying throat," offered Kunxilo.

"I will pay him a spear in his chest," said Rarapuna.

Xanxaniplo sighed and plumped down in front of his hut. Perhaps if he did nothing at all for an hour or so the two men would reconsider and cool down. He would have liked to spare the life of the one who was lying.

Wawanu's law was not much different from the old European custom of trial by ordeal. You might think trial by ordeal is a matter of faith but faith is a little vague. It would be more precise to say that it proceeds logically from a conception of the universe. Assume that the cosmos is not accidental or morally indifferent but organized and just, that all contingency is an illusion because there is a providence even in the fall of a sparrow. It follows that the world has been set in balance by some power who can be counted on to uphold truth and justice. One must not tempt this someone or annoy him over every trivial squabble; however, when nothing else will serve, then in a trial by ordeal the truth will infallibly be made known. First principles cannot be proved; but, given that of the Wawanu-Arapoi, the spear-trial was flawlessly logical. Yet if it is true that the practice depended on their conception of the world, then the obverse is no less true. That is, the Wawanu understanding of the world and the trial by ordeal hung together. To doubt one was to doubt the other.

Rarapuna's spear struck the tree just beside Kunxilo's left ear. Kunxilo's lodged in Rarapuna's stomach. No one removed it. Nobody even untied his left arm. Rarapuna took three hours to die, three hours of excruciating pain and incomprehensible dishonor. He did not say a word and, in fact, not even his brother attempted to speak to him. Malajola would have gone to him but she was forcibly prevented.

4.

PROMINENT on our eco-tour was a short, pale woman in her late twenties who looked out on the world through oversized glasses as though scrutinizing all she saw for microbes. Helen Henshaw seethed with laudable sentiments on several topics, especially Indians. Wherever we went she sought them out and with them her manner changed. Her customary smirks and moralistic ironies gave way to smiles and exaggerated bonhomie. Ms. Henshaw once said to me that she believed herself an Indian trapped in the body of a Scotch-Irishwoman from Pittsburgh. It was a pity to see that the Indians to whom she spoke did not recognize their solidarity; they appeared able to get along without her empathy. Perhaps if she had told them, as she repeatedly did her fellow travelers, that in a couple months she would be resuming her graduate program in anthropology they might have shown more deference. Helen was doing a sort of field work, scouting the terrain for future use, and was far more absorbed in observing Indians than by the variegated fauna and flora that were the putative object of our tour. She also took it upon herself to augment Francisco's admittedly misleading accounts of the natives, making it clear that she did not approve of our guide and adopting toward him a jovially truculent attitude, planting her feet wide and aiming her jaw at the vicinity of his nose. Though she may have known the truth in general—who didn't?—Helen Henshaw did not actually know many details and, to her credit, she was too scrupulous to fake them. The rest of us picked up on this and I am afraid she was often embarrassed by our questions. But if we were exasperating, her pride did not permit her to show it. She simply paid us back by delivering homilies, letting slip no opportunity to point out the sins committed against the Indians, ringing variations on her *idée fixe*. Whenever in our trip up river we happened by a logging camp or ranch, the Right Reverend Ms. Henshaw could be relied on to proffer, at the very least, a pointed comment, usually directed at poor Francisco.

One night we put in at the little river town of Matanmassas

where there was, Francisco promised, a cantina. After dinner a few of the men decided to go look for some bottled beer. Ms. Henshaw came along.

The hot spot turned out to be a cabin illuminated by a couple of 25-watt bulbs. It had the usual corrugated roof and its walls had been cobbled together out of crates; you could read the names of the companies where the naked boards were not covered by movie posters or religious calendars. But the place had its own generator and the beer was European and cold. The proprietor was a fat fellow, probably a mestizo, who called himself Don Pedro. His smooth face oozed kindness one minute, shrewdness the next. Don Pedro's throne was a padded stool behind the trestle that served as his bar and here he perched between his precious generator and a red Coca-Cola cooler. He welcomed us grandly and dispensed our beers as though each bottle were filled with a thrice-refined magic elixir.

The cantina had only four customers besides ourselves, all Indian men with terrific black eyes and thick hair that hung down over their immaculate white singlets. They stood up as we entered and nodded formally, as if we were in a Madrid salon. The salutation was intended chiefly for Helen who said "*Gracias, muchas gracias*" about half a dozen times before we got our beers and sat down on overturned bushel baskets around a Mitsubishi packing crate. Predictably, she tried to strike up a conversation with the Indians, asking them in her polished Spanish about their work and families. The Indians gave abrupt replies. They may have answered her precisely, but my own Spanish is rudimentary and it was hard to make out their dialect. Then Helen asked them the name of their tribe.

"*Buenos noches, Don Pedro*," said the oldest Indian suddenly. He motioned to the others and they all got up and walked out.

Poor Helen was distressed. "Why did they leave?" she inquired in general.

"Maybe they didn't want to talk," somebody said.

"Maybe they were here to drink," said another.

"Or it could be they don't care for gringas."

She pouted, dismissed our boyish teasing, and appealed to Don Pedro in English. "Did I offend them, Señor?"

Don Pedro's countenance shuttled from kind to shrewd. "They are Wawanu-Arapoi," he said, "or were once. Wawanu not like to talk with other peoples. Their way is funny, Señora. Very private. Not just you. Me too. Everybody."

"Why?"

Don Pedro shrugged. "*Quien sabe?* No like peoples. Cannot hold liquor either."

Ms. Henshaw sat up straighter and shot a cannonball of virtue across our host's bar. "Then you shouldn't sell them any."

Don Pedro narrowed his eyes at this impertinence and shifted on his stool. He would say no more to Ms. Henshaw who had violated the regulations of hospitality. We finished our beers and got up to leave. When I went up to pay the tab Don Pedro gestured for me to come closer.

"You want to know Wawanu," he whispered, "you go see Señor Grillo. The señor he is loco, but he know Arapoi. He know very much, even though he loco."

I wondered why the fellow thought I would be interested

and then, with a momentary shudder, I realized he must have assumed I was married to Ms. Henshaw. He had called her *señora*. I was not flattered but I decided to play along.

"Where is he, this loco Señor Grillo?"

"Outside town a little way. You ask for Hacienda Grillo. Everybody know where."

As I lay in my hammock that night the idea of one-upping Helen Henshaw, of doing precisely the thing that she would most like to do, appealed to me. No doubt it was an unchivalrous impulse but it was also an irresistible one. There would be time. Francisco, full of apologies, had been chain-smoking and waiting for us on deck. He was very sorry but there would be a slight delay in the morning, he said, while we waited for some necessity or other to arrive on the packet. I had already learned that a "slight" delay generally meant at least a day. Why shouldn't I take the opportunity to find this mad Grillo and fetch back some anecdote with which to regale everyone and especially to annoy the redoubtable Helen Henshaw? I determined to anthropologize.

5.

L ET'S try to imagine it together.

One or two women move about, a child whines. Most of the dogs and all of the people are still asleep, hung over from the two-day wedding blow-out. The village respires, snores, belches. Tan smoke rises from the dying fires, made paler by dawn glinting rosily off the river. Where the light isn't striking it, the river itself looks solid, like the thick glass of a two-hundred-year-old brandy bottle I once saw, midway between a dismal green and muddy brown.

The brother of Rarapuna had been beside himself at his brother's death; but who would be surprised by that? Rarapuna had proved a liar; his own honor was stained, his brother justly slain. There was no question of his showing his face at the wedding. Everybody presumed he had gone down river for a decent interval to fish and be alone and wait for things to blow over. But Rarapuna's brother was beset by even greater difficulties than familial dishonor. Two contradictory truths plucked at his well-tempered Wawanu soul. He wanted to run away not only from the village and the wedding, but even more from these two thoughts. They beset him like demons, like the demons who cut down trees and make fire from sticks and stink abominably and write advertising copy.

All on his own, then, he set out on a raid, a thing no one had dared since the days when Wawanu hunted alone. It was foolhardy, but Rarapuna's brother would not much have minded being killed. Even if he had the bad luck to be wounded, at least he would forget himself in action and pain. He had no interest in finding a woman, but if he were able to capture an Arunama man his damaged honor would be restored.

Now the mist is rising from the viscous river. The village is still drowsing when the brother of Rarapuna returns. He has a prisoner, a man he had found fishing with two boys. The boys had run away as soon as they heard his whoop. He fell on the man and knocked him into the river.

"Get up!" he is yelling. "Get up and look at the brother of Rarapuna!"

The village staggers to its feet. The dogs bark, the children fret and whine, the men curse. There is silence in the wedding hut because the night before Kunxilo has beaten Malajola to stop her interminable weeping.

Xanxaniplo totters out of his hut, before which Rarapuna's brother has been roaring. The shaman rubs his eyes and looks resentfully at the brother.

"What's all this noise, you monkey?"

The brother prods his prisoner with the butt of his spear and says proudly, "He is mine. Taken alone."

The prisoner looks at his feet.

The shaman rubs his eyes, strokes his chin. "No one is doubting you," he says. He feels compassion for the boy and admiration too. It is an unheard-of thing to carry out a night raid by oneself, to capture a man, a husband for a Wawanu woman, a convert for the god. There will be another wedding feast. Credit where credit is due. He is thinking the boy has now wiped his slate clean and propitiated Wawanu.

It is at this moment that Kunxilo emerges from the wedding hut to see what the fuss is about. Right behind him comes Malajola. The prisoner looks up and catches sight of her. He is not surprised to see her coming from the wedding hut but he is amazed to see her with Kunxilo and he says so.

"But where is the Wawanu you went with, Malajola?"

The brother of Rarapuna spins around.

6.

SEBASTIANO Grillo had a face like a tomahawk and blackened what remained of his hair, apparently with shoe polish. So narrow was his face that, seen from any angle, it looked two-dimensional. In addition to some ruined outbuildings, his "hacienda" consisted of a half-dozen lean-tos with a tropical verandah tacked on to hold the caboodle together. This porch still boasted four or five patches of blue paint; otherwise the wood was green or grey, depending on where something was growing on it. The surrounding acreage must once have been cleared for a farm or ranch, but the forest had surged back in. Huge palms were growing behind the house and their leaves spread over the verandah as if the whole place were about to be engulfed by a breaker. I was well sweated from my walk and the leaves made the porch appear green and cool.

It was on the verandah that I found Grillo. He was seated on a rattan rocker attended by two Indian women. One stood behind him kneading his neck; the other squatted by the screened door shoveling some kind of porridge into her mouth with her left hand from a huge wooden bowl dexterously balanced on her right. Grillo's eyes were closed. He was a gaunt man with a mean mouth, the lipless kind that looks like a gash. He reminded me of an inbred fanatic from the Bible Belt, but one who combed his remaining hair straight back like a cheap gambler or a crooked stockbroker.

"*Buenos dias, Señor,*" I said.

I'm sure he had watched me as I came down the narrow path

from the dirt road but he pretended to be surprised. He looked down at me and grunted. "What a dreadful accent you've got. Americano, no?"

Like any citizen of the United States, I was not pleased to be upbraided with my linguistic inadequacy; nevertheless, it was a relief that he spoke English.

"Don Pedro—"

"Ah, the big shot, the great man with the tiny refrigerator."

"Don Pedro suggested I speak to you."

"He did, did he? What about?"

"About the Arapoi, the Wawanu."

The two women froze in mid-knead, mid-munch.

With excruciating deliberation Grillo extricated a pack of cigarettes from the pocket of his faded shirt and tapped one out. With a surprisingly quick twist of his lean frame, the movement of an old knife-fighter I suppose, he slid a disposable lighter from his blue jeans then lit up.

"What for do you want to know about the Wawanu?"

I was still standing in the weeds below the porch so that I had to look up at him. Grillo seemed to relish making me feel like a supplicant. "What for?" I repeated with a dismissive laugh and, taking the measure of my audience, I answered, "To make a woman angry."

He laughed then coughed and stamped out his cigarette with a curse.

If Grillo were indeed loco his was the madness of morbidly meditating on one thing for too long. In this he was both like and unlike Ms. Henshaw with her own fixed ideas. Grillo's obsession was dark while hers was light, but both of them were inclined to be oratorical. My first impression had made me suppose it would be difficult to persuade such a tough old turkey to tell me anything except to go to Hell. In fact, it was as if he had been waiting there on his tumbledown verandah for me to show up so that he could unburden himself of the freight of his brooding. This he did, but he had to work his way up to it by delivering a detailed autobiography and he required the encouragement of a bottle of cheap rum from which, during the hour I spent with him, I also took a few sociable pulls.

His life had been as rough as his appearance suggested, varied too. His parents had come out from Calabria before the War to make a fortune but succeeded only in dying before he was twelve. Two years in a Catholic orphanage on the coast was his limit; he had run away. Thereafter he had been, by turns, logger, ranch hand, trapper, and hired killer—the last chiefly during his brief involvement in local politics, though he admitted to providing the same service for a couple of the big ranchers upriver. He once made a large sum from the drug trade, enough so that he thought of retiring. To hear him tell it, the three months he spent in the capital city were devoted entirely to getting rid of his money and fighting over women. It was after that respite in civilization that he returned to the forest and wound up in the vicinity of Matanmassas during what he called "the Arapoi land grab."

"As you see, Señor de la Norte, I am a *diablo*. But do not judge me too quickly for you are no better. You should keep this in mind as I tell you about the Wawanu."

Here he said something I couldn't understand to the women. They got up at once and went inside.

"I told them to leave. It is to spare them, you understand."

"Spare them?"

"They are Wawanu."

"I see."

It was then that he started in on Arapoi cosmogony and told me the story I have asked you to imagine, just as I pictured it on the ex-blue verandah of that arch-demon Grillo.

"You see," he said, "young Wawanu and Arunama didn't always meet during night raids. They often bathed together, fished, traded, played in the forest, socialized as we would say. Naturally, it sometimes happened that a Wawanu and an Arunama would fall in love but, in such a case, they would have to pretend, pretend that their marriage was a matter of force. It was a point of honor, a necessity both of tradition and religion. Wawanu and Arunama had at least to pretend to fight to keep up appearances, just as I used to go to confession in that infernal orphanage and pretend to repent for the fathers. Anyway, that was the case with Rarapuna and Malajola. They were in love. The night raid was a sham, all arranged in advance. But Kunxilo had seen them together; he was the snake in the grass, the serpent in the garden, a viper as full of venom as of envy. Desperation too. Rarapuna's love was deep but it was normal. Kunxilo's was something else again and, in his own way, he is no less tragic. You understand? He coveted Malajola so intensely that he was willing to stake his soul on the chance of getting her for himself or dying in the attempt, even to the point of tempting the judgment of Wawanu. Can you see the audacity of it? To me it is a crucial point that Kunxilo could not have expected to succeed. How amazed the fellow must have been when Rarapuna's spear missed him, when his found its mark.

"You understand? The man captured by the brother of Rarapuna was the cousin of Malajola. He was in on their secret and that is why he was astonished to see the girl come out of the wedding hut not with Rarapuna but with Kunxilo.

"It was only a week later that a bunch of us demons crossed the river for the first time."

7.

WE in the North are accustomed to a corrosion that results in disintegration; all that we learn is provisional, subject to daily upgrades. Here we are at the close of a century as thickly smeared with apocalypses as a New York bagel is with cream cheese and yet, though some of us still recoil in horror and revulsion, not one of our apocalypses has proved permanent. We are always moving on. History trumps eternity for us, even though we also believe that history is bunk. But imagine the first phase of the collapse, the doubt that burrows and illuminates, the shocking yet thrillingly opened horizons. Try to feel the sudden void at the core of an abrupt and perplexing multiplicity; figure to yourself the urgency of holding on at all costs, the need to reinterpret and so shore up what has been hopelessly undermined, to correct all those eccentric orbits, to argue away those fossils, to preserve the earth's age at no more than seven thousand years and fix it at the dead center of the cosmos.

Xanxaniplo must have felt it most, that pressure to deny and reassure, but also the harrowing tension of imminent collapse and inescapable doom.

The cousin of Malajola would not change his story. Even as he directed the torture, Xanxaniplo knew it was pointless, that he was only going through the motions. The law of Wawanu had not held. What could it mean? How had they sinned to make the god withdraw from them? The more half-hearted his defenses became, the more doubt seeped through the dikes, the more he redoubled his efforts to preserve his sense of things. Didn't he know, didn't they all know, of the fearful work of the demons, how they had been approaching ever closer to the river?

Around the fire he recited the old stories with a forlorn passion, stoking up the ashes of his faith, calling on Wawanu to return, to forgive, at least to show some sign. The people danced themselves into frenzies, smoked themselves into trances in which each dreamed his dream, each caught in his chamber of imagery. Xanxaniplo saw it all, saw plainly how the whole earth would be given over to the demons, heard the crashing of trees and the crack of the fires and guns, saw the tee-shirts and the music videos, heard the cattle and the radios, sniffed the smoldering of the forest and beheld the death and dispersion of the people. And yet, the demons could not win. In the abyss of his nightmare Xanxaniplo believed he foresaw what must happen: that a few of the human beings would survive—degraded, dispersed, despised, but nevertheless there, still alive, still Arapoi. He could not guess how many generations they would have to wait for the Apocalypse to come to pass but at the end of his dream he saw Wawanu returning in wrath, gathering up the last human beings and leading them in a great battle of redemption; he saw the god plunge through the ruins of the forest bearing his enormous war club, saw Arunama at his side, her great thighs parting the smoke, her feet splashing through blood, and how together the gods and the Arapoi drove all the demons into the river of the world where they would drown and then, after all this horror, a Golden Age would dawn for the Arapoi.

This was the dream of Xanxaniplo and he yearned to believe in it. That Wawanu had withdrawn was certain; that he would return was a promise, a threat, a wish. No one lacks the need, but how many are able to preserve the one belief that will satisfy it?

8.

SEBASTIANO Grillo crumpled his pack of cigarettes. The cellophane crackled like a fire.

"Xanxaniplo died fighting. I know because, you understand, I was the one who gave him his mortal wound and brought him to this place and helped him to die. He told me everything I have told you.

"I know what I have done, Señor. I am the worst of us demons, but I do not boast of it. I tell you this mouth deserves to be filled with river mud and the fish should pluck off this flesh. But you too are a demon and so are those among you—yes, I know them well—who blame their world for crushing the Wawanu and would smother them with sympathy. What is such misplaced compassion but a subtler form of our demonic pride? To presume that the Wawanu are our brothers and sisters really is devilish. You understand? We are not human beings; we are not fit to be brothers to such people. We are fit only to be their murderers."

I saw Ms. Henshaw in a new light.

Grillo set the rum bottle in his lap and began to rock himself like an autistic child.

"Those imbeciles in town like Don Pedro call my women Grillo's whores and say that it is through them that the mad old son of a dog keeps himself alive. The truth is that I am trying to protect them because they are Wawanu and it is only through Wawanu that this putrid world can be cleansed."

Grillo swallowed the last of the rum and hurled the empty bottle into the weeds. He smiled at me in a way that made his claim to be a demon particularly persuasive. "That is if, Señor, it is ever to be cleansed. You understand? *Quien sabe?*"

ACKNOWLEDGMENTS

"Heiberg's Twitch" and "Two Poets" first appeared in *The Literary Review*

"The Tale of Pu'i Chu-wo, from an Old Manuscript" first appeared in *The Write Room*

"Edith Fevrier" first appeared in *Grey Sparrow Journal*

"Lar" first appeared in *Eleven Eleven*

"Kolwitzer's Father" first appeared in *Sojourn*

"The Composer Mostov" first appeared in *First Intensity*

"Four Cinematic Episodes from the Life of Paul Bronn" first appeared in *Northwest Review*

"Kafka's Fountain Pen" and "Mesopotamia" first appeared in *Sou'wester*

"Eirene" first appeared in *Tryst*

"Ten-Minute Novel" first appeared in *BAP Quarterly*

"Urbs Fabula Sine Argumentum Est" first appeared in *Amarillo Bay*

"The Withdrawal of Wawanu" first appeared in *Lingo 7*

www.ingramcontent.com/pod-product-compliance
Lightning Source LLC
Chambersburg PA
CBHW020840020726
47497CB00005B/1184